Prestige of Hearts

A Novel

R. F. Whong

ISBN: 979-8-88904-005-7

Published by Vidasym Publishing
A Division of Vidasym, Inc.
5013 S. Louis Ave., #532
Sioux Falls, SD 57108

Table of Contents

Dedication

I dedicate this book, first and foremost, to my Savior, the Lord Jesus Christ, and furthermore, to my brothers and sisters in Christ who have supported us in our ministry over the years.

I wish to honor the numerous Christians in China and Hong Kong who remain steadfast under tremendous pressure and suffering even today.

Why I Wrote This Book

Since Xi Jinping ascended to power in China, his rule has had a significant impact on Hong Kong, particularly in terms of politics, economy, and civil liberties. The Chinese government has undertaken efforts to tighten control over the region, leading to widespread concerns about the erosion of Hong Kong's autonomy and the protection of its unique rights and freedoms. China has failed to uphold its pledge to respect Hong Kong's autonomy for five decades.

Furthermore, even after so many years, the Chinese government still hasn't admitted they did anything wrong with the Tiananmen Square Massacre in 1989.

In light of the uncertain future of the human rights movement in China, I crafted this book.

Note: This book was first published on Kindle Vella entitled *Crux of the Hear* [Episodes 1-24]. To acquaint readers with Hong Kong, I have included a map and a few pictures on the following page.

Discussion questions for book clubs

1. The letter that sends Grace to Hong Kong triggers decades of secrets to surface. How do hidden histories and withheld truths shape each character's destiny, and what does forgiveness look like once the full story is revealed?

2. Faith sits at the heart of many relationships here—from Grace's evangelism to Kevin's storm-tossed conversion and Mr. Lam's Bible study. Does the novel portray faith as rescue, community, control, or some mix of the three? Where do you see healthy conviction versus coercion?

3. Each potential suitor (Kevin, Christopher, Danny) seems to represent a different path—grief and redemption, privilege and legacy, political conviction and exile. What does Grace's navigation of this love triangle reveal about her agency, values, and limits?

4. Opulence and power permeate Mr. Lam's world. How do class and hierarchy shape choices and vulnerabilities in the mansion and the workplace, and how does this compare to other wealth-centric diaspora stories?

5. Tiananmen's aftermath and the 1997 Handover function almost like characters in the novel. How do public traumas mirror the private ones, and what do Kevin's book and the family's handover-night gathering suggest about memory, identity, and belonging?

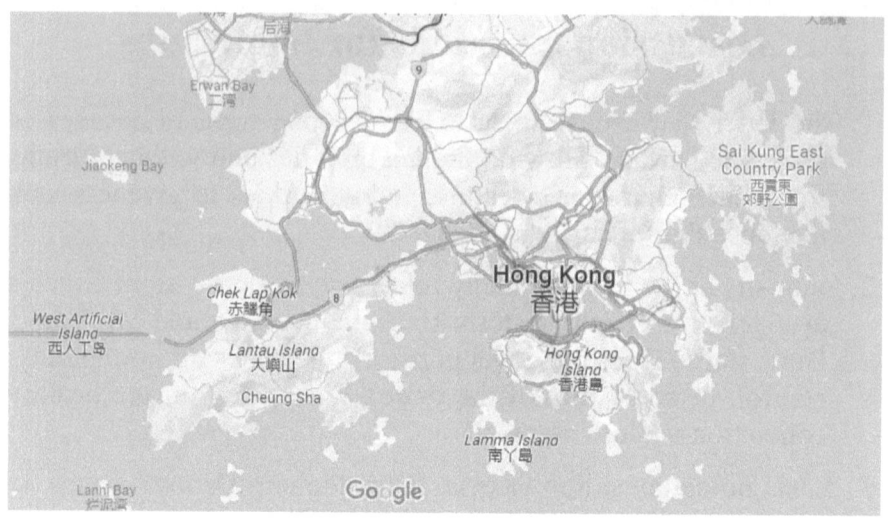

Chapter One

Hong Kong
Early summer 1992

Who was Mr. Samuel Lam? Why did Mom pen a letter from her deathbed to him?

With questions wound like a noose around her throat, Grace Feng grabbed a cab from the Kai-Tak Airport. As the sedan zigzagged through the busy streets, the driver kept glancing back at her.

He must be wondering why a girl clad in a cheap floral-print dress asked to go to the most affluent area in the whole of Hong Kong and Kowloon. She'd done her research. Her destination boasted the highest concentration of multimillionaire households in this group of British-ruled islands.

Her heart pounding, she wrapped her fingers around the gold cross pendant on her neck. *Lord, my future is in Your hand. I have little faith. Please help me.*

Gradually, individual houses replaced skyscrapers. The driver navigated a private road. She clutched her seat belt when he mumbled in Mandarin under his breath, "Wow, I've never seen this before. The lifestyle of wealthy people for sure differs from mine."

She nodded. "I..."

A magnificent iron gate blocked the way. Air whooshed from her chest, and her pulse quickened further. When did Mom know such a wealthy friend?

Grace fished the sealed envelope from her bag. It bore Susan Feng, her mother's name, as the sender and Mr. Samuel Lam as the recipient. Mom had told her that, after Mr. Lam read the letter, he

1

might ask her to stay in Hong Kong, and she must oblige—at least for a year.

When Grace inquired why, her mother, resting on the hospital bed, hadn't answered. Instead, she'd drawn Grace to her bosom and spoken in a mellow and languorous tone. "My precious Gracie, I won't be with you for long. I sincerely wish you'll stay near him. He'll have your best interests in mind."

Tears welled up. Why did Mom have to die and leave her alone in this scary world? Grace dabbed her eyes with a finger. If they'd loved each other less, would Mom's death be less painful?

"Miss?" The driver's bass rose, still speaking in Mandarin. "Miss, here you are. Eighty dollars, please."

Nice. Not even eleven US dollars. She handed over a hundred-dollar bill. "Keep the change."

A pleasant scent wafted in the air. She sucked in a deep breath, her nerves still jittery. Then she approached the guardhouse and, in English, asked to see Mr. Samuel Lam.

The man inside the booth gaped at her, his open perusal sending fresh flutters into her heart. "Do you have an appointment?" A heavy accent laced his English.

She needed an appointment to see her mother's friend? "I'm here to deliver a letter. Could you please send this in?"

After she dropped the envelope on the counter, the guy frowned at it. "Okay." He hurried inside.

Given a choice, she wouldn't have come to Hong Kong. She'd have moved right in with Nana Wang in the Chicago suburb and found a job. But she had to honor Mom's deathbed wish. Did Mom know about the guardhouse and the needed appointment to see this mysterious man?

Well, so be it.

Grace nodded. She'd booked a round-trip flight because of her tourist visa's requirement. Now she'd fulfilled her pledge. With the letter hand delivered, she'd return to Illinois and embrace the task of caring for Nana Wang in her old age.

She sidestepped her two heavy Pullman suitcases. The taxi had already left. She should've asked him to wait. Refusing to get ruffled, she planted her feet wide and savored being grounded after the long plane trip.

A shadow skimmed over her, and she tilted her face to follow the scarlet-bellied bird's flight. Higher up, cottony white clouds dotted the blue sky, while nearby pink flowers fluttered on the shrubs along the tranquil private road. Perhaps a stroll to the bus stop wouldn't be too troublesome. She sauntered near the closest bush, and the fragrant aroma grew more intense.

The gate rumbled open, and the same guard commanded, "Wait, miss."

She turned her head sideways. Her chest tightened. What did he want now?

"Miss Feng, Mr. Lam wants to see you." The lanky fellow strode to her side, then helped drag her luggage through the gate into a world alive with unique, colorful flowers. "Please, miss, come with me." He hustled her into the house and left her in a spacious room.

With her suitcases pulling on her arms, she edged past a magnificent couch and ornate side table, careful not to clatter into anything. She stopped below a six-foot-wide painting, the cube-shaped colors within its showy frame as vivid as the flowers she hadn't been allowed to assimilate.

Footsteps on the hardwood flooring had her turning. A man approached with one arm extended. His receding hairline and wrinkles around his eyes betrayed his age. Was he in his late forties?

As his gaze fell on her, his eyes widened.

Why would he look surprised to see her? She stretched out a hand. "Mr. Lam?"

"My name is Dave, Dave Cheung. I work for Mr. Lam." Mr. Cheung curled his lips into a small smile, a slight British accent hardening his English. "Please come with me. Mr. Lam is waiting for you in the study."

Yeah, Britain ruled Hong Kong. According to Mom, many people in Hong Kong studied abroad in different Commonwealth countries, former British colonies.

She left her suitcases and followed him into a room lined with tall bookcases. Once Mr. Cheung pulled out a chair for her and took his leave, she sat before the gorgeous mahogany desk and studied the man behind it.

Appearing tall and well-built, even seated in his fancy office chair, he must be in his midforties. Streaks of silver ran through his wavy, jet-black hair, but his simple blue polo shirt displayed the sculpted physique of a vital man. With fine bone structure on his chiseled face, a straight nose, and a sensual mouth, he made the word *handsome* an understatement.

He kept quiet, his brilliant eyes intense. Was he scrutinizing her as well?

She fidgeted and gripped the armrest, heat spreading from her neck to her cheeks.

"What year were you born?" A heavy Cantonese accent laced his Mandarin.

Such an odd opening question. Yet, his baritone sounded warm and gentle.

"In 1971." She replied in English.

He dipped his chin, his voice low, almost a whisper. "When did your mother pass away?"

"Less than a m–month ago. She died of pancreatic cancer a few days before I graduated from college." Grace's heart wrenched. Hard to believe a month had passed already. She touched her forehead, cringing over the months before that—months packed with hospital visits, insurance applications, budget concerns, and studies crammed into her spare time for her last semester at the University of Illinois.

"When did she find out she had cancer?"

Grace lowered her head, her vision blurry. She clenched her teeth. No way would she cry in front of a stranger. "Last December."

"What kind of treatment did she receive?"

"Chemo. But the doctor said it was too late." Moisture gathered behind her eyelids, and she squinted to hold it back.

"When did your father pass away?"

Her gaze jerked upward. "Before I was born."

Did Mr. Lam know her father? She'd never seen Papa's pictures. Mom had said she lost all their family photo albums during a move.

Every time Grace asked about Papa in her childhood, tears rushed into Mom's beautiful eyes. Her mom had worked so hard to provide a comfortable home. Grace learned not to bring up that subject. Still, it would be nice to know what he looked like.

Mr. Lam wheeled his office chair toward a floor-to-ceiling window overlooking the garden. Shadows flickered over a pond while the late afternoon sun shone on the blooming bushes.

An eerie hush stretched across the room, except for the birds chirping. She leaned forward, the wood beneath her fierce grip cutting into her fingers. Why did Mr. Lam behave like that?

At last, he rolled his chair back to face her, his eyes misty. "You said you've just graduated from college? What's your major? Where do you work?"

As she absorbed the concern deep in his eyes and the tender expressions of his voice, a perplexing question obtruded. Was he about to ask her to stay in Hong Kong as Mom had wished? *I hope not.* She had her return flight in a week. Surely, she'd be able to make it. "Finance. I haven't found a job yet. After I go home, I'll focus on my job-hunting."

With a small smile tugging at the corners of his mouth, he switched to English. "It so happens my company's chief financial analyst needs an assistant. Would you be interested?"

Oh no. He's offering me a job. Did she have to honor the second pledge she made to Mom and accept it? Her fingers clawed into the armrests. "I'm not allowed to work here. I'm on a tourist visa."

He waved Mom's letter. "I can arrange a work visa."

She stifled a sigh and scrunched her nose. "What company? What kind of pay are we talking about?"

He poured water for them. "In my hotel investment subsidiary. The pay—seventeen thousand Hong Kong dollars a month, equivalent to twenty-six thousand US dollars a year—is decent."

Grace furrowed her eyebrows. "Even with an entry-level position, I'll make more in the US."

He maintained steady eye contact. "First, you haven't found a job. Second, from our survey, the US entry-level annual salaries for finance majors range from twenty-two to thirty-two thousand dollars. I believe my offer is fair. Plus, the cost of living in Hong Kong is lower."

Quite persuasive. She narrowed her eyes. *Okay, one last try to decline.* "Isn't rent expensive in Hong Kong? Life in the US will be easier for me."

His expression turned blank. He sipped his water. When he spoke again, his eager tone drew her in. "You're right. The minimum rent for a modest one-bedroom apartment is about eight thousand Hong Kong dollars a month. How about I offer you free room and board in my house?"

She stifled a gasp at his beyond-generous offer. Why was he so persistent? "What do I need to do in exchange for free room and board?"

The man's sensual lips crinkled up. "Do you usually behave this way? Who taught you to haggle?"

I'm not haggling. I don't have any desire to stay in Hong Kong. I want to go home. Holding back the retort, she shook a finger at him with a grin. "Don't forget, I'm a finance major."

"And a good one." He inclined his head. "Do you know about 1997?"

Huh? What a switch in subjects. She blinked and tucked her hair behind her ears. "What about 1997?"

"Britain will give Hong Kong back to China in 1997, and we'll need to use Mandarin. As you can tell, I speak Mandarin with a strong Cantonese accent. So does my son." He spread out his hands. "Can you teach us to speak accent-free Mandarin? I'm not asking much. How about two hours every Saturday afternoon?"

That didn't sound appealing, but wasn't bad either. With the free room and board, she would make almost thirty-eight thousand US dollars a year, much better than a job she could find back in Illinois. "Your son? How old is he?"

"Christopher is a college freshman in California and will come home next week."

Grace stifled a sigh. Mom had wished for her to stay near Mr. Lam for a while. Maybe she could work in his company for a year to fulfill her second pledge. "I can't guarantee you'll get rid of the accent. The student's effort is more important than the teacher's skill."

He stood, shifted to her side, and seemed ready to hug her. Then he stretched out a palm. "Deal."

She shook his hand. "When do I start?"

He held her fingers a tad longer than expected. "Since you've just arrived, you may need time to rest and get over your jet lag. Plus, I'll need time to obtain your work visa." He twisted his watch into view. "Today is May twenty-second. It's customary here for a new employee to start on a Monday. How about June eighth, over two weeks from today? We can have our first Mandarin lesson on June thirteenth."

Another generous gesture. He didn't leave any room for her to turn down his offer.

"You've met Dave. He'll help you settle in." Mr. Lam picked up his desk phone and dialed a number.

Mr. Cheung came and guided Grace down a long winding hallway to enter a room, her new home. Her two Pullman suitcases had arrived before her. A navy-blue quilt covered the queen-size bed in the typical guest room. Next to it, a black phone sat on top of an antique-looking table with a matching chair. A wide dresser made of natural wood stood by the bathroom door.

He drew away the mint-green curtains, and light poured onto the floor.

She edged closer to the large window framed by azure walls. "Is that an Olympic-size swimming pool?"

"Yes. You're more than welcome to use it anytime."

"Too bad. I didn't bring my swimwear." She hugged her purse to her chest. "Does Mr. Lam usually treat guests this way?"

"What do you mean?"

"I mean—" She swallowed hard. "He's very generous."

Mr. Cheung shrugged. "Mr. Lam works in mysterious ways. I've been his butler and personal secretary for over a year and still haven't figured out what he likes and doesn't like to do."

"He asked me to teach him and his son to speak better Mandarin." She touched her throat, a knot tightening in her belly. "What is Christopher like?"

"No different from other kids of superwealthy families."

She dropped her purse on the bed. "How about Mrs. Lam?"

"I never met her. According to the tabloids, she died in a car accident a few years ago." He gave out a small cough. "I'll let you rest. Dinner is at seven thirty."

Reports from the tabloids about Mrs. Lam's death? What an unusual family.

He spun on his heels and trudged toward the door. Then, as if remembering something, he paused and gripped the doorframe. "Feel free to walk around the first floor and the garden. Just don't go to the second floor where Mr. Lam resides. He insists on privacy."

She dipped her chin. "Of course. I understand."

7

After Mr. Cheung left, she pushed her suitcases against the dresser, opened them, and unpacked. Not much to handle. Before she left Illinois, she'd donated most of their belongings to Goodwill and stored their family mementos at Nana Wang's house, except for the few items she brought with her.

A small glass bottle pendant fell out of its case. She snatched it and traced a finger along its smooth surface. All her pent-up emotions surged to the surface. She'd honored Mom's wish and buried her cremated remains with a young Japanese maple at the Chicago Botanic Garden, a program for people to dedicate a tree in memory of a loved one. The bottle in her hand contained a dash of Mom's ash as a keepsake.

Tears pooled in her eyes, and Mom's handwritten note seared her mind again.

> *Gracie, my dear daughter,*
>
> *I pray God will grant you courage and wisdom. Without me around, you'll live an abundant life, as promised by our Lord. Remember to ask this question in whatever you do—"Is it pleasing to God and helpful to others?" I've dreamed about taking you by the hand to lead you into the wedding ceremony one day. It's an impossible wish now. Yet, I've received confirmation from the Lord that He will always be with you.*
>
> *I know you want to stay with Nana Wang and care for her as she grows older. However, you need to hand deliver my letter to Mr. Samuel Lam as soon as possible. If he asks you to stay in Hong Kong, please oblige for my sake, at least for a year.*
>
> *Apart from my salvation, you're the greatest gift God's given me. Since childhood, you've always been kind, smart, and well-behaved.*
>
> *Look heavenward with hope. We'll meet again. I'm sure of it.*
>
> *Love,*
> *Mom*

She plopped into the nearby chair, covered her face, and burst out crying. *Mom, why did you have to die?*

And why did Mom instruct her to leave her familiar turf to come to this strange land? Even though Mom had taken her traveling around the world since childhood, they'd never visited Asia. From this point on, Grace had to live and work here. What an unexpected turn of life!

The clock struck seven. She jerked up her head and wiped her face with the back of a hand. Well, time to shower. The long flight rendered her a stinky mess.

She entered the bathroom and surveyed her reflection. A red smear marked her jaw from where she'd leaned on it earlier. Everybody told her she looked like her mother—fair skin, an oval face with almond-shaped eyes, and full lips. The only difference was the hair. While Mom's hair was straight, hers was naturally curly. She must've inherited it from Papa. What did he look like? Would Mr. Lam have pictures of her father?

With her chest tight, she stepped into the shower.

Perhaps this trip to Hong Kong wouldn't be in vain. At least she'd learn more about Papa from Mr. Lam.

Chapter Two

Kevin Cheung leaned against a wooden post in the spacious living room. Surrounded by gorgeous paintings and expensive furniture, he peeked into the plastic bag at hand—a woman's one-piece black swimsuit, size six, and a CD set, Cantonese for Mandarin Speakers.

"Ah, you're back." His father strolled in. "Did you get the stuff Mr. Lam requested?"

Kevin waved the bag.

Dad nodded, then his face contorted with a slight grimace. "How did your interview go today?"

His dad's countenance chilled him. Kevin shrugged. Did they have to go through this again?

"I told you to cut your hair short. You come across as untidy. No wonder you can't find a job. When are you going to settle down?" While he remained silent, Dad raised his voice. "Answer me."

Settle down. Why didn't Dad say outright that he wanted to become a grandpa?

Kevin ducked his head, the coldness creeping up his spine. "I'm trying my best."

"Trying isn't enough." Dad lowered his brows, the tendons standing out in his neck. "I paid for you to attend the University of Hong Kong and expected you to become independent as soon as you graduated. You've been idle for two years."

Dad was exaggerating again.

He hadn't been idle. Using his degree in English Literature, he translated documents for people to earn his way. A nine-to-five job didn't suit him. He needed time to write. Yeah, he remained an unpublished author, even though he'd submitted countless short

10

stories to the art and literature section of local magazines and newspapers since high school.

Enough proof to Dad that writing couldn't be a career. Only positions with a fixed monthly income met Dad's criteria.

Kevin adjusted his eyeglasses and bit his lip, clamping down his annoyance. "Almost seven thirty. Should we go to the dining room?"

Dad took a deep breath. "As long as you're not settled, I have to keep working. I'm not young anymore."

"You're only forty-eight." Kevin curled up his lips into a half smile. "You look like my brother, not my father."

Dad gave him a stern stare, then led the way forward.

In the oversized dining room, a fresh addition sat next to Mr. Lam at the custom-made table. A visitor didn't surprise him—they had guests often. But Kevin's jaw slackened at her appearance.

Beautiful, for sure. No, much more than that. Soft dark curls caressed her pale swanlike neck, and her creamy skin glowed in the chandelier light. With a delicate innocence in her countenance, she appeared like an angel depicted in storybooks.

Yet, she looked familiar. Had he seen her before? Where? On what occasion? If he'd ever seen such an alluring creature, he wouldn't have forgotten their meeting.

Mr. Lam glanced at them. "Dave, has Christopher called? Make sure you pick him up from the airport."

Odd. Why did Mr. Lam speak in English today? Perhaps their guest didn't understand Cantonese.

His father touched his forehead, a nervous habit. "He called and said he won't be back next week. He's going to Europe with friends and won't return until mid-June."

"This is the third time he's changed his plans." Mr. Lam frowned, then coughed. As he faced the newcomer, his expression softened. "Grace, let me introduce you to Kevin, Dave's son."

Kevin took the seat next to her. "Nice to meet you." After she flashed a gentle smile, he handed the bag to Dad's boss. "Dad asked me to buy these for you."

"Excellent. Thanks." Mr. Lam passed it to Grace. "This is to help you learn Cantonese. You may need to talk to clients in our local dialect. Also, a swimsuit for you in case you want to use the pool."

So, the items were for the young lady. What did Mr. Lam mean by meeting with clients?

The servants brought out the dishes. Crab cakes, clam chowder, seared scallops, and steamed lobsters...

Wow, seafood dinner, Kevin's favorite.

Mr. Lam placed a lobster on Grace's plate. "I remember your mother favored seafood, especially lobsters. I figure you love them too."

"Thank you. You're very kind." Unlike her smile and angelic appearance, her tone sounded modulated, strong. And her English was American.

Mr. Lam chuckled under his breath. "Make yourself at home. Whatever you need or want, let Dave or me know."

This person must be exceptional. Mr. Lam was kind, generous, and loved company. That was why he and Dad dined with the big boss every evening. But his attitude toward Grace was...

While Kevin chewed on the tender scallop, Mr. Lam turned to him. "Are you free in the next few days? Grace won't start her new job until June eighth. Can you show her around town? She's never been to Hong Kong before."

He gulped. That was beyond anything he'd known thus far about Dad's boss. Who was this young lady Mr. Lam doted on? "Of course. My pleasure." He let out a low whistle, audible only to himself. "How about we start tomorrow? Ten o'clock?"

Her grin rounded up her cheeks, and her eyes glowed above them. "Sure. Thanks."

After dinner, Kevin followed his father out of the dining room and couldn't help asking, "Dad, who is Grace? Where is she from?"

"She's from Illinois." Dad's steps slowed, and he lowered his voice to a whisper. "Mr. Lam has offered her a job as an assistant to the chief financial analyst. He's also providing her free room and board to teach him Mandarin."

Huh? Dad wasn't making any sense. "I don't get it."

"Mr. Lam said she just graduated from the University of Illinois, a finance major." Dad scanned around. "I know. It's an unusual arrangement, but it's also none of our business. Just be careful when you go out with her."

Careful of what?

A maid, Ah Tang, approached. "Ha, Kevin, I found you. I have a document to be translated into English. Could you please help?"

He bid Dad goodbye and followed her to the servants' quarters. Inside the enormous kitchen, his steps echoed on the tile as he crossed over to the pile of tabloids on the white marble countertop.

Yeah, weekly news about Hong Kong's superrich families. Dad's boss made his regular appearances on those magazine covers.

Ah Tang smirked, as if well pleased with herself. "You enjoy reading tabloids too? Look at this one. Mr. Lam danced with an actress named Lily Ching."

Kevin edged closer and studied the couple. Mr. Lam, in a black tuxedo, sported his usual amiable smile. The woman next to him raised her fingers to form a V sign as if claiming her victory over a date with Hong Kong's most eligible bachelor.

Wait.

He scrutinized Lily's face again. She looked like the girl he'd just met. He jabbed his hands into his pockets, clenching them against his nerves. "They have the same eyes."

Ah Tang cocked her head. "What did you say?"

"Nothing important." He swallowed hard as a sickening sensation spread throughout his body. He flipped through the tabloids. Another picture showed Mr. Lam holding hands with a different starlet. The woman had Grace's nose and mouth.

Grace looked like Mr. Lam's girlfriends. No, that wasn't accurate. Those women all looked like Grace in a certain way. No wonder he thought he'd seen her before. He'd seen her look-alikes on tabloid covers.

Did Mr. Lam offer Grace free room and board so he could seduce her? Did the newcomer know the scheme and go along with it?

He scrunched his nose, then pushed his glasses back up. None of his business. A college graduate, Grace should be able to take care of herself.

Still, his heart whimpered. No girl could resist Mr. Lam. He possessed everything a woman ever desired—charm, looks, money, and power. An exquisite, virtuous angel was about to fall. Or maybe this time Mr. Lam was serious about her. He'd invited none of his girlfriends to stay in his house. Grace was the first. Perhaps she would become Mrs. Lam.

Now, Kevin understood why Dad warned him to be careful when he spent time with Grace.

"Kevin, here's my document."

As Ah Tang handed it to him, he turned away from the pile of magazines. Okay, time to get to work.

After he returned to the room that he shared with Dad and translated Ah Tang's document, he went to bed early. The same dream, in an altered format, visited again. He and Wendy swam in the ocean. As a wave slammed into her face, she screamed. He moved toward her, but the torrent pushed him away. In an instant, Wendy disappeared.

"No..."

He jolted awake in a cold sweat, his chest heaving.

Although more than six years had passed since Wendy's accident, he still dreamed of her often. Lacing his fingers behind his head, he stifled a groan but couldn't stifle the unanswerable questions as they began their endless loop—again.

What made him invite Wendy out to the ocean on that fateful summer afternoon? Why did she insist on swimming toward the open water? Why was life so fragile?

He'd asked Dad and his friends those questions after she drowned. Some just stared at him, while others stated what he'd already known—death, like birth, was a part of human life.

Those answers didn't satisfy him. *Everyone dies sooner or later, and death is the end of everything.* What was the meaning of life? Why did most people want to live long?

The moon shadows on the ceiling faded. Faint sounds of water splashing disturbed him. Was that Grace? Why was she up so early? Ah, must be her jet lag.

Without disturbing Dad, he scrambled from his twin bed, changed, and dashed out.

The early morning sun shone on the swimming pool, deflecting light from its surface. An agile and strong figure emerged from the water, then sank again, propelling a slim, graceful body forward.

The summer breeze wafted a sweet scent into his nostrils. He fixed his gaze on the delightful scene. Grace swam back and forth, changing from freestyle to butterfly to backstroke, then to breaststroke.

14

As he approached, she glided to the edge near him. "Thank you for buying the swimsuit. It fits me well."

"I'm glad you like it." He sat and dipped his toes into the cool water. "You swim well. Where did you learn?"

She chuckled, grabbed the pool edge, and hurled herself out of the water. "My mother taught me when I was a kid."

As the morning sun stretched her shadow over him, he eyed her long, shapely legs, sensations of warmth spreading through him. *Calm down. Haven't you seen a woman in a swimsuit?* To hide his embarrassment, he handed her the towel. "You know so many strokes."

"Thank you." She wrapped the cloth around her waist like a sarong. "In high school, I was a varsity swim team member."

"Impressive." He met her laughing eyes, and his heart skipped a beat. Such an innocent-looking girl, yet with a curvaceous figure. And she was tall, maybe only slightly shorter than he was. Would she become Mr. Lam's mistress soon? "Where did you attend high school?"

"Libertyville High. Do you know where that is?"

Kevin shook his head, unable to turn away from the oval face glistening with water drops.

She lowered herself to sit beside him and flashed a smile as gentle as the morning breeze. Was that her signature smile?

"Yeah, nobody knows about Libertyville. It's a small town fifty miles north of downtown Chicago."

"Ha, now I know." He patted his forehead. "One year, my father and I visited Chicago. We drove north to Wisconsin. I might have seen an exit sign for your town."

Uh-oh. Why do I tell white lies to appease others?

"So, you've visited Chicago? How did you like it?" Her white, even teeth gleamed between her full lips.

Whew, she didn't ask why he could remember a random roadside sign. "It's a great city. I still like Hong Kong better. We have convenient public transportation and a lot more activities."

He didn't share the whole truth, either. His love for Hong Kong went beyond tangible reasons. His hometown, its combination of modernity and tradition, its hustling and bustling markets, its grand skyline, and its citizens' strong identity and pride captivated him. Dad had desired him to attend the University of Melbourne—Dad's alma mater—in Australia, but Kevin had chosen the University of Hong Kong to stay on his home turf.

An unexpected hush engulfed them. Had he said something offensive? Leaning forward, he scooped water in his palm and let it slip through his fingers, the dribbling sound filling their silence. He stole a glimpse of her. Grace's shoulders slumped, a solemn expression pulling down the corners of her mouth.

He cleared his throat, breaking the stillness. "Are you all right?"

She kicked the bare feet she'd dangled over the pool's edge, splashing shimmering water. "I'm fine. Thank you. I was thinking about our old house in Libertyville. I put it up for sale before I left."

"What happened? Why did you come to Hong Kong?"

Water dripped from her hair, and droplets traced the smooth line of her cheek and jaw, enticing his fingers to flick them away. She gripped the tiles on either side of her and bit down on her bottom lip as if deciding what to say. "My mom passed away. She asked me to deliver a letter to Mr. Lam in person."

"I'm so sorry to hear that." He patted her bare shoulder and almost flinched as a sudden rush of heat sent tingles down his body. "Why did your mother send you all the way here with a letter? Couldn't you have mailed it instead?"

She shrugged, hesitation marking her tone. "I'm not sure. She wished for me to stay near Mr. Lam for a while."

So, Mr. Lam must have close ties with her family. Still, why did all his girlfriends look like Grace?

Well, it wasn't his business to know.

He wrapped his arms around his knees to conceal any sign of his discomfort.

No matter how much he tried, he was no different from other men. Attractive women like Grace aroused him. Pure physiological reactions, right? Discipline had been his pride. Unlike some of his friends, he'd avoided visiting call girls so far. Also, different from most of his friends, he hadn't found a stable job to have spare cash.

You idiot. Don't behave like a teenager. His lack of sleep must have weakened his mind.

He checked his watch. Not even six thirty. "It's early. I plan to go back to bed. Should we still meet at ten? Where do you want to go today?"

As he yawned, she yawned too. Yarning was definitely contagious.

"I need your help to run errands." She hopped to her feet and fingered through her wet hair. "Are banks open today? I have to open a checking account. I also need to buy an international phone card."

As they left the pool, his gaze fell on a second-floor window. A man's silhouette stood partially shielded by the curtain.

Yeah, Mr. Lam's living quarters. Was the big boss watching them? Again, it didn't concern him. "Sure. Whatever you need to do, I'll try my best to help."

"Thank you." She shaded her eyes from the sun in the eastern sky, scanning the surroundings. "How big is this house? Looks enormous."

"Besides the study, office, game room, den, and others, the house has nine bedrooms, not counting the servants' area. The lot is about an acre." He pointed toward the other end of the yard. "Do you play tennis? The tennis court is on the other side."

"Imposing. I noticed a koi pond outside Mr. Lam's study as well." She released an audible breath. "This must be Hong Kong's largest estate. I heard it's expensive even to own an apartment here."

A chuckle rumbled from his chest. "That's why my dad decided to work here. Free room and board for both of us." He waved back at the swimming pool. "And I get to enjoy all the amenities."

"Do you need to do anything in exchange?" Grace tipped up her face.

He grinned. "No. Nothing other than running errands for Mr. Lam from time to time, like buying those things for you."

"What do you do for a living?"

He rubbed the back of his neck. "I translate documents from Chinese to English for my clients. I majored in English Literature in college."

"No wonder you speak such good English." Her laughter was so sweet that his heart skipped a beat. "Do you make enough to survive in this superexpensive city?"

He raised a brow. "Are you always so straightforward?"

"Sorry." She dipped her chin, exposing her swanlike neck. "I was just curious how young people make do here."

"Curiosity will kill a cat." Shaking a finger at her, he twisted the corners of his lips. "How about you? I heard you're going to teach Mr. Lam Mandarin. Didn't you grow up in the US? Where did you learn to speak such fluent Mandarin?"

"My mother taught me to read, write, and speak Chinese. But she only knew Mandarin, not Cantonese. She also sent me to a Saturday Chinese school run by our church." As though uncomfortable with the conversation, she yawned again. "Okay, I'd better get back to my room and take a nap. See you later."

Kevin watched her stroll away, stood still, and couldn't help whistling the tune, "Speak Softly, Love."

It'd been a long time since he thought of the song.

Chapter Three

After exiting the electronics store with Grace, Kevin scanned the busy street scene. "I'm glad you found what you needed."

"Wow, an international phone card is much cheaper here." She flashed a bright smile and checked her watch. "Two o'clock? It's midnight in Chicago. I'll have to wait at least until eight to call my friend."

What friend was she referring to? Must be her boyfriend. Otherwise, why would she be so eager to call?

Good luck to Mr. Lam. Maybe he wouldn't make Grace his mistress easily. "Are you hungry? I know an excellent dumpling joint in Mongkok." He led the way down Nathan Road in Tsim Sha Tsui. "I suppose you haven't been there. Mongkok is a major shopping area for locals on the Kowloon side."

Cars, minibuses, and double-deckers weaved the narrow streets. Bright sunshine cast warm rays on pedestrians. Merchants shouted to attract passersby.

Kevin halted at a dingy little restaurant. "This place is famous for dumplings."

She craned her neck to peek into the dark interior, then followed him inside to sit on the only two remaining seats at a shabby wooden table shared by a group of strangers.

As soon as the server brought their orders, Grace devoured hers and chuckled. "Delicious. Excellent."

Her laugh was a soothing salve, the sweetest sound he'd heard in a while.

Two men across from them trained their bold gazes on her. Perhaps her hearty appetite stunned them. Kevin ignored the others and reciprocated with a smile, his heart aflutter.

What was going on with him? Since Wendy's death, he shunned dating and struggled to meet new girls. *Wait.* He'd met Grace only yesterday. The time may have come for him to move on with someone new and make Dad proud.

Whoa. Where'd *that* thought come from?

He crooked up one corner of his mouth. "I'm glad you liked it. The food back at Mr. Lam's mansion is even better. How come you didn't eat like this?"

Crimson crept up to her oval face. "Eat like this in front of Mr. Lam and your father? You must be kidding."

So, Grace wasn't as straightforward as he thought. She behaved differently on different occasions. Did she feel at ease in his presence? Must be. A soothing warmth enveloped him. "Are you done? Do you want to go to the Peak? It's the most iconic tourist attraction here."

"Sure. I've heard of it. Let's go."

They took the Star Ferry across Victoria Harbour back to the Hong Kong Island side. From the pier, he guided her toward the tram. "Too bad I don't own a car. Otherwise, I'd take you to Repulse Bay. It has a beautiful white-sand beach."

"No hurry. I may stay here for a while." She tucked a tress behind her ear.

A simple movement, yet she did it with such charm. He couldn't turn away his gaze.

"Are you okay?"

"Yeah, I'm fine." Heat crept up to his cheeks. He scratched his forehead to shade his blush.

They trekked behind foreigners to Victoria Peak and stopped to take in the panoramic landscape.

"Such a gorgeous sight." She took out her camera to snap photos. "No wonder this place is the tourists' favorite attraction."

His chest swelled as they overlooked the stunning view stretching from Victoria Harbour to Kai-Tak Airport to sites beyond Kowloon. Yes, one of the many reasons he loved Hong Kong.

A man approached them. "Do you want me to take a picture of you two together?"

"Sure." Grace glanced at Kevin. "If it's okay with you."

Wow, was that the difference between growing up in the US versus Hong Kong? Local girls would think twice about having pictures taken with someone they barely knew. But she seemed unconcerned.

The man took her camera. "Come on. Stand closer. Sir, wrap your arm around her waist."

Even after her encouraging nod, Kevin hesitated. But why not? As he placed his palm on her narrow waist, a tingling sensation zipped through his arm, and his heart rate picked up.

Watch out. You can't afford to lose the free room and board.

Grace seemed not to notice his unease. She slipped away, retrieved her camera, and straightened her blouse where he'd rumpled it. "This is fun. Hong Kong is an awesome place."

He curled his fingers into a fist, resisting the urge to slip them around her waist again. Why did he respond like a juvenile fool? *Cool down. You're taking care of her for Mr. Lam.* "Anywhere else you want to go?"

Her headshake shook her soft curls, their bounce around her cheeks mesmerizing. "Not today. Mr. Lam said we should get back before seven. He wants to dine with us and has something to discuss with me after dinner."

Kevin narrowed his eyes. For sure, Mr. Lam wasn't wasting any time. *Grace, be careful.* He bit his lip hard to swallow the unspoken words. It was none of his business. "How about tomorrow? What do you have in mind?"

She twirled a curl around her fingers. "Do you know any church that has an English or Mandarin worship service?"

He stretched his eyes wide. Was she a Christian? "I have a friend from Mainland China who goes to church. I'll try to call him tonight."

"Thank you." She flashed another of her signature gentle smiles.

He sucked in a breath. "Did you go to church in Chicago? Was it a Chinese church? I heard there're many ethnic churches in the US."

"Yeah." She inclined her head. "My mom and I attended a Chinese church in Chicago's north suburbs."

Kevin raised his brows, detecting a flutter in his stomach. "What was it like growing up in the US?"

Her smile vanished. She folded her arms across her chest and cocked her head. "Not fun. We lived in a Caucasian town. I was the only Chinese throughout elementary school. Oh, my class did have a Korean girl. We were like two ugly ducklings. Our classmates made fun of our appearance all the time. Our skin was too yellow, our eyes too small, and our noses not high enough."

Her speech was straightforward. But could she be serious? An ugly duckling? She was more beautiful than any movie star in Hong Kong.

He kept quiet.

She retrieved a pair of oversized sunglasses from her bag and slid them on. "How about you? Did you grow up in Hong Kong? What was it like?"

He touched his nose, debating whether to delve into his troubled childhood. She didn't hold back, though, so shouldn't he share as much? "Not an easy time in my life, either. My mother passed away when I was two. At every parent-teacher conference, I envied my classmates. They had their dads and moms with them. I had only my father."

Yet, when his classmates looked down on him, Wendy—and only Wendy—showed him kindness. Yes, he'd known her since first grade.

Grace didn't respond and adjusted her sunglasses.

He hesitated, then pulled a picture from his wallet. "Me with my mom when I was a baby."

She tipped the photo to catch the sunlight. "At least you know what your mother looked like. My dad passed away before I was born, and I've never seen his picture."

How dreadful. Kevin pressed his lips tight and blinked as his head buzzed.

In his elementary school days, whenever the teacher assigned them to write an essay about their mothers, he and Dad would sit together and go over Mom's pictures. Without ever seeing her father's photo, how would Grace have written her articles about her dad? It must've been a tough experience. Or maybe the US teachers didn't give students that sort of assignment.

"Um..." At last, he took back the photo and traced Mom's kind face with his index finger. "What happened to your family's pictures?"

22

She fingered through her curly mane. "My mom lost all her albums during a move."

Ouch. What a terrible loss. He adjusted his glasses. "Have you reached out to family members who may have photos or memories of your father?"

Her hand pinned down one side of her hair, stopping the wind from teasing it into her eyes. "My mom was an only child, and my grandparents passed away before I was born."

He drew a heavy breath, held it in, then released it. "I'm so sorry."

She raised her gaze toward a puppy-shaped cloud. "It seems Mr. Lam was a good friend of my mom's. He may have known my papa. Is it okay if I ask him whether he has pictures of my parents? Perhaps he'll lend them to me, and I can have a shop to make duplicates."

"It won't hurt to ask. The worst you can get is a no."

"You're very kind." Grace touched his arm.

He flinched as if scorched by a flame. *Cool it. You just met her yesterday.* Yet, he found solace in her company, and their similar childhood experiences made him feel safe and secure. Should he open up and talk about Wendy? "We'd better leave now. It'll take us a while by tram and bus to get back."

***

Grace checked the wall clock. Seven ten. She massaged her temples. Five ten in the morning Chicago time. Too early to call Nana Wang. She'd have to call later.

At seven thirty, she strolled into the dining room and took her assigned seat.

Still the same group of people.

Mr. Lam fixed his gaze on her. "How did your day go?"

"Fine." She stole a glimpse of Kevin. With high cheekbones, a cleft chin, and shoulder-length hair, except for the pair of thick glasses, he looked like Jonathan Poon, the most popular boy in her Illinois church's youth group. "Kevin is an excellent guide. He helped me run errands and took me to the Peak."

She stifled a sigh at the thought of Jonathan. They'd dated in high school. When he went to the East Coast for college, they continued their long-distance relationship for another two years and tried to make it work by talking on the phone and seeing each other in person

23

as much as possible. Was the distance too much for them to sustain their puppy love? They soon drifted apart.

"Ah, the Peak." Mr. Lam shifted his focus to Kevin. "Did you and Grace have lunch at the Peak restaurant?"

A flush spread across Kevin's cheeks. He winced. "It's way beyond our budget."

"I see." Mr. Lam pulled a card from his pocket. "Starting tomorrow, charge all Grace's expenses to this."

Kevin's eyes stretched wide.

She leaned over to peek at the card. Just a normal-looking credit or debit card. Why did Kevin seem astonished? It wouldn't be free, for sure. She'd pay Mr. Lam back once she started working.

The servants brought out the dishes. Wow, another splendid dinner comprised seafood soup, stir-fried littlenecks, sea bass steamed with ginger and green onion... A delightful aroma drifted around the room.

"This is good. You'll like it." Mr. Lam forked a chunk of fish onto Grace's plate, then turned around to Mr. Cheung. "Dave, please cancel my appointment with Lily Ching. I plan to stay home tomorrow night."

"Yes, sir." Mr. Cheung retrieved a notebook from his pocket and jotted it down. "Anything else?"

"No, that's all." Mr. Lam sipped his merlot. "Grace, do you like lamb?"

She bobbed her head. "Very much."

"Ha, you're like me." Mr. Lam gave out a hearty laugh. "Make sure the kitchen prepares lamb chops tomorrow."

"Of course." Mr. Cheung nodded.

Lily Ching? Who was she? Brushing aside the questions, Grace focused on eating. The chef had seasoned the sea bass with a mixture of herbs, creating a delicious flavor. Its flaky texture paired well with spinach cooked in garlic. So light and refreshing.

She wiped her mouth with a napkin and sank back in her seat.

Mr. Lam checked his watch. "Grace, remember to come to my study at nine."

Her lips curled up even further, her heartbeat jittering. Would she see her papa's pictures? "Sure. See you soon."

Back in her room, she glanced at the clock. Eight forty-five. Not enough time to call Nana Wang to have a decent conversation.

She strolled out to the hallway and peered into the garden. The sun had set. Yet, a remaining glow cast a rosy hue across the lawn. An almost electrical current of excitement pulsed through her veins. Tonight, she might learn what Papa looked like. Did he have curly hair like her? Mom had claimed Grace's thick mane took after Papa.

"What are you looking at?" Kevin's voice sounded behind her.

She spun around, a hand to her chest. "You scared me."

"I'm sorry." He directed his gaze between her and the dark garden. "I didn't see much out there."

"I wasn't looking at anything." She let out a breath. "Mr. Lam spoke of Lily Ching. Who is she?"

"A famous movie star in Hong Kong." He leaned toward her. "You ought to read the tabloids. Mr. Lam appears on their covers frequently."

Huh? Why was Mr. Lam linked to movie stars and tabloids? "Isn't he a businessman?"

"He is, and more." Kevin twisted his watch into view. "Are you meeting with him at nine? It's almost time. You'd better go."

Grace waved him good night and ambled down the hallway. The knot in her stomach tightened. At the study, she knocked, then pushed open its ajar door. Mr. Lam didn't sit behind the enormous desk like before. Instead, he guided her to the sitting area with a black leather sofa.

Why didn't she notice such a plush and luxurious couch before? She might have been too nervous yesterday.

"Let's sit here. It's more comfortable." He poured tea for them. "What do you think about Hong Kong?"

With him close by, his woody and spicy scent clogged her nostrils.

"So far, so good." She forced a smile. Deep down, homesickness gripped her, and her heart ached for the familiar sights and sounds of her hometown and Nana Wang. "It's my second day here. I may be able to give you a more thorough report as time goes by."

He tapped his porcelain cup, his expression somber. "Tell me more about your mother. When did she move to Chicago?"

Move to Chicago? Hadn't Mom always lived in Illinois?

"You look puzzled." From his wallet, Mr. Lam retrieved a black-and-white picture. Inside, a couple, both glowing in happiness, stood in front of a tall tower adorned with a tiled roof.

Grace scrutinized it. The girl looked like her, except for her shoulder-length straight hair. And the young man... She blurted out, "You and my mom?"

His lips curled into a wobbly smile, the glow in his eyes dimming. "Yes."

"Where were you?" She brushed her fingers over the photo's cold surface.

"In front of the Hoover Tower at Stanford University." He reclaimed the picture and, his hand trembling slightly, tucked it in his wallet.

Mom had graduated from the University of Illinois. Was she visiting California when the picture was taken? Why did Mr. Lam treasure it so much to carry in his wallet?

He took a sip of his tea. "Your mother and I both attended Stanford. I was one year her senior."

She slackened her jaw, unsure of which she felt more—surprise or unease. "Mom never mentioned that to me. I assumed she spent all her school years in Chicago."

He shook his head but kept quiet.

She almost reached for his arm. Instead, she curled both hands around her teacup, holding on so tight she might break the delicate thing. "You met my mother at Stanford?"

"Even earlier. We became good friends when we attended a boarding high school in the Bay Area." He directed his gaze toward the yard beyond the floor-to-ceiling window. Night had thickened like a sable curtain, blanketing the lawn. The lampposts around the koi pond cast mystifying shadows from the nearby trees.

One more tidbit she didn't know. Had Mom's family been wealthy? Otherwise, how could they have afforded to send her to a boarding school?

"Although your mother was a year younger, she was more mature and took care of me. Back then, I acted like a spoiled, rebellious brat. Nobody at school liked me, except your mother." Mr. Lam's lips seemed to cling to the small smile he kept in place.

She scooted to the edge of the sofa and clamped her hands on her knees. "Do you know my father? Do you have pictures of him?"

"I–I—" He set down his cup and looked away. "Sorry, I don't know him."

So he hadn't crossed paths with Papa. She slumped back onto the sofa.

A crease formed between his brows. "Enough for tonight. I shouldn't take up too much of your time. You must need to go to bed early to overcome your jet lag."

He rose from the sofa, a clear sign of dismissal.

But why send her away so soon? Didn't *he* ask to see *her*? They'd only talked for a few minutes, and so many unasked questions remained. She swallowed back her suffocating disappointment. Well, she could always ask him later.

Back in her room, she sat by the table and slid a photo from her purse. In it, Mom and she smiled in front of their church's sanctuary.

That day, her Sunday school teacher complained to Mom that Grace argued with her about creation versus evolution. Yeah, in middle school, she began to doubt the Christian faith she'd learned since childhood. Different ideas taught at school challenged her to reexamine her beliefs. Mom didn't get upset but encouraged her to delve deeper for more understanding of the Bible.

After worship, Nana Wang took this picture. It'd become one of Grace's favorite keepsakes and a constant reminder of Mom's loving guidance through her rebellious years.

As a scientist, Mom had gone through a long thinking process on her faith journey. Her words echoed even now. "For years, I struggled with the debate between creation and evolution. In the end, God's irresistible grace fell on me, and the debate no longer bothers me. You can always ask God about anything. If you have a sincere attitude, He'll answer and guide you."

Mom, I miss you so much.

Her pent-up emotions—disappointment over not seeing Papa's pictures, dread over the unfamiliar environment, fear over the unknown, and sadness over being left alone in this terrifying world—broke free. She covered her face with both hands and gulped down soft sobs.

The clock struck ten.

She jerked up her head and wiped her face with a hand. Time to call it a day. Tomorrow, she'd face a new beginning, no matter what.

Wait. She forgot to call Nana Wang. At least she still had her beloved friend who loved her as if she were her granddaughter.

With a glance at the clock again, Grace frowned. Nana Wang must have already left for her Saturday morning Bible study group. Well, she'd call tomorrow.

Chapter Four

The sounds began as a low rumble and grew more intense until they erupted into a deafening explosion. The earth shook as lava poured down the side of the mountain, lighting up the night sky....

Grace opened her eyes. All was tranquil.

Did the noises occur in her dreams? Where was she?

Sunrays penetrated the mint-green curtains and shone on her face. She sat up and checked the clock. Six twenty.

Right. She was inside Mr. Lam's guest bedroom in Hong Kong.

For the first time since Mom's death, she'd slept for a few hours with no disturbance.

After freshening up, she took out her Bible for her daily devotion time. No Bible No Breakfast. Since high school, she'd followed Mom's example and practiced No B No B every day.

She finished her prayers as the clock struck seven.

Kevin told her breakfast and lunch were buffet-style in the dining room. Yesterday, she didn't go because of her nap.

Should she go now? Maybe not. Five in the afternoon in Chicago. Perfect time for a call.

She sat at the antique ebony table and dialed the familiar number. "Nana Wang, it's me."

"Hey, girl." Her beloved friend's merry tone rang in her ear. "I've been waiting for your call since you left. How's everything?"

"Very well. I arrived with no delay. After I delivered Mom's letter to Mr. Lam, he offered me a position in his company. I'll start my job on June eighth." Grace stood up and leaned against the wall. "A hectic day yesterday. I went into town to run errands and rushed back to have dinner with Mr. Lam. Then he wanted to talk to me.

By the time I finished my meeting with him, I figured you'd gone to church. So, I didn't call you until now."

Her dear friend asked her more about her flight, her new surroundings, and her meetings with Mr. Lam.

She inhaled and exhaled to relax her body. Yeah, she'd omitted some details. No point in talking about her emotional state lest she worry Nana Wang. Still, she couldn't help releasing a heavy breath. Her audible sigh must have given her away.

"Are you all right?" Nana Wang asked. "Did Mr. Lam treat you well? I didn't support your mother's idea of sending you all the way to Hong Kong, but she insisted."

A rustle came through the phone. What was her friend doing?

"Mr. Lam is very kind. He not only offered me a job but also free room and board in his mansion. I feel the presence of the Lord all the time." Her spirit perked up as a renewed sense of hopeful determination crept in. Perhaps that was why Mom wanted her to come—to experience God's guidance in a strange land.

"That's incredibly generous."

Grace chuckled. "You must come to visit me here. This place is beyond anything I've ever seen." Gushing now, she went to great lengths to share her impression of the house and its amenities.

"That's great."

But something muffled Nana Wang's voice. Was she crying? Grace sprang to her feet as if she could rush to her friend's side. "Are you well?" She paced the length of the phone cord. "Did you just choke up?"

"I'm fine. I'm relieved to hear it worked out well. I admit I had doubts about whether Mr. Lam would see you. After all, your mom hadn't been in touch with him for years."

"He mentioned many things I didn't know about Mom. Why didn't she ever mention Mr. Lam until she asked me to deliver her letter?" Curling the phone cord around her finger, Grace returned to her seat. "From the way he talked, he and Mom knew each other well. He even kept a picture of them in his wallet."

"Did he?" Another swish reached her ears.

Was Nana Wang dabbing her eyes with tissue paper? Grace palmed her forehead. "Did you know they became friends while attending a boarding high school in the Bay Area?"

The other end kept quiet. At last, Nana Wang spoke. "It's almost time for me to go. I'm meeting someone from church for dinner tonight. I'd better get ready. Let's talk later."

The line dropped.

Okay. Grace got it. Nana Wang knew something about Mom's relationship with Mr. Lam but didn't want to talk about it.

Someone tapped on the door.

"Who is it?" Grace stowed her Bible in the table's drawer and changed out of her pajamas.

The knock persisted, followed by Kevin's voice. "It's me."

She pulled the door open. "You're early. Have you had breakfast?"

Kevin checked his watch. "Seven forty-nine. I forgot to tell you. My friend, Danny, wants to have dim sum with us before church."

"Dim sum in the morning?" She threw a questioning glance at him. "Is the restaurant open?"

He nudged his glasses up, their shadow falling on his high cheekbones. His eyes glowed behind them. "In Hong Kong, some dim sum restaurants open at five in the morning for people who need to go to work early."

"Indeed? I had no idea." His bright smile coaxed her to crinkle her lips. "We have dim sum restaurants in Chicago's Chinatown. They usually won't open until eleven."

Her new friend looked her up and down. "You're all dressed up. The green dress fits you well."

"Aren't we going to church? Since childhood, my mom insisted on dressing me up for Sunday worship." She grabbed her purse. "Okay. Let's go."

The moment they reached the waiting area, Bus 56A came by. Twenty minutes later, they got off, and Kevin guided her into a crowded restaurant.

How was it possible to find an empty table?

"Ah, Danny is over there. He must have come super early to secure a spot." Kevin rushed over and spoke against the excessive noise from diners and clattering plates. "This is Grace. She's interested in going to your church."

Danny stood to pull out a chair for her. The tall young man drew his long, thick brows tight, his soulful midnight-black eyes adding a trace of mystery to his melancholy expression. Why did the guy look so sad?

"I heard you're staying in the same mansion as Kevin." Danny's baritone vibrated, his Mandarin laced with a distinct Peking accent. "Lucky you. Do you know where I lived when I first arrived in Hong Kong?"

Was he from Beijing? She shook her head and remained quiet.

"I could only afford a cot that offered barely enough space for me to lie down. The sole separation between my bunk and the next was a pile of old newspapers."

Kevin poured tea for her and Danny. "Now you own your studio. Unlike me. I'm still a hermit crab—without my shell."

She couldn't help laughing. The more familiar she became with Kevin, the better she enjoyed his company. Yesterday, he'd told her about his childhood. Even growing up in different countries, they shared similar experiences—both felt like misfits among their peers. And he liked her. She was sure of it. Yet, how could she think about dating and courtship? He wasn't a Christian, and her goal, God willing, was to get back to the US next year. Since Mom's death, she'd vowed to tend to Nana Wang's needs in her old age. She would take her shopping and help with household chores and doctor appointments. That was the least she could do to repay her beloved friend for all the love and support she'd shown Mom and her over the years.

Unease creeping in, she sipped her tea, letting the warm liquid soothe the chill creeping into her chest.

The server came by with a cart, and Kevin ordered in Cantonese for them.

Grace raised her chopsticks with no delay and devoured a BBQ pork bun, two shrimp dumplings, and a spoonful of tripe steamed with ginger and green onion. With a satisfied sigh, she leaned back in her chair. "Wow. Much better than what I was used to eating in Chicago."

Kevin gaped at her, his shiny dark eyes wide behind his glasses. "You ate as if you came from a famine. So, besides seafood and lamb, you also like dim sum?"

Heat flushed her face. She even forgot to pray before the meal. As Mom had told her before, one of these days her craving for

Chinese food would cause her downfall. "Sorry. I *love, love, love* dim sum. But I should have waited for us to start together."

A smile broke Danny's somber expression. "No worries. Let's order more."

While the three of them finished a few more dishes, Grace shared about her job offer from Mr. Lam. Afterward, Danny braced his elbows on the table. "Kevin..." He dragged his friend's name out, his tone serious. "Is your dad still bugging you to find a regular job?"

Kevin dipped his chin. "Almost every day."

"We have an opening. Are you interested?"

"I–I—" Kevin's jaw slackened. "I don't think I can handle it."

What kind of job was that? She nudged her plate aside and scooted to the edge of her chair. "Danny, what do you do for a living?"

"I'm an embalmer." He chewed on a pork bun, avoiding eye contact. "Do you know anything about what embalmers do?"

She brought a palm to her mouth as moisture blurred her vision.

"Are you okay?" The two men asked in unison, their Cantonese and Mandarin blending.

"I just thought of my mother. She passed away a month ago." She swallowed hard. "The embalmer did an excellent job. She looked so peaceful, like in a deep sleep."

Kevin patted her arm. "I'm sorry."

Danny muttered under his breath. "The longer I work as an embalmer, the more I see through life and death."

"'Life and death are one thread, the same line viewed from different sides.'" Kevin squinted.

Was that a poem? Somehow, his mellow chant, like a balm, brought comfort to her heart. Grace regained her composure. "That sounds poetic. Who said it?"

"You never heard of it?" He raised a brow, its dark arc sliding up beneath his long bangs. "It's one of Lao Zi's most famous sayings."

"Who's Lao Zi?" She had to speak louder as those at a nearby table argued.

"I forgot you grew up in the US. Your Chinese is good, but not to the level of understanding our forefathers' philosophy." He tugged on an ear. "Lao Zi was considered the founder of philosophical and religious Taoism. He lived about three thousand years ago."

"Right. Mom often said I had a lot to learn about Chinese culture." She turned her head sideways and changed the subject. "Danny, do you speak Cantonese? Is it very different from Mandarin?"

"Just as Chinese is distinct from Japanese." Danny's voice wobbled. "It's a difficult dialect to master. Since my arrival, I've been attending our church's Cantonese class. I still can't converse freely with the locals. My job doesn't require me to talk much."

Kevin laughed. "Isn't it odd that we Chinese don't understand each other's speech? But we can when we jot the words down."

Yeah. How come she hadn't thought about that? "Do you know why?"

His face scrunched. "The fault of our first emperor, Qin Shihuang. He unified the written language. Unfortunately, he couldn't go to each home to force everyone to speak Mandarin."

"True." Danny tapped his teacup. "Kevin, seriously, have you thought about what you want from life? If you didn't have to worry about money, what would you like to do?"

"I want to become a full-time writer." Articulating his idea, Kevin waved both hands.

Caught up in his excitement, Grace sat up straighter. "What story do you have in mind?"

"I've written lots of short stories, none of them published yet." He winked at Danny. "My first full-length book will be about you and your friends."

What sort of experiences had Danny gone through? He looked like any other ordinary young guy, except for his melancholy expression.

The three obnoxious guests to their right took leave, and the place quieted down.

Danny scowled. "Kevin, don't daydream. Nobody will be interested."

"Now you've got me curious." She set down her chopsticks to sip tea, and its tangy steam swirled around her face. "Besides being an embalmer, what else have you done?"

Kevin gripped his friend's shoulder, his voice soft. "Should I tell her?"

A shudder shook Danny before he inclined his head.

Thumping the table, Kevin drew a deep breath as if filling up with courage. "No doubt, you've heard about the Tiananmen Square Massacre in 1989. Danny's two best friends died in that incident, and he came to Hong Kong afterward."

"Whoa." She couldn't stifle a small cry. How horrid. In her home church, one woman's husband also died on that fateful day. "Were you there on June Fourth?"

"My friends and I—" Eyes closed, Danny rubbed his forehead, the action brushing his thick brows out of line. "We love our motherland and would do anything for her. It wasn't our intention to overthrow the government. We just wanted more reforms and a better future for all of us. But..."

Moisture gleamed in his deep-set eyes.

A waiter came to clean up the vacated table as the hostess led a group of four individuals over.

"It's okay." Kevin patted Danny's back. "If you aren't ready to talk about it, don't force yourself."

"Sorry." Danny grabbed a napkin to wipe his face.

"Well, doesn't your worship service start at ten?" Kevin twisted his watch into view. "It's almost nine thirty."

With his lips downturned, Danny remained seated and drew his brows tight. A glazed expression left his eyes shiny.

Kevin was right. Time to go. She clattered her teacup back to the rosewood-like table and pushed back her chair. "Where is the church?"

At last, Danny lifted his gaze. "It's right here in Causeway Bay. Kevin, are you coming with us?"

Kevin's headshake swayed his long hair. "Are you joking? Of course not. I'm an atheist."

Was he? Grace placed a palm on her heart, capturing the burden for his soul as it pulsed there. "Why are you an atheist?"

"Because I don't believe God exists." He waved in the air around them, then upward before pointing at Danny and her. "You—show me where God is, and I'll believe."

Such a typical response. Her heated debates with Mom about the Bible weren't in vain. Her heartbeat thudded beneath her hand, picking up speed. "If God doesn't exist, then why has a whole ethnic group of people for generations claimed to be God's chosen people?

The descendants of the Jews who compiled the Old Testament are still with us today."

"Interesting. I never pondered the God stuff from that angle." Kevin narrowed his eyes. "It isn't convincing enough."

"What would convince you?"

"I don't know." He shrugged. "Maybe a personal experience of God."

Ha, a stubborn soul. *Lord, please grant me patience and understanding.* "From my faith journey, I can tell you God exists and works in my life."

As Kevin remained mute, Danny stood up. "We'd better go now. The church is just around the corner, but we should arrive early to prepare our hearts for worship."

Kevin took his leave in silence.

While she and Danny navigated the busy street, her curiosity wriggled free. "Why did you become an embalmer? Do you like your job?"

A group of teenagers approached, laughing and yelling in Cantonese. Danny pulled her into a convenience store by the road. Inside, the smell of freshly brewed coffee swirled in the air, and a soft hum of refrigerators and freezers provided a calming background noise. "It was the highest-paying job I could find at that time. In the beginning, I hated it. Every time I prepared a body for burial, I became nauseous and would vomit afterward. Later, I learned to appreciate my job. People often thank me for making their loved ones appear like in a peaceful sleep. I now take pride in the work I do."

"Yes, it's important work." Her eyes misted up. She shaded her eyes to hide her unbridled emotions. "I also felt comforted when I saw Mom in the casket. Her serene appearance reaffirmed we would meet again as Mom mentioned in her last note to me."

They resumed their steps and soon entered the church's modest sanctuary. Danny guided her toward a pew, and she sang along with the worship team before the pastor—Pastor Hong—cited Romans 3:23–24 and preached about sin and redemption by Christ.

After the benediction, when she rose to leave, she spun on her heels and rushed to Kevin in the last row. "I thought you'd left us."

He palmed the back of his neck. "I remembered I promised Mr. Lam to take you to a pleasant restaurant for lunch."

Lunch? What about their recent dim sum brunch? "I'm not hungry." She brushed stray curls away from her face. "What did you think about today's sermon?"

"Not very good." He started walking. "The pastor didn't know what he was talking about. I'm not a sinner. I've never stolen, robbed, or done anything really bad."

Sidestepping a mother with a toddler, she leaned toward him and switched to English. "I think you're confusing sin with crime."

Kevin bypassed Danny to walk alongside her as the three of them strolled toward the exit. "Humor me with your explanation."

A woman in her late thirties approached. "Danny, are you leaving? Ah, are these new friends? Please introduce them to me."

"They're my friends, Grace Feng and Kevin Cheung." Danny waved. "Ms. Zhou is a nurse. She's been here for a long while."

"Call me Angela." A cheerful smile crinkled up the sides of Ms. Zhou's kind eyes. "Nice to have you here today. Hope you'll come again next week."

Such an amiable sister in Christ. Warmth flooded Grace's heart. "I shall indeed. This place..." She touched the nearby pew at the back of the midsize church, her hand lingering as if on an old friend's shoulder. "It feels so homey and welcoming."

"Good." Angela beamed, her sisterly affection encompassing Grace as she patted her hand before leaving.

Danny led the way out of the door. Outside, the midday summer sun reflected off the uneven cement walkway into the massive crowds.

Kevin tilted his head sideways. "Grace, you still owe me an explanation."

She retrieved her white sunglasses from her purse and put them on, letting the dark shades shield her unease. *Lord, please give me wisdom.* "In English, sin and crime are two distinct words, but we Chinese have only one word for the two divergent concepts. That's why most folks mix them up."

Kevin wagged a finger at her. "You've confused me even more. Explain yourself."

She sucked in a quick breath. "Sin is not honoring God, not doing things according to His will. Crime is doing something against the law."

"Well said." Danny scratched his forehead, then smoothed his askew eyebrows into line. "I've been attending church for a while. Every time the pastor talks about sin, I feel offended. Like Kevin, I consider myself a decent person."

"I'm still not convinced." Kevin crossed his arms over his chest and tilted his face toward the blue sky. "I don't believe in God's existence. act in line with my conscience, so I should be fine."

Lord, what to say next? Letting them stride ahead of her, she touched her throat to ease the tightness lodged there. Her fingertips brushed the cross at her neck, and the familiar metal bolstered her. "Our consciences can misguide us."

Danny grasped Kevin's arm. "Now that I think of it. Didn't the news report a murder case last week? The taxi driver who killed a prostitute said he was just following his conscience to remove a parasite from our society."

"We're way off track in our discussion." Kevin freed himself from Danny. "If you guys aren't hungry, should we go shopping? Grace, I don't believe you've been to the Ladies' Market, have you?"

"The Ladies' Market?" She skipped a step, scooting closer to the guys. "What's that?"

Danny grinned. "You ought to go. It's a sight to behold."

Okay. For sure, she could find another time to speak with Kevin more about God and the Bible since they lived under the same roof. Releasing her grip on the cross, she twitched her fingers around her purse strap. "Let's go."

Chapter Five

Sleep eluded Grace again last night. Was it the jet lag or something else? Yesterday when she returned to her room, an ornate porcelain vase, likely an antique, holding an enormous bouquet of yellow roses welcomed her. She'd searched unsuccessfully for a note to indicate the reason for the gift.

Who'd sent it?

Yellow roses were Mom's favorite, but Grace preferred drought-resistant plants. Unlike flowers, they didn't wilt easily. She smiled as her mom's words and laughter echoed in her mind. "My dear Gracie, you're such a practical and rational girl."

After her morning devotion, she pushed open the French doors at the end of the long hallway and walked down the steps. Flowering shrubs surrounded the spacious courtyard. On the path lined with a rainbow of blooming plants stood a solitary figure—Mr. Lam.

He raised his head toward her. For a moment, he seemed frozen, but his twinkling eyes betrayed him.

Dirt on my face? She wiped her cheeks with the back of her hand. Did she forget to wash it this morning?

Mr. Lam trudged forward and reached out to touch her hair. Then, in slow motion, he brushed a loose curl away from her temple.

Bewildered, she took a step back. "Mr. Lam..."

He placed a finger on his lips, and his gaze never wandered from her.

Unease creeping up, she swallowed hard and edged back another step. Yet, his eyes appeared so sad and fatherly, she couldn't fear he had indecent intentions. "Are you all right?"

He dropped his hand and slid it into a pocket. "You look so much like your mother." Speaking in a low voice, he continued to survey her. "You're not only beautiful but also smart, aren't you? Susan did an excellent job raising such a daughter. She must have been proud of you."

His soft tone cast a hypnotic effect. What kind of man was he? So handsome and masculine, yet so gentle.

A new tenderness, such as she'd never felt toward anyone except her mother, loosened her tensed muscles. Meanwhile, a calm voice emerged in her mind. *Flee the evil desires of youth, and pursue righteousness, faith, love, and peace.*

She blurted out, "Second Timothy two twenty-two."

"What did you say?" He frowned, his warmth vanishing. "Do you often talk such nonsense?"

"I'm sorry." She touched her forehead, thankful the awkward moment passed. *Lord, thank You for the reminder of the Holy Spirit.*

"Do you have a few minutes?" He gestured toward the garden bench nearby. "Tell me more about your mother. What did she do to support you?"

She took the seat next to him where the fragrance from the surrounding shrubs overpowered his woody and spicy scent. "Mom worked for a pharmaceutical company a few miles away from our house. She was a chemist."

"She majored in chemistry at Stanford." Mr. Lam nodded. "Was she a technician in the lab?"

Her chest swelled, pride buoying her. "My mom received a PhD from the University of Illinois. She worked as a principal scientist and supervised a group of technicians."

His eyes opened wide. "Indeed? How did she manage to earn a PhD while taking care of you?"

She stilled. "Do you know Nana Wang?"

"Who?"

So, he knew nothing about Mom's life after she moved to Illinois. "Nana Wang is a doctor in our church. She's single and retired early because of health issues. Before my mom found her job at the pharmaceutical company, we lived with Nana Wang. Even after we got our place, she took care of me when Mom was busy."

She hugged her arms around herself, aching for her childhood home—Nana Wang's house. Nana Wang loved gardening. During the Midwest's brief summer, Grace helped her beloved friend fill the spacious backyard vegetable patch with tomatoes, cucumbers, and squashes. In the front yard, they planted various peonies. Every spring, the flowers popped up and scented the air.

"Why didn't your mother remarry?"

As his unexpected question interrupted her reverie, she shrugged. "Some uncles from church came to visit from time to time, but Mom never went out with any of them."

He sank into quietness.

What other questions did he have in mind? Fidgety, she checked her watch. "Kevin told me to meet him in the dining room for breakfast at eight. If you don't need me anymore, may I be excused?"

He waved and remained in his sitting position, like a stone statue.

As she ambled back into the hallway, Kevin leaned against the wall. "I saw Mr. Lam touch you."

She scrunched her nose. "What are you talking about?"

"When you met him on the walkway before you two sat down, didn't he cup your face with his palm like this?" He moved to her side and stretched out his hand toward her face.

"You're yakking nonsense." She brushed away his arm, a hot annoyance simmering. "He didn't do anything improper. Even if he did, what has it to do with you? It's none of your business."

"Grace." His voice was lower than usual. "I care about you. I don't want to see you get hurt."

She lifted her chin, the annoyed heat flushing through her body. "Didn't we meet only three days ago? What made you so concerned about my welfare?"

"I–I—" His shoulders slumped. He spun and dashed away.

She winced at his back.

Lord, forgive me.

Why had she gotten so angry? He was just trying to be kind.

She unlocked her room, a knot in her stomach. With today's run-in, how could she expect Kevin to listen to her testimony about Jesus? She liked him a lot, but his behavior toward her was...

Should she go to breakfast? Originally, Kevin planned to take her hiking on Lantau Island today. Would he cancel the trip?

She'd better call Nana Wang.

On the first ring, her beloved friend answered. "Hi, girl, how was Sunday?"

The gentleness in her tone brought comfort to Grace's heart, and her shoulders loosened. "Interesting." She described her new friends, Kevin and Danny, as well as the midsize church. "I plan to go again this week."

"I'm glad you found a church so soon." Nana Wang laughed. "On our spiritual journey in this world, it's necessary to get together with brothers and sisters."

"Yeah, very true." Grace's mind circled back to her conversation with Mr. Lam. "Do you know Mr. Lam personally?"

"Why do you ask?"

She flipped through her Bible on the table. "I had a chat with him this morning. He said he didn't know you. It surprised me. He seems ignorant of anything about Mom beyond her days in California. I wonder why."

The other end lapsed into silence.

"Are you still there?"

"I am." A whoosh whispered through the receiver. Did Nana Wang sigh? "I've never met Mr. Lam. Everything I know about him was from your mother."

So, Mom had told Nana Wang about her past with Mr. Lam. "Why didn't Mom tell me about him before?"

"Your mother must have had her reasons."

What sort of reasons? Grace palmed her forehead. "Were they close?"

"They grew up together when both were in boarding school." Another rustle came over the line. "Well, I'm hungry and need to cook my dinner. Next time, let me call you."

Like yesterday, Nana Wang tried to dodge her questions. Grace clutched the receiver tighter. One way or the other, she'd ferret out the facts. "Okay. Talk to you later."

After hanging up, she changed into her swimsuit and strolled to the pool. Right. She'd skip breakfast to avoid facing Kevin.

***

Kevin charged into the dining room, his shoulders growing tighter by the minute.

Why did he act like a fool? As Grace pointed out, he'd known her for only three days. Yet, somehow, she'd filled the hollowness in his heart since Wendy's death.

As usual, eggs, yogurt with fruit, and cottage cheese together with Chinese dishes including congee, pork buns, and stir-fried vegetables burdened the enormous irregular-shaped rosewood table.

A pleasant aroma swirled around the spacious room, yet he held his plate and stood still. Food no longer stimulated his appetite.

"Are you well?" Dad reached for another piece of toast. "You don't look good."

Kevin plopped into the seat next to Dad. "Do you believe in love at first sight?"

Dad jerked his head up, a grin crinkling his still-youthful face. "Are you dating? When can I meet her?"

Whoops. Dad was so eager for him to settle down. Kevin swallowed hard. "No, not yet. I like a girl but haven't mustered up the nerve to ask her out."

"Why don't you take action?" Dad's smile vanished, and his brows contracted. "Are you worried she'll say no because you don't have a regular job? That's why I urged you..."

Couldn't Dad treat him like an adult and have a man-to-man conversation? "Please, just listen to me, for once."

Dad stopped spreading butter on his toast. "Okay. Tell me."

"I've never asked you this before." Kevin huffed to loosen the tightness in his chest. "After Mom died, why didn't you remarry?"

"Because—" Dad dropped the toast back onto his plate. "Who would marry a poor widower with a toddler?"

Life wasn't fair.

Even the dining table in front of him served as a reminder that Dad and Mr. Lam belonged to different worlds. The tabloids reported that Dad's boss was a friend of the famous Japanese-American architect and furniture maker, George Katsutoshi Nakashima, who handpicked the wood to craft the piece for his buddy. Money not only bought Mr. Lam the rosewood table but also turned him into Hong Kong's most eligible bachelor.

Did all women act alike and want only handsome, well-built, and superwealthy men? Although tall and good-looking, Dad wasn't rich. "How about love? Is it possible for someone to, ugh, love you as who you are regardless of what you have?"

Dad touched his temple. "I haven't met such a person since your mother passed away."

"Do all relationships harbor a hidden agenda?" Kevin muttered under his breath, tasting bitterness in his mouth. "Does true love exist in this world?"

"Your mom and I loved each other when we owned nothing."

Yeah, both Dad and Mom came from blue-collar families. Yet, Dad managed to obtain a scholarship to study in Australia.

"So, maybe I shouldn't find a regular job." Kevin made a face with a cross between a smile and a frown to tease Dad. "A girl who is willing to accept me now must love me for who I am."

"If such a girl exists." Dad pressed his lips tight.

Was Grace that girl? Could he make her fall in love with him? "Do you think that's why Mr. Lam never considers remarriage? He's associated with so many beautiful women. Are they all more interested in his money than him as a person?"

"In his situation and with his intelligence, it'd be tough for him to find true love." Dad hitched a breath. "I often wonder if he, like everyone else, is still searching for that special someone who loves him as he is."

Dad couldn't be referring to Grace, right? Why did Kevin's mind circle back to her? Still, he had to ask. "Do you think Mr. Lam is interested in Grace? Is that why he offered her free room and board here?"

Dad gave him a stern glance. "It's none of our business. Just be careful when you show Grace around town."

"Now that you've reminded me, I promised to take her to Lantau Island today." He took several pork buns and nestled them in a carryout box. "I'll go check on her."

Grace might still be furious with him. Instead of going straight to her room, he strolled to the outside lounge by the pool, plopped onto the plush sofa, and took out a pork bun. As he munched it down, the flavors and spices danced on his taste buds, and the tranquil moment calmed his edginess.

A splashing disturbed the peace. In the pool, Grace's lithe body sliced through the water, emerged for an instant, then sank back in with her smooth strokes.

The stillness returned and continued.

Why didn't she come up?

A horrific idea crawled into his head. He flung away the carryout box, rushed to the poolside, and fixated on the still, clear water. The sunlight reflected a distorted figure in his sight. Grace's palms appeared to press against the bottom of the pool, her hair floating around her.

Kevin pushed his feet off the edge and jumped in. His glasses flew away in the cold water. Still, his clothes, shoes, and leather belt hindered his movement.

Stay calm.

He kicked his legs hard to propel his body toward his target. Then he seized Grace and threw an arm across her shoulder. With her weight hung upon him, he swam back to the poolside.

Once he hoisted her onto the dry land, he placed her on her back, pressed the heel of one hand on the center of her chest, and pushed down with the other hand.

Fear gripped him. Memories—how he watched lifeguards searching the ocean for Wendy on that fateful summer day—intruded.

Please. Don't die.

He took a deep breath and forced himself to concentrate. Following the chest compressions, he lifted her chin, pinched her nostrils shut, and covered her mouth with his to provide two rescue breaths.

After thirty additional chest compressions, her body stirred. She opened her eyes, wheezed, and spluttered water.

"Kevin?" She sat up, her body heaving and shuddering as she coughed. "You saved my life."

He wrapped the towel around her with trembling hands, then slumped back onto the hard tiles, his legs giving him away. "What happened? One moment, you were swimming. The next, you sank."

"I should have warmed up before jumping in." She massaged the muscle below her left knee. "I had a terrible cramp here. That never happened before."

"Grace, you ought to be more careful." He pushed himself up, and seeing the carryout box, he reached for it. "Are you hungry? I brought you a few pork buns."

After he handed her the box, she opened it and stared at the four squished, deformed buns. He stretched out his hand to take it back. "I flung the box away too hard. They're no good."

"No. I like them." She tore a small piece off a bun and stuck it in her mouth. As she chewed, her eyes turned misty.

Now, what was wrong with her? Perhaps the near-death experience had shocked her. "Are you okay?"

"I'm fine." She set the box aside, sniffling. "The buns reminded me of my mom. Whenever she went to dim sum with a friend, she'd bring back these for me. She knew I enjoyed them."

"Oh, Grace." Tender feelings flooded him. He moved to her side and hugged her.

"Why is life so fragile?" She leaned against his wet shirt. "My mom passed away. A moment ago, I almost drowned."

He held her close, feeling the warmth of her body against his. Desire pulsed through his veins, and the discomfort against the damp fabric of his shorts brought heat to his face.

Uh-oh.

A gentleman should never take advantage of an emotionally vulnerable girl. Resisting the temptation to kiss away her tears, he gave her back a gentle pat.

A clatter of familiar footsteps rose behind them. "Kevin and Grace, what are you two doing here?"

"Mr. Lam!" She jerked away from him. "I developed a muscle cramp and almost drowned. Kevin saved me."

"Are you all right now?" Mr. Lam stooped to examine her.

She nodded.

"Well, I'm glad Kevin is by your side. Kevin, take care of Grace for me, will you?" He glanced at his watch. "I'd better get going. I'm meeting a client at the office today."

What did Mr. Lam mean? Didn't he want Grace for himself? Kevin watched him stroll away, the questions roiling him.

After Mr. Lam was out of sight, Grace's almond-shaped eyes blinked up at him, all dewy. Water droplets still slipped down her delicate face—or were those tears? "Thank you again for your help. Sorry, I got angry with you earlier."

The trust in her expression caused his heart to tumble over, like a stone falling off a cliff. He rubbed his temples, and words toppled out before he could stop them. "So, did Mr. Lam touch you this morning?"

Grace squinted. "He brushed away a loose hair from my face like a father. That was all."

His spirit perked up. As an old friend of her mom, Mr. Lam treated Grace like his daughter. So, Dad had misjudged, and his warning was groundless. "Do you feel well enough for a hike on Lantau Island?"

"Maybe not right now. I should be fine after an hour or so." She stood and wrapped the towel tighter around her waist, her shadow falling across his feet. "Tell me what's so exciting about Lantau?"

"There's a temple called Po Lin Monastery. You're in luck. Last year, they completed the Big Buddha, a colossal bronze statue. It has become a popular tourist attraction." Oh no. He kneaded his brows against an unfortunate thought. As a Christian, she might not be interested in seeing the Big Buddha.

She dropped back into her seat and patted his hand. "Are you thinking Christians can't visit Buddhist temples?"

Her touch sent a tingling sensation up his arm. He stretched his eyes wide. "You read my mind."

She grinned. "The Bible has this teaching, 'Everything is permissible, but not everything is beneficial. Everything is permissible, but not everything is constructive.' Christians are free to do many things, as long as we maintain God's sovereignty in our lives."

What did she mean? He combed his wet hair with his fingers. "Aren't religions all the same? Lots of rules and regulations."

"True Christianity isn't a set of rules and regulations." She paused as if searching for the proper words. "Church traditions can become legalism or even an idol. As a Christian, the key is to establish a genuine relationship with God."

A relationship with God? What if God didn't exist? "This is news to me."

"I understand." She heaved out a breath. "Will you be interested in attending church with me again this Sunday?"

"Today is only Monday. I'll let you know when the time comes." He shot to his feet. Religious talks made him jittery. "Are you sure you still want to go hiking? We'll need to take a bus and catch a ferry to reach Lantau Island...."

Before he finished speaking, Grace pointed at him. "What happened to your glasses?"

He'd forgotten about them. "Must be still in the water."

"Let me go get them for you." She edged toward the pool.

"Don't worry about it. I'll ask the gardener to fish them out for me. I also have a spare pair." Resisting the urge to grasp her arm, he led the way toward the house. "Is an hour enough for you? Let's meet back here."

Chapter Six

Kevin sat on Bus 56A and peeked at the lovely girl next to him from time to time. Since the pool incident, they seemed to have developed a new connection.

During their hike—just the two of them—on Lantau Island yesterday, he'd needed every ounce of his willpower not to wrap his arms around her narrow waist. Such a stupid move might jeopardize their relationship. Still, he couldn't help but ask her whether she had a boyfriend. Joy had diffused throughout his whole person when she'd answered no without hesitation.

Today, she'd invited Danny to join their outing to Cheung Chau Island. Why did she do that? Didn't she enjoy going out alone with him?

After they exited the bus, he guided Grace into Central Ferry Pier 5. "Did Danny tell you he'd buy the ferry tickets for us?"

"Yes." She put on her sunglasses. "The summer sun is quite bothersome."

The morning wind ruffled her hair. Kevin stretched out a hand, then dropped it. To suppress a powerful urge to tuck her curls behind her ear, he wrapped his fingers around his backpack strap. "Today is Tuesday. Doesn't Danny have to work?"

"He worked overtime last weekend, and the boss gave him comp time." She glided onto her tiptoes. "There he is."

"Hi, Grace. That teal T-shirt matches your jeans so well." A broad smile eclipsed Danny's usual melancholy expression. "Hi, Kevin."

Was his friend interested in Grace as well? Must be. Otherwise, why would Danny call her last night, not him? They'd known each other for years, while Danny had just met Grace a few days ago.

Kevin tapped his khaki shorts, unease tingling at the back of his neck. Going after the same girl with a friend wasn't an appealing idea. Maybe Grace preferred him. After all, they lived under the same roof.

The PA system announced their ferry number, pushing his last question aside.

They took their seats in uncomfortable plastic chairs, he and Danny flanking Grace.

She slid her sunglasses into her backpack and tucked it between her feet, her hair slithering over one shoulder before she shook it back. "Kevin, you were telling me something on the bus about Mr. Lam's business. How did he make his fortune?"

Why did stories about Mr. Lam engross Grace? Did she, like all the other women, find him attractive? A tremor ran through Kevin's lips, but he steadied them to speak. "Everything I know about him is from the tabloids. Not sure how accurate the information is."

"No problem." She patted his arm. "I'm just curious."

A prickle shot through his body. He adjusted his glasses to calm down. "Have you heard about the Hong Kong riots in the spring of 1966?"

Loose curls danced across her cheeks with her quick headshake. She brushed them away from her face.

"Well, it's a complicated story. The outcome was unequivocal, though. Many people emigrated out of Hong Kong and the housing prices plummeted." Kevin's chest tightened. His friend appeared listening, yet his gaze kept flashing toward Grace. What a clear sign. Danny was after her.

Grace's well-shaped eyebrows creased. "Yeah? What does that have to do with Mr. Lam?"

Kevin leaned forward, contending with a flutter in his stomach. "Mr. Lam's father worked in construction. The tabloids said he was already quite well-to-do. He sought the opportunity and racked up dozens of distressed buildings all over Hong Kong and Kowloon."

"So, Mr. Lam inherited his father's fortune and lives off the wealth?" Incredulity flashed across Grace's face. "What a waste of his talents."

"You jumped to your conclusion too soon because you don't know Hong Kong well enough." Danny chuckled, pushing into the conversation. "Samuel Lam is the most respected architect here. Almost all the tall buildings you see bear his touch."

Her jaw dropped. "I had no idea."

"Mr. Lam graduated from Stanford with a degree in Architectural Design." Danny inclined his head. "The tabloids even said that, instead of five years, he graduated in four."

"I've heard all architects draw well." She fidgeted in her seat. "Mr. Lam must be an excellent painter."

Why did Danny take over? Kevin swallowed his rising annoyance. "Now that you've mentioned it. My dad once saw a woman's half-finished portrait in Mr. Lam's bedroom. He said Mr. Lam painted it."

Dad had also commented that the subject looked very much like Lily Ching. At the time, Kevin brushed it off since it was natural for the big boss to paint someone he was dating. Could it be... No, that was absurd, impossible.

The ferry docked. Everyone streamed toward the exit.

"Watch out." Danny held out a hand for Grace. "The gangway is a bit unstable."

"Thank you very much." She grasped his arm.

The waves crashed along the rocks lining the shore. Kevin followed them and pressed his lips tight. Why hadn't he thought of helping Grace? Later today, when they went fishing on the charter boat, he'd make sure to give her his hand.

Once on solid ground, she moved away from Danny and came to walk by him. "What's wrong? You look unhappy."

"Nothing." Kevin gestured to a vendor selling shells. "Have you ever listened to a shell?"

She cocked her head, giving him a questioning glance.

He hurried to purchase a shell as large as his fist. "For you. Hold it up to your ear. Tell me what you hear."

She obliged. "So far, nothing." She squinted as if in deep concentration. "I still can't hear anything."

"You're so unromantic." Danny laughed. "Didn't you hear Kevin whisper your name?"

Kevin gave Danny a stern glance. *Why did he joke at my expense?*

"No, just silence." She handed the shell back, her innocent expression adorable. "I suppose my mom was right. I'm too practical."

"Well, our appointment with the charter boat is still two hours away." Kevin stifled a groan but couldn't suppress his irritation. "Are you interested in visiting a natural cave where the famous Guangdong pirate Cheung Po Tsai was said to keep his treasures?"

"Pirate? Sounds intriguing. Let's go." She put on her sunglasses again.

"That's the spirit." Danny clapped Kevin on the back. "I like the idea."

The cave held nothing inside, but an enormous rock stood nearby. They sat together on the boulder as waves crawled to the shore. From his bag, Kevin retrieved the pork buns he'd saved from breakfast.

Grace chewed on one side of a bun. "So tranquil here. Nice place."

Danny directed his gaze toward the horizon. "The sea can be tempestuous and unpredictable."

"It sounds like you've experienced rough seas before." She turned the bun around and nibbled the other side.

Warmth swirled inside Kevin's heart. She was like a little girl, saving the best till the last minute.

Danny lowered his chin. "I have."

"Tell us." Grace devoured the rest of the bun, her voice muffled. "What happened?"

Kevin clenched his teeth, a sourness flooding his mouth despite the pork bun's savory taste. Danny hadn't shared much of his past. With Grace, would he talk? No matter what, Kevin wanted to expand his knowledge of the Tiananmen Square Massacre. Nothing would stop him from someday penning a book on the subject.

Danny lifted his head toward the blue sky. "After the incident, I bid my parents farewell and started my escape. A friend and I boarded a train south. We transferred to a car, then made a few more transfers by train and bus until we arrived at a village by the Pearl River in Guangdong. Across the river, the gleaming evening lights of Hong Kong beckoned us to go over."

Kevin couldn't help interrupting. "So, you crossed the river to come to Hong Kong?"

"I wish it were so simple." Danny's face contorted. "We waited till the middle of the night and jumped into the river. The current was much stronger than I'd expected and swept us toward the open sea. My friend and I got separated. A piece of wood bumped into me, and I grabbed it. The evening dragged on to morning, then to night again. At one point, a swarm of something surrounded me. Fortunately, nothing bit me. At last, a faint twinkle flashed at a far distance. I let go of the log and swam toward the light. Under the cover of darkness, I dragged my body to the riverbank in Macau."

"Macau?" Grace gripped her cross pendant, her tone higher than usual. "How about your friend?"

"Yes, Macau. That was how far I'd drifted." Danny gripped his knees, his knuckles whitening. "I never saw my friend again."

"You think he might..." Moisture glistened in Grace's beautiful eyes. She tugged the pendant back and forth on its gold chain.

A tenderness rose in Kevin's chest. She had a compassionate heart. The more he knew her, the better he liked her. *No, maybe more than like.*

"I don't know." Danny twisted his grip on his knees.

Kevin patted his friend's hand. With so much sorrow in Danny's expression, comforting words were scarce for him. He racked his brain. But his literature degree failed him, and he could only ask, "How did you move from Macau to Hong Kong?"

"Through a local church's help. The pastor there took me in and arranged for someone to transport me to Hong Kong. He said the Hong Kong government is more tolerant toward fugitives like me."

"An incredible yet touching story." She reached out to hug Danny. "Is that why you started to attend church?"

"Yes." Danny extracted a sheet of tissue paper from his bag and wiped his face. "You probably heard about this before. In China, we're taught religion is the people's opium. I used to believe communism would build a utopia in this world. The Tiananmen Square Student Movement crushed my dream. Then I found in Macau that, unlike what the government told us, Christians showed genuine kindness toward me, even though they knew I had no way to pay them back. I wanted to know what made Christians different."

Kevin's gentle emotion vanished. He gritted his teeth. "Not all Christians are kind, as you've described." He crossed his arms, his chin jutting up. "I've known quite a few who are even more terrible than non-Christians."

"Have you indeed?" She shifted her whole body to face him, her expression open, not a bit defensive. "Tell us about them."

He swallowed hard. "Well, a college classmate claimed to be a devout Christian, but he cheated on every exam and dated two girls at the same time. I'm a much better person than him."

"I'm sorry to hear about that." She blew a loose curl away from her face. "Although many people claim to be Christians, they may not have any connection with God. If someone doesn't have a genuine relationship with God through Jesus Christ, then at best he's a nominal or cultural Christian."

Kevin kneaded his temples. "You're confusing me with all the Christian jargon again."

"Sorry. My fault." She flashed her pearly whites. "A Christian isn't someone who receives baptism, attends church, or reads the Bible often. If it were that simple, all the Pharisees of Jesus' time would be Christians."

"Well said." Danny sprang to his feet, stooped, and scooped up a handful of pebbles. Then he jiggled them and let them slip through his open fingers. "I've always wondered why Jesus was so critical of those Pharisees. Your explanation makes sense."

Who were the Pharisees? Such nonsense. Kevin didn't care about what a Christian was or wasn't. He rolled his eyes and raised a palm. "I'm fed up with our religious discussions. Can we talk about something else?"

Danny brushed sand from his fingers, then twisted his watch into view. "About time to go to the pier, anyway. Are you both excited about fishing? Hope we can catch lots of fish today."

They walked back to the dock where the chartered boat awaited them.

"Watch your step." Kevin grasped Grace's arm and guided her onto the ladder connecting the land and the boat. Although itching to move his hand to her waist, he'd better not. It would be embarrassing if she pushed him away. So he settled for guiding her to the boat's spacious seating area, big enough for the three of them.

A crew member, his skin as tanned as the brown faux leather lining the seat, came forward. "Are you the Cheung party?

Welcome. My name is Fabian. Please pay first. Will you be paying with cash or credit card?"

Kevin handed over Mr. Lam's credit card and gaped when the fellow ran it through a machine. Wow, he didn't know even sailors were into high-tech. "Grace, next time you should ask Mr. Lam to let us use his yacht."

"Does he own a yacht?" She tilted her head toward him.

He chuckled. "He owns every kind of toy a man could want. I've seen pictures of him with movie stars on his yacht."

The other crew member started the engine. As soon as the boat reached a good distance away from the shore, Fabian gave them each a fishing pole. "Have you all fished before?" When Grace shook her head, Fabian took her pole back. "No problem. I'll hook the bait for you."

The wind blew her hair across her face again. Kevin tightened his grip on the pole so hard his knuckles turned white. No way would she let him brush the strayed curls away from her cheeks.

After she dipped her bait into the water, the rod bent down and pulsed as the line sang off the spool. "Whoa. What happened?"

Fabian rushed over. "You've hooked a fish. Adjust your drag and reel in."

"I can't," Grace yelled against the blowing wind.

"Let me try." Kevin grabbed the pole. "The fish must be humongous."

For a moment that stretched like an eternity, he struggled with the fish's long runs and broad dodges. After a huge swirl and tail splash, a bronze flank glowed below the surface.

Fabian grabbed an enormous net and dropped it into the water. "Splendid, maybe thirty pounds."

The summer sun beat down hot, and seagulls squeaked in the distance. At last, they hauled it out of the water.

Grace stooped to survey the swashing beauty on the deck. "What kind of fish is this?"

"The best kind. A sea bass." Fabian grinned. "Truly beginner's luck."

"For real?" She turned up the corners of her mouth. "I had no clue. What kinds of fish do you have down there?"

Fabian unhooked the fish from the line. "We have more than a hundred and fifty species in the Hong Kong waters. You can catch croaker, sea bass, grouper, snapper, parrotfish, or even baby shark."

"Wow." Grace tugged on an ear. "That's awesome."

Danny came over. "With this sea bass, our mission is accomplished. We should try to find a seafood restaurant in Cheung Chau for them to cook this fish."

"Well, we haven't used up our two hours." Kevin untangled the fishing line. No way would he stop now. He'd at least catch something. "Don't waste Mr. Lam's money."

"It's not Mr. Lam's money." Grace wagged a finger at him. "I'll pay him back once I start work."

"Whatever." Kevin walked away and resumed his fishing position, his mood remaining in the ditch. Why did today's trip deflate and frustrate him so much? He should get excited about her big catch, right?

Another hour passed. Except for a small croaker, he didn't catch anything else. "Not a lucky day for me."

"At least I got this like you." Danny raised another croaker.

Fabian collected their poles. "Time to go."

"Yeah." Grace picked up her backpack. "Kevin, you've got to help me carry the fish back home. Didn't we have sea bass the other day? Perhaps Ah Tang can cook it for us."

Danny's face dropped. "Aren't we having dinner together?"

Kevin touched his throat, then let out a rush of air. *Be kind. Let Grace know non-Christians can be good people.* "Mr. Lam asks to have dinner with Grace. Danny, do you want to come too? I'm sure Mr. Lam won't mind."

With a fierce competitor like Danny vying for Grace's affection, what did Kevin have to lose by being nice?

As the three of them walked off together, a spark ignited. Yeah, he had an advantage over Danny. He and Grace stayed under the same roof. Sooner or later, he'd find a way to her heart.

Chapter Seven

Grace leaned back in the bus's hard, blue seat. After their fishing trip, she'd spent the past three days investigating New Territories and other outlying islands with Kevin. Just the two of them. Yesterday, they'd spent hours hiking in the Sai Kung Country Park with a magnificent view over the surrounding bay.

Was their relationship moving in a new direction since her pool accident? But exactly what?

She stole a glimpse of Kevin sitting next to her. A complex person—caring, idealistic, and intelligent. With high cheekbones and a cleft chin, he was handsome in his unique way. His eyes, full of life with occasional melancholy, intrigued her.

He adored her—now she was certain of it. Also attracted to him, she wanted to know him better.

Should she encourage him and pursue a relationship?

Yet, he wasn't a Christian, and she planned to return to the US a year from now.

No, it wouldn't be fair to him.

During her last call with Nana Wang, her dear friend brought up that Jonathan Poon broke off with his current girlfriend. "He asked me for your new phone number and address. Should I tell him?"

Grace had said no. They were now in different stages of their lives. If it didn't work out when she was in Illinois and he on the East Coast, how could it work with the Pacific Ocean between them?

After she inquired whether it was okay to date while in mourning, Nana Wang had laughed in her delightful way. "Your mom would love to see you settled. Why are you asking, though? Have you met anyone interesting?" While Grace hesitated, Nana Wang put her at ease. "It's about time for you to think about courtship. Your mom was always worried about whether you'd get married. She said you didn't date anyone after Jonathan. Try to soften your bluntness. Men like demure women. Don't argue your point too much."

Did her straightforwardness impede her from having a boyfriend—or was Nana Wang speaking of her own lifetime of single status?

With a weight pressing down on her spirit, Grace mentioned Kevin and his being an atheist.

Her friend had chuckled. "Who was born a Christian? Even you, growing up in a Christian family, went through your soul-searching process."

Yeah, in middle school, she'd developed doubts about the Bible and engaged in heated debates with her mother, Nana Wang, and even her Sunday school teachers. In the end, she connected with God. No, to be precise, God found her.

The bus stopped.

Best just to enjoy the moment and not think too much.

She exited with Kevin, letting him reach up and grip her hand as he steadied her on the bus steps. The sweet scent of magnolia blossoms, with a hint of citrus, drifted around them. "What's the name of the island we're heading to today? Tai something. I forgot. Cantonese is so difficult."

"Tai O." Kevin guided her toward Central Pier, his palm warm on the small of her back. "It's dubbed the Venice of Hong Kong."

Venice? "During one of my trips with Mom, we visited Venice. I'd never experienced anything like it—the St. Mark's Square, the narrow streets, the gondola ride..." She quickened her pace enough to move away from Kevin's touch while keeping her voice steady. "I'll never forget how the gondolier, in black pants and a striped shirt, asked us in his limited English with a charming accent"—she tried to mimic his dulcet tones—"'Beautiful ladies, do you know this song, "Santa Lucia"?'"

Before they even responded, the young fellow's baritone voice lilted in the air, swirling around them, lifting them. The eager singer finished but let the last note resonate throughout the canal. Mom clapped with moisture in her beautiful eyes. That precious moment had remained on Grace's mind ever since.

She pressed her lips tight. No use thinking about it now. Mom had wanted her to move on and live her life in the present.

"A penny for your thoughts." Kevin tapped her arm.

"Nothing." She forced a smile and edged her arm away. When had he gotten so bold to keep touching her? Innocent touches, yes, but too many. "Tell me more about Tai O."

"You'll see stilt houses built right over the waterway. There's a cable ferry. We may see the famous pink dolphins, and the fabulous sunset is well-known too." As a woman with a cart zipped by them, Kevin pulled Grace aside. "Boy, it's dangerous on these streets."

He didn't release his hold on her waist. While they passed by a bookstore, Nana Wang's suggestion popped into her mind. Grace scooted free. "May I go get something?"

Without waiting for a reply, she hurried inside and grabbed a Chinese-English Bible from the religion section.

Kevin trailed her. "Don't you have a Bible already?"

She went to the checkout, paid, and gave him the gift. "Kevin, thank you again for saving my life the other day. This is a small token to show my appreciation. I hope you'll accept it."

"I–I..." He glanced down at it, then at her. "Of course, I'll accept it. I'll even read it. Thanks."

Whew. Not as difficult as she'd thought. Her taut muscles loosened up. *Lord, I pray for Your mercy to fall on him soon.*

After he placed the book into his backpack, he grasped her hand again. "Let's go. Otherwise, we'll miss the ferry. The next one is an hour away."

His fingers, warm and strong, wrapped around hers. She raised her gaze to his, a tinge of heat rising to her neck. *Is he just protecting me from the crowd?*

Not seeming to notice her unease, he guided her forward. As they entered Central Ferry Pier 7, his hand moved to her back to draw her closer. "Wow, look at the crowd. Today is Saturday. No wonder."

He stood so close, his breath tickling her ear. She drew in his spicy scent, and warmth spread through her body.

Nice to have someone like him by her side. But he wasn't a Christian. They wouldn't share the same values about life.

A shiver coursed down her spine.

Even if he became a Christian, entering a courtship with him wouldn't be prudent, right? He belonged to Hong Kong. She didn't.

She stepped away, yet the surrounding people pushed her back. She exhaled, blowing a wayward curl off her face. What was more unsettling? The crowd, her hair, or his hand on her back?

Take it easy, Grace.

Kevin was just being kind. He'd do the same for any girl in their situation, wouldn't he? She shook her head, knowing he wasn't just being kind.

He liked her.

The other day, when he'd asked whether she had a boyfriend and she'd answered no, he'd let out a merry laugh, and his grin reached from one ear to the other.

As expected, they didn't find empty seats when they entered the ferry.

"The weather is gorgeous today." He hooked his arm with hers. "Let's go to the upper deck."

The beautiful waters reflected the blue sky. A soft wind blew over her, tickling her curls across her face. The sun's rays made everything feel cheerful—a reminder to appreciate the moment and be thankful.

As he tucked a strand of hair behind her ear, an avalanche of unbridled emotion overwhelmed her, and uncensored words burst out. "What type of girl interests you?"

Despite her low voice and the surrounding noise, Kevin heard her and chuckled. "Someone like you."

Heat burned her cheeks. Why had she asked such a silly question?

His proximity felt so good, like a comforting salve. "Have you dated before?"

His hand dropped to his side, his tender smile vanishing.

What happened?

"Sorry." Her shoulders stiffened. "Did I say something wrong?"

"No." He tilted his face toward the azure sky dotted with cotton-candy clouds. "I don't know how to explain it. Wendy and I knew each other since elementary school. I suppose we did date in high school."

"Is Wendy your girlfriend?" A knot tightened in her stomach. Grace took a step back and leaned against the hard iron railing, farther away. "Where is she?"

"She died six years ago."

His words burst out like fireballs, and their scorching pain seared her. She brought a palm to her mouth. "I'm terribly sorry."

He kept quiet.

The misery in his eyes touched something in her heart, a feeling she hadn't experienced before. "Care to tell me more about Wendy?"

An unnerving silence lurked as Kevin faced the far horizon as if seeing something she didn't—something she'd never be able to see with him.

Then the ferryboat rocked hard, letting out a long moaning noise. She lost her footing and slammed into him.

His large hands caught her waist. "Are you all right?"

Their gazes tangled, his dark and unreadable.

"I'm fine. Thank you." She tried to wiggle away, but he didn't let go. Once again, unedited words flew from her lips. "Do you still love her?"

A knot of muscle trembled above his cleft chin.

"Wendy will always occupy a part of my life, but six years is a long time." He spoke in a muffled tone. His whisper tickled her ear, tenderness softening his expression. "I need to move on. I believe my heart has room for another person."

Was he hinting at something more than friendship? She searched her heart and dared not face the answer. It wouldn't work. He wasn't a Christian, and she planned to go back to the US.

After breaking their eye contact, she freed herself. "The ferry is about to dock. We'd better go down."

Yeah, it was prudent this way. She'd better maintain a safe distance from him.

***

Kevin walked side by side with Grace on the narrow street toward the cable ferry, their sneakers scuffling along the cobblestones. The crowd had dispersed. With nobody around, he longed to wrap his arms around her waist again. Yet she'd pulled away on the ferry. Had his story with Wendy scared her? Or perhaps Dad was right, and Grace, like most women, only dated men with a stable job and fixed income.

Her countenance remained pleasant, but distant.

Why was he attracted to her? For years, he'd guarded his heart so he wouldn't fall under the spell of love. Would he now be hurt again? When did his fortified walls crumble?

He racked his brain for something to talk about. Yeah, the Bible. He cleared his throat. "I took a course in college about the Bible to study its influence, language, and artistic legacy."

"For real?" She scooted away from him around a pothole. "Did you enjoy the course?"

"Well." He slid his hands into the pockets of his khaki shorts. "Our teacher was a die-hard atheist. One of the class activities was to go to the library and move all the books related to the Bible to the fiction section. He said we should read the Bible as a novel."

"Hideous." She raised a well-shaped brow. "Is that why you're an atheist?"

Good question. Did his college professor exert such a profound influence? "Um..." He raked through his hair, unsure how to respond. A tangle in the long strands snagged his fingers. "I remember the Old Testament is a compilation of various Jewish writings. It's difficult to understand the connection between the different books."

"Yeah. If you view the Bible like a fiction book, it's easy to get lost." She touched her chin. A simple gesture, yet so alluring and sweet. "My mom taught me to keep one theme in mind while reading the Old Testament—the preparation for the coming of the Messiah."

He slowed his steps and waved, haziness clogging his mind. "Why so?"

"Different books of the Old Testament record all sorts of events, including the Jews' rebellion. But the central theme is consistent. God called Abraham from the beginning with one clear goal. In the future, all nations and people would receive God's blessings through Abraham's one offspring."

As she paused, the midmorning sun shone on her, casting a shadow of her slender body on the ground. He couldn't turn his gaze away. The entire world seemed frozen in an instant.

"Are you okay?" She tugged at his sleeve. "Did my Christian jargon baffle you again?"

He jerked himself back to his senses. *Okay, try to focus.* The sun beamed into his eyes, and he squinted against its atypical brightness on this small island. "Hmm, I suppose when I read the Old Testament again, I should keep your point in mind."

"So, you'll read the Bible I gave you?" She swung her backpack around to her other shoulder and beamed, her smile brighter than the sunlight. "One more thing. Have you heard of the Dead Sea Scrolls?"

He nodded. "Of course. Isn't that one of the most important archaeological finds in our century?"

"Yes." Her fingers wrapped around the bag's strap. "Except for the book of Esther, all the other Old Testament books were found in the Dead Sea Scrolls. Experts have dated many of them as far back as 100 BCE, long before Jesus was born. When one compares those manuscripts with the editions we have now, the difference is negligible, less than one percent."

"Is there any significance in what you've just said?" He resumed his speed.

Trailing him now, she spoke behind him. "It's important because over three hundred prophecies from the Old Testament were fulfilled in Jesus Christ. My mom often said, 'As a scientist, I try to keep an open mind. If anyone could point to ancient books that prophesied his coming—and if he was also willing to die for my sin—then I'd take a serious look at him.'"

She almost bumped into him when he turned around. "Are you trying to convince me the Old Testament makes Jesus unique?"

"I believe you'll find that out yourself." Grace also halted. She wrinkled her nose as if struck by a sudden thought. "If you're serious about reading the Bible, you ought to read the New Testament first, beginning with the Gospel of John."

Her expression was earnest, yet a touch of cuteness enhanced her adorable charm. With her face so close, a faint jasmine scent teased his nostrils. Her perfume? No, she didn't look like a girl who wore perfume. Must be her shampoo.

Heat rushed through his body. *Not again.*

Resisting the urge to pull her into his arms, he took a step back to subdue the desire pulsing at his core.

"You look confused again." She scratched her forehead. "I hope I didn't overwhelm you with extra information."

Confused? *Bewitched* would be a more accurate description of his physiological reaction. "Sorry, you were talking about the New Testament. What about it again?"

"Start with the Gospel of John when you read the Bible." Her full lips curled up. "If you have questions, don't hesitate to ask me. I'd be more than happy to study the Bible with you."

"In your room?" Uh-oh. Not the right thing to say.

"You're comical." She waved as if brushing away a silly joke. "Mr. Lam's mansion is vast. We can find a suitable spot for Bible study."

Yeah, right. Enough religious talk. "Let's change topics. I'm curious about your childhood in the US."

"What do you want to know?" The sunshine caught the loops of her curls as she tilted her head.

He tapped his fingers against his shorts, a warmth tingling in his chest as his eyes bored into hers. "What was your most fun memory from when you were a kid?"

"Um... So many of them." She pressed a hand to her cheek. "Yes, fireflies. In the summer, fireflies flickered at dusk in our small backyard. I loved to sit on the lawn and count them with my mom. The most we've ever counted was ninety-three. Their blinking light fascinated me as if countless stories of adventure and mystery were woven together in their glowing bodies."

Wow. What a beautiful and poetic image of mother and daughter sitting together, surrounded by tiny flying lightbulbs. Perhaps he could write a scene like that into his next short story.

Moisture glistened in her eyes. She must have thought of her mom's death again. Her expression, with so much sorrow and tenderness, plucked at his heart. His gaze fell on her teal T-shirt and blue jeans, so delicate and strong at the same time. He almost reached a comforting hand to her shoulder, but he'd better not.

She wiped her face with a hand and flashed a tentative smile. "How about you? Any fun anecdote to share?"

He frowned. Did he have any memorable and pleasant experiences other than his friendship with Wendy? Well, maybe reading. He spent most of his spare time reading, usually alone in a bookstore or a library. Sitting with Dad and going over Mom's pictures was nice. But fun wasn't the correct word to describe that.

Dad always lapsed into silence whenever things reminded him of Mom.

He started walking. "We'd better hurry. I bet you'll enjoy the cable ferry."

Chapter Eight

Grace entered the dining room and froze. What was going on? Everybody, including Mr. Lam, was present for breakfast.

"Hi, Grace." Kevin pulled out a chair for her. "We're just talking about you."

Unease crept up the back of her neck as she sat. Maybe Mr. Lam found someone more suitable for the financial position and rescinded his job offer. Not a bad thing, because she could go home right away. "Did I do something wrong?"

"Not at all." Mr. Lam coiled up his sensual mouth. "Kevin was telling us you plan to go to a Mandarin-speaking church today. I would like to go with you. It's an excellent way to get used to being around Mandarin-speaking people."

"You... going to church with me?" She brought a palm to her chest.

Kevin chuckled. "My dad and I will go too."

"But..." She scratched her cheek, then fumbled with the chopsticks on her plate. "Kevin, didn't you say church bores you?"

"Um." He let out a small cough. "It never hurts to learn something new. Last night, I started reading the Bible you gave me. I might be biased before."

Was the Holy Spirit working in her new friends? Lord, please shine Your mercy on everyone who is going to church with me today.

"Let's finish breakfast." Mr. Lam checked his watch. "Dave, make sure Old Moy drives the Mercedes-Benz SUV so we can all fit."

Grace sampled the pickled cucumbers, distinct questions racing through her mind. Driving? How could they find a parking spot in Causeway Bay? It was such a crowded area. And everyone in Hong Kong seemed to know Mr. Lam. What would people at church think when such an entourage arrived?

As if understanding her thoughts, he patted her arm. "Don't worry. Old Moy will drop us off, and I'll sit in the last row so nobody will notice me."

How did Mr. Lam read her mind so accurately? His intense eyes bored into hers, and she dipped her chin. Heat crept from her neck to her ears as she stole another glimpse of the handsome profile next to her.

She touched her forehead, her thoughts spinning in circles. Was it apprehension or confusion? Somehow, Mr. Lam unsettled her. He didn't attract her as Kevin did, yet she felt a draw to get closer to him. Maybe because of his fatherly care. *Watch out, Grace. Don't play with fire.*

Kevin placed the two remaining pork buns on her plate. "For you. I know you like them."

She blinked. Both men were paying her extra attention. Yeah, their interest in her flattered her ego. In the US, she never considered herself attractive. Well, most of the time she thought herself ugly, especially in the presence of her Caucasian friends. Besides, Mom always emphasized that appearance wasn't important. The inside was.

Mr. Lam waited for her to finish eating, then stood. "Let's meet by the guardhouse."

On their way to church, Mr. Lam sat with her in the second row, while Kevin and Mr. Cheung stayed at the back. With Mr. Lam so close, she sucked in his woody and spicy scent, wondering what brand of cologne or aftershave it was. It smelled so good. Must be something superexpensive.

"Tell me, Grace." One of his long legs bumped into hers. "Was your mom a Christian? When did she become one?"

"I went to church with Mom since childhood." She shifted toward the window, away from him. "Why? When you met her in California, wasn't she already a Christian?"

"No." His reflection caught on the dark glass. He smoothed back the sides of his hair, silver strands ruffling over his fingertips as he brushed them to mesh with wavy black. "One of our favorite activities was clamming on Sunday."

Clamming? What was that?

His lips crinkled up. "Your mom loved clamming. We'd drive to a town in East Bay, near where a river merged into the sea. After removing our shoes, we dug our toes into the wet sand to search for the littlenecks buried underneath. Sometimes, we gathered a whole bucket of harvest in one morning. After we went home, your mom would make spaghetti with clams and garlic sauce."

Grace couldn't help chuckling at the picture of her mom digging her toes into the sand. When Mom found her clams, did she giggle like she often did when she encountered a pleasant surprise?

A gentle smile curved his lips while the sorrow etched the lines on his face. "Did you know your mom was an excellent cook?"

The word *was* sunk deep into her heart like a dagger.

Mom's words and merry laughter echoed even now. "Of course. I'm a superb cook. Cooking isn't much different from carrying out a chemical reaction."

The vision of Mom in their kitchen flashed across her mind. All the meals her mom had prepared for her, the unique recipes only she knew how to make...

But Mom could never cook for her again. Ever.

That knifelike pain thrust deeper into her chest, and moisture gathered behind her eyelids.

Perhaps sensing her mood change, Mr. Lam chuffed a breath. "I'm sorry to bring up the past. Did your mom ever mention her love of clamming?"

"No. Mom never even hinted she used to live in California."

Mom, why? Was that part of her life so heartbreaking that she tried to forget?

Grace sucked in a breath to calm down. "Please tell me more. Besides clamming, what did she do with you?"

"Your mom was an excellent piano performer." Mr. Lam fidgeted. "I play the violin. So, we often played duets for fun and also for others on special occasions like the Chinese New Year."

Right. Mom taught her to play when she turned six. She and Mom did a piano duet for their church one year during the Christmas celebration event. She grinned, imagining Mr. Lam and Mom playing on a similar occasion. They must have looked great.

So, Mr. Lam was Mom's boyfriend back then? Otherwise, how could she explain all those constant meetings? What caused them to break up? Why didn't Mom ever mention him before her deathbed?

Kevin's voice rose from the back. "We're here."

As they entered the church, Danny joined them. "Wow, you brought the whole household."

He tried to lead them toward the second pew, but Grace glanced back at her friends. They'd all settled in the last row. "Danny"—she kept her voice low—"maybe we should keep our visitors company."

With obvious reluctance, Danny followed her to the back.

Pastor Hong cited 1 Corinthians 15:14–19 and preached about why Christ's resurrection was Christianity's central message.

Grace's eyes misted again. The sermon resurrected Mom's words: "My dear Gracie, look heavenward with hope. We'll meet again. I'm sure of it."

She smiled through her tears. *Yes, Mom. How glorious it'll be on that day when I see you in heaven.*

After the benediction, a few church members formed a circle around them. A woman in her upper thirties with a pair of intelligent eyes raised a hand. "Are you Mr. Samuel Lam, the famous architect?"

Angela Zhou came over. "Dear all, let's welcome our newcomers and let them introduce themselves."

Mr. Lam smiled and stated his name. "Very nice to meet you all. Sorry, I'll need to take leave right away."

He waved to Mr. Cheung, and they left together.

Angela frowned. "I hope we didn't scare away our visitors."

Grace narrowed her eyes, detecting a knot in her stomach. It wasn't easy being rich and famous. Poor Mr. Lam. Would he ever come to church again?

A burden for his soul fell on her, and she pressed against her chest. *Lord, please let Mr. Lam have the chance to know You.*

The small crowd dispersed, but before leaving with the others, Angela grasped Grace's hand. "I'm so glad you came again today. Our fellowship group for young people meets every Saturday evening at church. Are you interested? Can I have your phone number? I'll call you to share more information."

Grace gave her the number in her room, and Angela ambled away.

Kevin tapped her shoulder. "Shall we leave now? Since you love dim sum, let's go to that same restaurant we visited last week."

"We won't find any empty seats there now." Danny wagged a finger. "It's still early. Why don't we cross over to the Kowloon side? I know a great little restaurant."

Grace trailed her two companions toward the metro station. As the subtropical summer sun beat down on her, beads of sweat formed on her forehead. She put on her sunglasses and pressed her lips tight. Being rich had its advantage. Wouldn't it be nice to have a chauffeur drive her around in a Mercedes-Benz?

Then a soft voice emerged in her mind. What good will it be for a man if he gains the whole world, yet forfeits his soul? Or what can a man give in exchange for his soul?

She mumbled under her breath, "Matthew sixteen twenty-six."

"Did you say something?" Kevin halted.

"No. Nothing." Lord, thank You again for the Holy Spirit's reminder.

Danny also slowed down his steps. "Kevin, what did you think about today's sermon?"

"Do you truly believe a dead man could come back to life and is still living today?"

"I–I—" At Kevin's query, Danny glanced back at Grace. "I used to have doubt, but now I'm fully convinced. There's no other way to explain the dramatic changes in Jesus' disciples' behavior."

Kevin shifted closer to her. "Grace, do you also believe that?"

She adjusted her sunglasses, her muscles tightening. *Lord, please give me proper words.* "Of course, I do. All Christians do."

"Humor me with your explanation." He almost stepped in her way, blocking her.

She blinked. Did he truly want to know? Or was he mocking her?

"All four Gospels described Jesus' crucifixion and resurrection in significant detail. His disciples, most of them uneducated, blue-collar men, morphed from cowards before Jesus' resurrection to martyrs who willingly laid down their lives instead of renouncing their beliefs. If Jesus had not resurrected and appeared to them, that would have been impossible." Danny clasped his hands together, as though in prayer. "Besides, when the Gospel books were written and circulated, many people around Jesus' time were still alive. If Jesus' disciples weren't speaking the truth about the resurrection, then their contemporaries would have said something to dispute their claims."

A gust of warmth traveled from Grace's neck to her cheeks as they resumed their pace. Wow. Danny had spent time and effort studying the Bible.

Kevin led them down the escalator to board the train.

The Mass Transit Railway didn't have a mob today. Right. It was Sunday noon. Most people probably already reached their destinations for lunch.

Once seated, Kevin turned to face her. "Did other documents outside the Bible around that time talk about Jesus?"

"Yes." She returned his gaze, even as he pushed into her space. "The writing by the first-century Jewish historian, Flavius Josephus, talked about what happened to Jesus. Josephus wasn't a Christian." Was Kevin convinced? Unlikely. "Have you heard about the Shroud of Turin?"

The two men flanking her shook their heads.

Perhaps she shouldn't talk about that. Too late. "It's the linen cloth many believe was used to wrap Jesus' body after His crucifixion. You should read books about it. It's fascinating."

"Sure. I'll research it. But I don't think it's important." Danny touched his chin. "To me, Jesus is alive today because His promise about the Holy Spirit is true. Since the Tiananmen Square incident, whenever the memories of that day haunt me, I receive comfort from the Holy Spirit."

As Danny's face contorted with so much emotion—longing, fear, and rage—Grace touched his shoulder. "You've gone through so much. I'm glad the Holy Spirit works in you."

"You guys are confusing me with all the jargon again." Kevin kneaded his brows. "The Holy Spirit? What is it? How does it work? If you can show me how, I may put aside my skepticism."

"First, the Holy Spirit is not an *it*. He is one of the three persons in the Triune God." Grace tapped her fingertips together. "The Holy Spirit was with God even at the time of creation and is still working today. All Christians experience Him."

"The three persons? The Triune God?" Kevin lowered his hand, but his brows scrunched up further into his long bangs. "You confuse me even more."

"Let's not go into the theology side." Danny sank back in his seat, folded his arms over his chest, and crossed his legs. "The most important work of the Holy Spirit is to let us recognize our sins. I may consider myself a decent person. When the Holy Spirit enters my heart, I see all the sins within me."

Leaning around her to speak to his friend, Kevin scoffed. "That's just a form of autosuggestion."

But Danny remained relaxed as he clamped both hands on the knee he'd crossed over the other. "Unlike autosuggestion, in which one taps into his own strength to become more confident or to feel better, the Holy Spirit points out our defects. All Christians share the same experience."

Grace's toes tingled inside her sneakers, her chest feeling lighter. He said it so well. What a brother in Christ.

The train slowed. A few passengers shot to their feet and hurried toward the door. So typical of Hong Kong locals. Always in a rush to go somewhere. Grace followed her friends to exit the metro station, and they ambled to Mongkok. In front of the restaurant, she blurted out, "Hey, Kevin. Isn't this where we had lunch together the other day?"

"You remember?" He flashed a bright smile.

"Of course. It's excellent." Like last time, once the server brought her order of dumplings, she devoured them. "I love, love these."

The corners of Danny's mouth curled up as he watched her eat. "Are you free tomorrow? We can come here again. I want to introduce you to a friend."

Was he paying her extra attention as well? Before she came to Hong Kong, she'd prayed for finding new friends here but never thought about courtship.

Lord, please grant me wisdom.

They were all so kind. What should she do to maintain the friendship without hurting anyone? "What time? Lunch like today?"

Kevin raised a hand. "How about me? Can I come too?"

"Of course. Yeah. Let's meet back here at noon tomorrow." Danny wiped his face with a napkin. Before taking his leave, he retrieved a notebook from his backpack. "Kevin, this is for you. You've been asking me to tell you more about my experience from that fateful day. I compiled something for you."

After Danny left, Grace followed Kevin back to the metro. Then they transferred to Bus 56A.

Kevin drew her to sit together. "I overheard your conversation with Mr. Lam this morning. Your mother seemed very close to him. I suspect she and Mr. Lam used to date. Don't you think?"

So he'd drawn the same deduction. Or maybe anyone would have, based on Mr. Lam's words. "I would think so. I'm confused. Why didn't my mother ever mention him or California?"

"Really? Your mother never talked about him?"

"No." She wiggled her toes in her sneakers, something heavy creeping into her heart. *Mom, why?* "The first time I learned about him was when she asked me to deliver a letter to him."

"Perhaps you should ask Mr. Lam directly."

Should she? It was worth a try. But what was the use? Mom was no longer around. Tears welled up, and she turned her head toward the scene outside the bus window.

"Are you all right?"

"Yeah." She nodded as the mansions flashed by.

Oh, Mom. How much I miss you.

Chapter Nine

Back in Mongkok the next day, Kevin weaved through the busy sidewalk with Grace. The noon sun beat down from the cloudless sky. Grace's rosy cheeks glowed, and her upturned lips drew his attention.

"It's hot, isn't it?" He rubbed the back of his neck, unable to shift his gaze from her face. "We'll enjoy the air-conditioning in the restaurant soon."

She adjusted her sunglasses. "I wonder whom Danny plans to introduce us to. He sounded mysterious."

"Not sure." Kevin squinted. His eyes tightened further at the corners over how he met Danny.

June fourth, 1990, the first anniversary of the Tiananmen Square Massacre. The organization, Hong Kong Alliance in Support of Patriotic Democratic Movements of China, held a candlelight vigil on the soccer fields of Victoria Park, with more than a hundred thousand people in attendance.

Someone to his left yelled in Cantonese, "Release the prodemocracy activists! Rehabilitate the prodemocracy movement! End the one-party dictatorship! Build a democratic China!"

The young man to his right narrowed his soulful midnight-black eyes and mumbled in Mandarin. "The Beijing government still denies anything ever happened at Tiananmen."

Kevin introduced himself. Since then, he and Danny had kept in touch.

"Are you okay?" Grace's voice snapped him out of his contemplation. Sunlight caught the loops of her curls as she tilted her chin up. "Did my question upset you?"

He shook his head. "No, not at all. Our meeting with Danny and his friend may have something to do with the candlelight vigil scheduled for this Thursday in Victoria Park."

Grace shaded her eyes from the sun's glare, the light also casting a sheen on her skin. "The candlelight vigil? What's it about?"

He adjusted his eyeglasses. Did young people of Chinese descent in the US know nothing about the biggest annual event in Hong Kong since the Tiananmen Square Massacre? Maybe he shouldn't be surprised. The Beijing Student Movement shocked everyone in his circle. In five years, Britain would return the colony to China. For the first time in Hong Kong's history, the British subjects fully awakened to their Chinese identity and harbored mixed feelings toward China, their soon-to-be motherland.

As if standing on a threshold, he, along with many in Hong Kong, pondered what the future held. But they couldn't find a way back to the past. Why did political events beyond anyone's control threaten the prosperity of "The Pearl of the Orient" and its inhabitants? Did people outside of Hong Kong care? It seemed someone like Grace, born and raised in the US, wouldn't understand. "Remember when we talked about the 1989 Tiananmen Square Massacre the other day? The candlelight vigil helps us remember those killed in the incident. Does the US have similar activities?"

"Although I've heard about protests organized in DC, I don't know the details." She scrunched her nose. "Isn't Victoria Park right next to our church? Will you go on Thursday?"

Kevin eyed her cute expression. His lips curled up as he thought of how her jasmine-scented body pressed against his when she almost fell on the ferryboat. They'd locked eyes. A magical moment. Yet, later, she'd pulled away from him.

Before he responded, they approached the restaurant. Grace tucked her sunglasses in her hair and used them to pull the curls back from her face.

In front of the restaurant, Danny awaited with a carryout bag. "Yan and I decided to eat at home. Safer and easier for our conversation."

So, the friend's name was Yan. Was that his first or last name?

Danny led them to his studio apartment in Waterloo. Once inside, he called toward a skinny guy with ultrashort hair. "Yan, meet my friends, Grace and Kevin."

Were they all on a first-name basis? Kevin sucked in a breath. Right. They'd better take safety precautions just in case.

The Chinese government still publicized the list of the twenty-one most wanted student leaders, even though it had been three years since the Tiananmen incident. Kevin's friends had said that Hong Kong activists and the triad, a transnational organized crime syndicate, worked together to coordinate Operation Yellow Bird to smuggle the dissidents from China to safety in the British colony.

Was Yan on that list?

Grace took a seat at the small round table. "Can we eat now? I'm famished."

Yan's brows shot up on his youthful tan forehead, the vicissitude in his expression diminishing a bit.

Somehow, Grace's lack of pretense lessened any situation's seriousness. Girls growing up in Hong Kong would think twice before showing their true selves to prospective beaus. Perhaps that was why she intrigued Danny and him so much.

Kevin scanned the area for where to sit. Then he gave in to the magnetic pull and took the seat beside her. "Didn't we have breakfast?"

She lowered her lashes and remained quiet.

Danny chuckled. "No problem."

Like before, she devoured the dumplings faster than the others did. "So good. I can never get enough of these things."

Yan stared at her, his lips twitching and his eyes twinkling.

The image of Grace enjoying breakfast in Mr. Lam's dining room earlier today tickled Kevin's heart. He scooted forward in his chair, speaking in her place. "Grace came to Hong Kong not long ago. She craves authentic Chinese food."

"Sorry, I didn't wait for you guys." She flashed a timid smile. "We don't have dumplings like these in Chicago."

"You're from the US?" Yan dropped his chopsticks. "I may go to the US soon."

"Really?" The three of them asked in unison, their English, Mandarin, and Cantonese blending.

Yan inclined his head. "Yes. Operation Yellow Bird is applying for a special visa for me."

Grace squinted. "What's Operation Yellow Bird?"

After Danny explained, Kevin raised a hand. "Yan, could you tell me what happened before you came to Hong Kong? I'm in the process of writing a book about the Tiananmen incident."

The desolation returned to Yan's narrow face, and his chin jerked up higher like a soldier at attention. "They seized me in late June 1989 at Datong. Believe it or not, hundreds of armed soldiers transported me back to Beijing as if I were a VIP." A bitter smile distorted his lips. "They detained me in a maximum-security prison for nineteen months."

He halted as a knot of muscle twitched in his jaw.

Grace brought a palm to her mouth, her eyes misty.

Danny finished for him. "Eventually, they released Yan but stripped away all his identification documents. By God's mercy, he met a member of an underground church and got in touch with Operation Yellow Bird. He arrived here last week."

"Are you a Christian?" Grace spoke in a breathless whisper.

Yan nodded. "I accepted Christ as my Savior after a brother from the underground church shared the gospel with me."

Kevin cocked his head. "I've heard Operation Yellow Bird smuggled at least ten of the twenty-one most wanted and also many other dissidents out of China." Different questions raced through his mind. How did they accomplish the almost impossible mission? "Did you meet people from Operation Yellow Bird? Are they all from Hong Kong?"

"I think so, although I can't be sure." Yan still sat stiffly in his seat, his back ramrod straight and his angular jaw tight. "They were equipped with scrambler devices, night-vision goggles, and infrared signalers. Some of them might've been makeup artists. They helped disguise me and never introduced themselves."

He drew a breath and gaped into the distance, lost in thought.

Danny tapped the table, breaking the stillness. "Any news about others on the most wanted list?"

Kevin stood to pour himself a cup of ice water, then sat back down. Yan, indeed, must be one of the twenty-one.

Yan's posture slumped. "Dan, Gang, and a few others remain in prison. Kaixi was in Hong Kong for a while but may have gone to the US."

"Yan, are your parents still in China?" Grace lifted her glass, condensation dripping from it onto the white top she'd tucked into her crisp blue shorts. "Will the government persecute them because of you?"

Kevin suppressed a shudder and ran his fingers through his long hair, raking the parts at his nape the wrong way. The government wouldn't leave Yan's parents or other family members alone. In Chinese history, anytime a person committed a crime against the emperor, the punishment was to eradicate not only the offender but also the entire family line.

An eerie hush fell again. Then Danny sucked in a breath. "We can only pray."

At his friend's sad expression, Kevin clamped his teeth into his lower lip to prevent his mouth from asking offensive questions. Still, sarcastic words rolled off his tongue. "Would prayers help in such a dire situation? If God existed, why didn't He do something to stop injustice against good people?"

Uh-oh. Did his questions upset Grace? He stole a glimpse of her.

Ice tinkled as she set the glass on the table. Flicking the condensation from her fingertips, she sat up straighter. "God exists, and He cares about each of us. Otherwise, He wouldn't have sent His only begotten Son into this treacherous world. On earth, Jesus braved intense hardships, including crucifixion, the most terrible form of death. He understands our difficulties and will walk with us through life's darkest valleys."

Kevin leaned forward, searching her face in the ambient lighting for a clue to her emotion. Good. She looked calm, composed. Yeah, she'd encouraged him to raise questions about Christianity, stating if he asked with a sincere attitude, God would answer and guide him. "It may sound good, but the reality is different." He couldn't prevent mockery from souring his tone. "Whether Jesus walks with us through tough times doesn't make any difference to the suffering we experience."

Yan closed his eyes, rubbed his temples, and whispered into his bowl of uneaten dumplings. "I admit God seems distant when I feel helpless. During the past few months, I've learned to count on the promises in the Bible. At the most painful moment, fellowship from the Holy Spirit comforts me."

Moisture glistened in Danny's deep-set eyes. "It does make a difference knowing Jesus walks by my side in my tribulation. I don't understand why tragedies happen. I'm convinced the Lord is aware of my pain. He's promised to walk with me regardless of my circumstances."

Kevin's palm glided along the chair's armrest. He lowered his chin, and his hair fell over his forehead. "That doesn't solve what will happen to your family members."

While the others kept quiet, Grace patted Danny's hand. "The Bible tells us suffering refines us like fine gold, making us closer to God."

Kevin tapped his fingers against his knee. Maybe he shouldn't ask too many questions. He peeked at her, his shoulders stiffening against the tension, and doubts burning through him. "How about miscarriages and the death of babies? They don't have the luxury to live their lives and be refined by suffering. What does the pain of death mean to them?"

"I can't provide a satisfactory answer." She hugged her arms. "If there were only the material world, the lives of many like those you've mentioned would be utterly meaningless. In the spiritual realm, God, together with thousands of angels, sees the existence of fetuses and babies who die prematurely. To the Almighty, suffering, no matter in what form, is always meaningful."

An excellent response. Still, doubts lingered. With a jerk of his chin, Kevin flung his hair away from his face. Then he adjusted the eyeglasses he'd jostled. "Do you really believe there's something beyond the material world?"

Danny blinked, then dabbed his eyes with a finger. "If you believe humans have souls, then you have to believe in the spiritual realm."

What a statement. Souls...

Yan turned his somber gaze toward Kevin. "Why do humans, limited by space and time, have the concept of eternity? Likely, God planted it in our hearts so we would seek Him."

Another incredible assertion!

The many stories about the emperors in Chinese history brought a shudder to Kevin's spine. Yeah, they all sought to live forever. The most extreme of them was Qin Shihuang.

The first emperor, obsessed with immortality, sent his generals to the eastern seas to search for secret concoctions that would help him live forever. Besides, he ordered everyone to search for immortality substances from frontier regions. In his desperate rush to avoid the grave, he died at forty-nine. Instead of living for a millennium, he only made it to middle age, leaving behind a massive terracotta army to guard a tomb he worked very hard to avoid occupying.

Ironic and tragic, yet undeniable that, since the very beginning, mankind fathomed the limited spectrum of human life and yearned for something more.

Why?

Unable to find answers, Kevin exhaled hard, the puff of air ruffling his bangs. "Back to my question about the family members you left behind. Have you heard anything from them?"

"The June Fourth incident roused widespread attention from Western countries. Otherwise, the government wouldn't have released me. As long as the international pressure continues, my family may be okay." A warmth came into Yan's eyes. "People from the underground church and Operation Yellow Bird have also been taking care of my parents."

Danny pressed his fingers together. "Same here."

Kevin sucked in a quick breath. Compared to these friends, he was most fortunate to live in Hong Kong with his dad beside him. And with Grace in the same house now, life was good. Could it last? After Britain gave Hong Kong back to China, would China keep the promise to let Hong Kong remain a free special administrative region? And if he could find a way into Grace's heart...

Too many vague questions to focus on. He waved but couldn't brush aside the uncertainties. "Are you all going to the candlelight vigil this Thursday?"

"No."

His jaw dropped at Yan's response. "You're not going?"

Yan touched his nose. "To me, the date June Fourth will always be linked to the massacre. I think we should focus on the prodemocracy movement in China, not the tragedy of that day."

Was there a difference?

The more Kevin thought about it, the better he respected Yan, a deep thinker. Yes, the efforts should go to promote future democracy. Yet, the vigil would get people motivated in seeking a better future for Hong Kong. "I'm going. How about you two?"

Danny turned away his gaze. "I can't go this year. I have to work."

Grace shook her head. "I'll start my new job next Monday. Mr. Lam has given me lots of documents to read."

Did a cultural gap exist between him and his friends? Unlike him, they didn't seem to have a strong attachment to his beloved hometown. Not that he could blame them. None of them grew up in this city. He'd do whatever it took to ensure a better future for Hong Kong, but the city was only a transient, temporary stop to them.

He bowed his head. What would happen between him and Grace? To find a way to her heart, what did he have to do besides seek a regular job?

Chapter Ten

In his makeshift office, Kevin squinted at his computer screen. Dad had let him set up his writing desk in the spacious walk-in closet. Recently, a few magazines changed their policies and now only accepted electronic submissions. Good news to him since he preferred the paperless approach. The only problem? His computer was too old, and he didn't have money to replace it.

He pivoted his chair from the computer and frowned at Danny's notebook.

April 21, 1989: It has been six days since General Secretary Hu Yaobang passed away. Hundreds of thousands of students went on strike and gathered in Tiananmen Square, waiting overnight for his memorial service tomorrow. Many of my classmates, including my best friends Chong and Jintao, joined the strike. I didn't go.

May 12, 1989: I've decided to join Chong and Jintao on the hunger strike. Since Peking University students filed the seven-point petition in April urging the government to correct corruption and nepotism, they've been bugging me to take part in the strikes. Chong joked about whether my sweetheart wouldn't permit me to go. He and Jintao both have steady girlfriends and will become engaged as soon as they graduate. No, I'm not dating. So far, I haven't participated in any of their activities because I don't want my parents to worry. But the hunger strike seems benign enough. We'll just ask for two things: (1) A specific dialogue between the government and Beijing universities on equal footing, and (2) recognition from the government that the student movement is patriotic for the purpose of achieving a better future for everyone.

May 13, 1989: I don't know how many of us are here. Tiananmen Square is abuzz with students. I mimicked my friends and wrapped a white band around my head. We put up a handmade sign, "Hunger strike oath: I swear, for the prosperity of the country, I voluntarily go on a hunger strike and will not give up until the goal is achieved." In the evening, Chong's and Jintao's girlfriends, Wei and Lyn-Lyn, stopped by. They stayed with us until almost midnight. We talked about our goals and resolved to make our voices heard. A feeling of camaraderie and hope surrounded us. This is the first time I've ever taken part in a protest, and I'm filled with excitement, fear, and determination.

Kevin tugged on an ear. How could he convert Danny's news-like accounts of the Tiananmen Square incidents into a truthful, engaging fiction book? To add emotions to the main character, he'd had to ask Danny what went through his mind back then.

Images of the crowd from last Thursday's candlelight vigil remained fresh. Participants still packed the soccer fields in Victoria Park, yet the news reported a drastically reduced number, almost half of last year's attendance. By the year 1997, would the Hong Kong folks forget the Tiananmen incident?

Neither Danny nor Grace had attended the vigil, but they'd made time to go to yesterday's fellowship group meeting. Where were their priorities?

Familiar footsteps sounded, and Dad peeked in at him.

At his unsettled expression, Kevin pushed aside Danny's notebook. "What's up? Why are you looking at me like that?"

Dad tapped the doorframe. "I noticed you paid Grace special attention at church today."

"Um." Heat crept up to his cheeks. "Was it so obvious?"

"Yes. Even Mr. Lam commented about it on our drive home." Dad shifted to the desk, braced a hip against it, and scratched his forehead. "I was wrong about my boss. He seemed pleased you're showing an interest in Grace. He even said she'd make a superb match for you."

Kevin's head jerked up, his long bangs whipping across his eyes. Did he have blessings from both Dad and Mr. Lam to court Grace? If only he could find a way to her heart... He shifted in his seat, needing to move, to pace—anything—to expel the burst of energy. "I don't know how to gain her affection. I've tried everything I can think of."

Dad smiled. "Maybe you should find a proper job."

Not again. Kevin clamped his fists in his lap. "I know, Dad. I've been looking. Nothing seems to fit."

Uh-oh, he hadn't been completely truthful. This afternoon, Mr. Lam had cornered him and asked him whether he would be interested in joining his company's PR team. The big boss sounded eager. "The primary task is to write press releases. Your degree in English Literature will come in handy. You'd do an excellent job."

Odd. He'd lived under Mr. Lam's roof for over a year. Although Mr. Lam was kind and generous, he never mentioned any openings in his company. Could this offer have something to do with Grace?

Giving up my dream so I can write press releases? At his silence, Mr. Lam didn't push the subject but told him to think about it before they talked further.

Dad patted his shoulder. "I'm glad you're looking. Once you decide to try, you'll find a job. In the meantime, why don't you show Grace how much you care about her? Do things to make her feel unique. Show her you're patient and kind. These qualities will help you win her heart."

Hadn't he done all that and more? Perhaps Grace favored Danny over him... Kevin slumped under the weight of Dad's hand and muttered under his breath, "I wish it were so easy."

Releasing his grip, Dad raised his eyebrows. "What did you say, son?"

"Nothing." Kevin blinked to brush aside the unpleasant subject and straightened up. "What did you think about Pastor Hong's sermon?"

"About heaven and eternal life?"

"Yeah." He shook his long bangs back from his forehead.

"Quite intriguing. He said the Bible doesn't define eternal life by time." Dad pursed his lips. "He also explained that heaven isn't a physical place."

"Just to confirm, I came home and read the Gospel of John. He was right that the Bible states, 'This is eternal life: that they may know you, the only true God, and Jesus Christ, whom you have sent.'" Kevin narrowed his eyes. "And heaven is where God is, not a physical place."

"Interesting, right?" Dad inclined his head, his cheeks turning crimson. "Angela invited Mr. Lam and me to her Bible study group."

"Really?" Kevin searched Dad's face. Why was he embarrassed? "Are you going?"

"I'll go with my boss this Saturday." Dad tilted his head away. "Well, I'd better get going. I need to talk to the gardeners. See you at dinner."

Dad halted at the door again. "Since Grace starts her job tomorrow, you won't need Mr. Lam's credit card anymore. Don't forget to return it."

"I already have." Kevin waved and sucked in a breath. Did Dad have to treat him like a child all the time?

Dad strolled away, his enthusiasm for attending the Bible study group confusing. He'd never been religious. And he'd blushed.

What was going on?

And what about his own Bible study group? His shoulders stiffened. Last night, when he asked an honest question about an incident recorded in the Bible, the woman who led the study didn't know how to answer, and Grace growled at him.

What was the woman's name again? Li something. Most folks in Hong Kong adopted English names to make themselves more memorable to the surrounding British. Why would that woman keep her Chinese name?

Music floated in the air, and his musing went awry. Someone was playing the piano.

As if lured by hypnotic power, he left the desk and strolled toward the source.

Mr. Lam stood behind the pianist, blocking Kevin's view. It must be Grace because he'd heard the hymn earlier at church, "It Is Well with My Soul."

She played with such tenderness and sorrow that the melody, like a rainbow ribbon engrossing him, drew him across a bridge into a peaceful land. Moisture built up in his eyes as something tugged at his soul.

Grace finished the last note and stood.

Mr. Lam applauded. "Both lyrics and music are so sad yet so full of hope. I wonder who wrote the song."

"It was written..." Grace's gaze fell on Kevin. She waved, beckoning him closer.

He rubbed a palm against his khakis and crossed the room. "Didn't we hear this song during worship this morning?"

"Ah, you recognized it." She flashed her signature gentle smile.

As he gazed at her full lips, heat spread from his chest through his torso, flowing outward to his limbs.

Calm down. Don't behave like a lovestruck idiot in front of Mr. Lam.

Mr. Lam guided them toward the sofa and patted the seat beside him. "Grace, you were about to tell me who wrote the song."

"Oh yes." She sat and adjusted her wrinkled skirt. "I can't remember who composed the music, but the story behind the lyrics is very sad and related to Chicago where I came from."

Kevin took the seat next to her. As his leg brushed against hers, a pleasant tingling sensation traveled from the back of his scalp to the base of his spine.

Why did she affect him so much?

She laced her fingers on her lap. "An attorney and real estate investor in the nineteenth century lost a fortune in the great Chicago fire. Then his four-year-old son died of scarlet fever. The family decided to take a vacation to Europe. His wife and four daughters went first. He stayed behind to take care of his business before joining them. The ship carrying his family sunk. Many lost their lives, including his four daughters. His wife survived and sent him a two-word telegram—'Saved alone.' At once, he set sail for England. While they came upon the spot of the shipwreck, sorrow, mingled with hope from God, overtook him. He wrote these lyrics."

"Wow, what a tragedy." His expression somber, Mr. Lam strolled to the piano, retrieved the music sheet, and read aloud. "'When peace like a river attendeth my way, when sorrows like sea billows roll—whatever my lot, thou hast taught me to know. It is well, it is well with my soul.' I wonder what enabled him to say, 'It is well with my soul.'"

"It was because of his Christian faith."

A knot tightened Kevin's stomach. His palm cupped the back of his neck. "If God exists, why does He allow tragedies to fall on Christians? Shouldn't He take care of those who believe in Him?"

Grace's eyes grew moist. Did she think of her mother? Maybe he shouldn't have asked. He swallowed hard, but couldn't gulp back the question. "I'm sorry—"

She dipped her chin. "It's okay. You asked a similar question the other day. Suffering is an unsolvable problem for us humans since ancient times. Tragedy befalls unsuspecting individuals all the time. I can only reiterate that, on this earth, Jesus encountered intense suffering, including crucifixion. He understands my pain and walks with me, regardless of my circumstances."

Mr. Lam fixated his gaze on Grace. "Did Jesus walk with you after your mom fell ill?"

She nodded without hesitation. "Yes, He accompanied me through the deepest, darkest valley. In addition, many people in our church helped me and stayed by my side."

"Grace, you're a courageous girl. Your mom must have been very proud of you." Mr. Lam's mouth curled up.

"Thank you." She wiped her face.

Mr. Lam twisted his watch into view. "I have some errands to take care of. See you two around."

After their host left, Kevin picked up the music sheet from the sofa. "Where did you get this?"

"Mr. Lam gave it to me." She slid it from his grasp and brought it to the piano. After placing it on the music stand, she let her fingers dance over the keys, their trill resounding before she spun toward Kevin again. "He might have asked the pastor for it after today's worship. It was nice that he went to church with us again and nobody bothered him."

Kevin let out a small chuckle. "Perhaps Angela Zhou requested the others leave him alone. Still, that same woman came by and introduced herself. Amelia Zhou, right?"

"Yes. Angela's sister, the nephrologist who works in Queen Mary Hospital." Grace licked her lips. "She's gorgeous. Don't you think?"

Not as gorgeous as you. The words almost rolled off his tongue, but he stopped them, not wanting to offend her. Instead, he gave her an inquiring glance. "Were you upset with me last night when I asked my question?"

"About how Jesus preached from the boat to thousands standing on the shore without electricity and a microphone?" She traced a finger along the curve of the piano. "No."

"You frowned."

"Did I?" She tipped her head, letting her hands fall to her sides. "I was debating whether to chime in and explain but decided against it. I'm glad our group leader promised to do some research and get back to us this Saturday. Will you come again?"

"I will." How could he say no? He wanted to be a part of her life. Besides, the people there appeared kind, even though he asked tough questions. "You mentioned you were tempted to explain. Do you know the answer?"

"I do." She inclined her head. "I had the same question about the verses in the Gospel of Mark before I visited Israel."

His jaw went limp. "You visited Israel? When?"

She lifted her chin. "Four years ago when I graduated from high school. It was my mom's gift to me. We joined a tour group and traveled together."

He snapped his jaw closed. Could a believable answer exist to his question? "Tell me what you learned."

"Our guide took us to a place by the Sea of Galilee, a cove with the appearance of a natural amphitheater. The article he gave us described how two scientists conducted an experiment to test the location's acoustic effects. After their study, they concluded that, because of the bowl-like setting there, a few thousand could see and hear Jesus who sat in a boat a short distance away without any problem."

Kevin widened his eyes. "So, you're saying that, even without a microphone, a large group of people could hear Jesus' words clearly?"

"Yes." Her grin broadened. "I was skeptical, and the guide did a test for us. He drove us to a nearby road, about a hundred yards away. Then he returned to the lakeshore and called my name from there. I heard his voice as clearly as if he were talking to me face-to-face."

"Unbelievable." He lifted a hand to his mouth. "Must be an awesome experience. What else did you see over there?"

"Many sites depicted in the Bible. It was amazing that we could still see and experience the places Jesus Christ and His disciples used to live and tread."

What must it have been like for the mother-daughter duo traveling together through Israel? A warmth stirred his chest. "You were very close to your mom?"

"Yes." Her eyes glistened. "I miss her so much."

How he longed to draw her into his arms. But he dared not. What could he do or say under the circumstances?

Amid great pain, human language became feeble and inadequate.

His stomach lurched as he thought of the interminable months following Wendy's death. Darkness swallowed his entire being, and hopelessness hissed at him. For weeks, he didn't eat or sleep well. Besides grief, he battled unspeakable regret and guilt. Dad took him to see a psychiatrist. Fortunately, he recovered enough to attend his first day at the University of Hong Kong.

In comparison, Grace seemed to handle the grieving process much better than he did. Of course, the situation was different.

At last, he squeezed out a few syllables, his tone strained. "It's tough to lose someone we love."

Her expressive eyes bored into his. "Are you thinking of your friend Wendy? Care to tell me more about her? What caused her death at such a young age?"

Could he bare his soul and tell her about the accident? Uncertain thoughts came in and out of focus as his stomach fluttered. "We went swimming in the ocean, and she drowned."

His vision blurred, and his throat seized up. Feeling as if he were sinking underwater, he shook his head hard but couldn't shake off the agony sluicing over him.

"Oh no. How terrible." She squeezed his hand. "Don't force yourself to share things you don't want to."

Her touch soothed like a salve on his old wound. He sucked in a deep breath. "I often wonder... If I hadn't invited her to go swimming that day, would she still be around?"

An awkward stillness followed. Then she laced her fingers through his. "It's not your fault that Wendy drowned."

He closed his grip around Grace's. "Everyone, including my dad and even Wendy's parents, said the same thing. In my rational thoughts, I agree with them." He fixed his gaze on the ceiling. "Still, I can't get rid of the guilt in my heart."

Her firm hold grounded him. "You may not believe in God and the spiritual realm. From my experience, Satan uses all sorts of methods to enslave us. One of them is guilt. Do you want me to pray for you now?"

Did he? He held his breath. No, not yet. Despite her sincerity, he wasn't ready. "Maybe not."

"No problem." She slid her hand free. "I understand. I'll pray for you in my personal prayers."

The spectacular cuckoo clock in the music room called out the hour. Seven o'clock.

She stood up. "I'd better return to my room and get ready for dinner. See you soon."

He watched her stroll away. Somehow, the heaviness in his chest and the weariness in his limbs eased a little. Definitely soothing to share his burden with someone who cared about him.

Chapter Eleven

All day, Grace occupied his mind. How was she handling her first day at work? Dad had mentioned that Wilma, the chief financial analyst at Mr. Lam's hotel subsidiary, was difficult to get along with.

Okay. Admit it. You're in love with Grace.

Otherwise, why would he care so much about what happened to her?

If he professed his love, would he scare her off?

He groaned, grabbed Danny's notebook, and trudged out toward the koi pond.

After he sat on the garden bench, Ah Tang approached from the other side. "Kevin, here's a letter for you." She took the empty seat beside him. "Looks like from the same magazine."

He ripped it open. Another rejection note. What stories did they want?

Ah Tang craned into his space, a tender gleam in her eyes. "Don't give up. Sooner or later, they'll discover your talents and publish your work."

What did she know? Didn't she only read tabloids and meaningless romance novels?

Air bubbles popped up as a group of golden koi swam by the moon bridge connecting the path across the pond. A blackbird circled in, dipped one wing into the water, and looped away. The startled fish scattered.

Conflict. Discord. Fear. Kevin frowned harder at the little drama playing out in the pond.

Ah Tang patted his shoulder. "You ought to write about Mr. Lam's romance with all those women. It'll sell." She winked. "People enjoy love stories, especially if you spice them up with steamy sex."

Was she joking? No way would he do that for the sake of making money. He muttered under his breath, "They aren't love stories. There's no love in those affairs. Only sex in exchange for expensive gifts."

She raised her painted brow. "How do you know? Have you been reading the tabloids as well?"

He adjusted his glasses and didn't bother to respond.

"What do you think about this newcomer, Grace F..." She scratched her forehead. "I forgot what her last name is."

"Feng, Grace Feng."

"Right. She's more beautiful than any movie star and so innocent-looking." Ah Tang wrinkled her nose. "Everyone is wondering why Mr. Lam asked her to stay here."

Were all the servants gossiping about Grace and Mr. Lam? Kevin took a deep breath, ready to set the record straight. "Grace's mom and Mr. Lam knew each other for years. Her mom passed away recently. It's nothing special for Mr. Lam to take care of an old friend's daughter."

"Really? We didn't know that." She giggled. "I must tell everyone. They've been guessing when Grace will become Mrs. Lam."

How sick were those groundless rumors! A heat simmered in his gut as he spoke through clenched teeth. "You folks have too much free time. I ought to ask Dad to add more chores to keep your team busy."

"Why are you angry?" Her jaw slackened. "I've known you for over a year and have never seen you so upset before. Are you—?"

Her gaze bored into his. Then she slapped his shoulder. "Ha, you care about that girl."

An uncomfortable stillness ensued. Heat flushed his cheeks, and he tilted his head away.

A frog jumped onto the lily pad near them, and his croak broke the silence.

"Love is such a complex thing." Ah Tang slumped back in her seat and tucked her elbows on the backrest. "Do you know how Christopher's mother died?"

"Mrs. Lisa Lam?" Kevin gave her a questioning glance. "The tabloids said she died in a car accident."

"So, you do read the tabloids." Ah Tang nudged him with her shoulder before resuming her relaxed stance. She crossed her legs at the ankles and lowered her voice. "It's even more complicated. I believe she died of a broken heart."

Was she yakking nonsense? Could someone die of a broken heart?

"That would be a good story for you to write about." She stood to examine the croaking frog. "Shortly after she and Mr. Lam got married, she found out Mr. Lam was in love with someone else."

A gentle wind blew, rustling the leaves of the nearby shrubs. Kevin followed her to the edge of the pond. "With whom was Mr. Lam in love?"

"A classmate of his while he was studying in California."

Grace's mom? Kevin's interest heightened. "Why didn't he marry her?"

"Christopher's mom told me the girl died. That was why. But Mr. Lam never forgot her." Ah Tang returned to the bench.

Surely, that girl wasn't Grace's mom. Her mom passed away a month ago, not some twenty years prior.

His heart ached for Mr. Lam. For six years, Kevin couldn't get Wendy out of his mind. Mr. Lam, like him, might have encased himself in a fortified castle to avoid getting hurt again.

After Kevin met Grace, that protective wall crumbled. Yes, he'd opened up to her in ways he hadn't before, and they'd formed a connection.

Perhaps Mr. Lam hadn't met the right person to help him deal with his haunted past. "How did Mr. Lam marry his wife?"

"Through their parents. The union was a merger of two powerful families possessing multiple properties in Hong Kong. Mr. Lam's father arranged the marriage when he returned from California. He resisted the idea. Then his father suffered a stroke. According to Cantonese folk belief, a family member's wedding brings the sick person comfort and even a cure. As the only son, Mr. Lam had no choice but to oblige. Connie Dong, Lisa's mother, became a board member in the merged company. Unfortunately, his father still passed away two years later."

Even though it made little sense, Kevin was aware of the age-old Chinese tradition. He stood by Ah Tang. "You know a lot about the Lams. How many years have you been here?"

"I came here shortly after Mr. Lam got married. They had Christopher before Mr. Lam's father passed away. While Mr. Lam worked, Mrs. Lam kept busy with parties. I, together with some of my colleagues, raised the poor child." She let out an exaggerated sigh. "That's why he's attached to me. He called me last night and said he'd come home later this week."

Kevin met Christopher last summer. He didn't look like a poor child at all. A replica of his father, he knew how to charm girls. During his few weeks' stay at home, he'd organized pool parties, and the tabloids featured him on their covers with his girlfriends, all from superwealthy families.

Ah Tang rose. "I'd better get going. The kitchen needs me."

Once she left, Kevin sat and flipped open Danny's notebook.

May 19, 1989: It's been a week since we started the hunger strike. Today is the last day. The government has done nothing. Instead, ambulances from different hospitals came to help us, and many citizens stopped by to show their support. Wei and Lyn-Lyn swung by again and told us the student demonstrations have spread to twenty cities across the country. In Beijing alone, more than a million people joined the protests.

The Soviet leader, Gorbachev, and his officials are visiting Beijing. Because of our hunger strike, the original plan to receive the Soviet delegation with a grand ceremony at Tiananmen has been canceled. Some students around us made banners hailing Gorbachev as "The Ambassador of Democracy." Not sure I agree.

I've promised Chong and Jintao to continue to take part in the student movement after the hunger strike.

Familiar footsteps squeaked from the walkway and halted. Grace's calm tone sounded. "Kevin, what are you doing here?"

He lifted his gaze. Her tailored blazer and matching skirt clashed with her regular sneakers, making her look like a child playing dress-up in business attire. "Nothing. I'm reading Danny's notebook about his Tiananmen Square experience." Even in a mix-and-match attire, she appeared stunning. His mouth went dry. He licked his lips, ready to praise her. Instead, he blurted out, "Your shoes don't match your clothes."

"I know." She slid onto the empty seat by him. "I don't like wearing high heels for the hike home."

"How's your day?" A pleasant scent wafted in the air. Was it from the blooming shrubs or her? Was she wearing makeup today? He scanned her face. No, no cosmetics. Her natural beauty shone like always.

"Not good." She fumbled through her purse to retrieve a packet of tissues. "I'm too inexperienced, and Wilma is tough."

Oh, poor Grace.

He clutched the bench seat alongside him against the urge to pull her into his arms. "Only day one. I'm sure it'll get easier."

"I hope so." She inclined her ear. "What's that sound?"

Ah, the buzz and hum of insects from the underbrush. The girl who couldn't hear anything from a seashell was listening to the late afternoon sound in the garden. He crinkled up his lips. "The setting here is wonderful, isn't it?"

She nodded. "Nice to be rich. At the same time, money can never buy happiness."

Indeed. "Yeah. Ah Tang just told me something about Mr. Lam. No wonder he always sports a trace of desolation in his expression, even though he's loaded."

Her gaze jerked up. "What do you mean?"

He couldn't help releasing a heavy breath after relaying Mrs. Lam's death. "From what Ah Tang said, the woman Mr. Lam loved died young, and he's never forgotten her."

"So..." Grace's eyes opened wide, and her full lips formed an enticing *O*. "You don't think he used to date my mom when they were in California?"

He tightened his grip further on the bench seat and averted his gaze from that kissable mouth. "Well, it's possible he dated your mom after that girl died. When your mom learned he still loved the other woman, she was devastated." The more he thought about it, the more convinced he was about this new theory. "Maybe that was why your mom left him and moved to Chicago."

"Sounds logical enough. Like Mrs. Lam, my mom must have felt heartbroken. It would explain why she never talked about Mr. Lam and California."

But how did that explain why Grace's mom suddenly remembered Mr. Lam on her deathbed and sent her daughter all the way here?

Very puzzling. He scratched his forehead, a flutter rising in his stomach.

Grace stuck the packet of tissues back into her purse. "When did Mrs. Lam have her car accident?"

"The tabloids said about three or four years ago. I..." A thrusting sound in the water caught his attention. He stood to survey the reeds. A snake slithered through the decaying leaves.

"Kevin, what's that?"

Not wanting to alarm her, he sat back down. "Nothing."

"Was Mrs. Lam alone in the car?"

"Yes." He pushed Danny's notebook aside and edged closer to Grace. "She and Mr. Lam seemed to have led separate lives. He worked nonstop, and she entertained herself by attending parties. The report said she was drunk at the time of the accident."

"How horrible." Grace brought a palm to her mouth. "For sure, money can't buy happiness."

He shifted his body. His arm brushed against hers, and heat spread through him. He crossed his legs. "Have you read 'Faust' by the eighteenth-century German novelist, Johann Wolfgang von Goethe?"

"No. I don't usually read fiction books." She flashed a modest smile. "What's it about?"

"In essence, it's about how excessive longing can lead to one's doom. The story depicts someone who became obsessed with gaining knowledge and experience to the point that he willingly struck a deal with the devil. In the end, his soul was lost forever."

Grace scrunched her delicate, upturned nose. "That's horrid. Why would anyone do such a thing?"

After a glance at her impossibly full lips and perfectly arched brows, Kevin squeezed his legs together but couldn't subdue his physical reaction. *Why can't I control my desire?* "You ought to read von Goethe's books—Tolstoy's as well. He has similar themes. I think they might have been Christians."

"I'll try." Grace let out an enormous yawn. "Boy, I'm exhausted. I'd better go to my room and get ready for dinner. See you soon."

As she strolled away, Kevin's gaze followed her. I've got to find a way to confess my feelings toward her.

Chapter Twelve

Grace sucked in a deep breath and hit send. Within seconds, Wilma's email pinged hers. "Instead of emailing me about the project, just walk down the hall and work out the details in person."

Lord, please help me.

Day three on her new job, and she'd already experienced issues— constant yelling from her boss and sniggers from colleagues, sleepless nights, headaches, and stomach pain. She hadn't shared her difficulties with anyone except Nana Wang, although Kevin asked about her job every day.

She let out an audible sigh and fumbled with a pen.

"Trouble again?" Speaking in singsong, Mary leaned over the thin wall separating their cubicles. "What did you do wrong this time?"

Grace bit down on her lower lip, stifling the array of emotions. Despite only spending a few days in Mary's presence, Grace sensed her colleague loved to see her in trouble.

She should have taken a job in the US. If her current situation worsened, she'd have no choice but to pack up and return to her home turf. That would be a good thing. Nana Wang in her old age would need someone to take care of her.

"You know your problem?" Mary continued. "You're too beautiful. Besides, you came in through Mr. Lam's recommendation."

Lord, please give me wisdom. "Thank you for your concern and compliment." Grace forced a smile. "You know, back home in Illinois, all my friends considered me ugly."

"Indeed?" Mary came to stand by her and looked her up and down. "You came from the US?"

"Yes." Grace swallowed hard and drilled calmness into her voice. "Most of my friends have porcelainlike white skin, beautiful blue or green eyes, and golden hair. In comparison, I'm brown and coarse."

"How dreadful." Mary's eyes softened a bit. "About Mr. Lam. What's your relationship with him?"

"He's a family friend." Grace glanced at the clock. Almost four thirty. "I'd better go to Wilma's office. She's expecting me."

"Good luck."

Wonder of wonders, Mary sounded sincere. And wonders didn't cease there. The meeting with Wilma turned out better than Grace anticipated. Yeah, she was careless and messed up a few numbers on the Excel sheet. When she apologized for causing inconvenience, her boss didn't yell at her like in the previous two days and simply nodded. "Make sure you double- and triple-check every time you deal with numbers."

Then they worked together to fix the errors.

Whew. What a relief.

By the time she returned to her cubicle, all her colleagues, including Mary, had already left. She twisted her watch into view. Last night, Mr. Lam said he and Mr. Cheung wouldn't be home for dinner.

So, she would dine alone with Kevin if she went back now.

She brought a hand to her chest, the heavy thumps beneath her palm betraying her anxious state. Right, she'd better avoid Kevin. Even with her busy schedule since starting her job, she thought of him too often. It would be nice to have him by her side. His smart remarks always cracked her up. How did he manage to find a way into her heart in such a short time? But... he wasn't a Christian, and she still planned to leave Hong Kong soon.

With a groan, she reached for the phone and left a message for Ah Tang that she wouldn't be back for dinner.

After changing into her sneakers, Grace wandered into a nearby Beijing-style restaurant to enjoy half of a BBQ duck by herself. Yeah, the beauty of living in Hong Kong. So many different kinds of food from all over the world. She ignored the patrons around her and licked her fingers as much as she wanted.

Afterward, she took the bus to her stop and hiked the private road back to the mansion. As she entered the living room, Mr. Lam was standing in front of an enormous, ancient Chinese painting. "You're back. I just came home a few minutes before you."

"When did the servants change the decor?" As if drawn by an invisible force, she crossed the spacious room to his side. "Who are the two individuals depicted in the painting beneath the full moon?"

Mr. Lam curled up his lips. "Do you know the story of Han Xin in Chinese history?"

Heat creeping up her neck, Grace shook her head. "I know very little about Chinese culture and history."

"I see." He gestured for her to sit on the plush black leather sofa. "Han Xin was a military strategist in the early Han Dynasty of China. Although a talented young man, he lived in poverty. During the Peasant War at the end of the Qin Dynasty when various generals, including Liu Bang, fought to gain control of the country, Liu's advisor Xiao He tried to recruit Han. Because Liu didn't like him, Han left. Xiao told Liu that they couldn't win the war without Han. Xiao then hopped on a horse and, under the pale moonlight, chased after him."

What a fascinating story. She eyed the two men on horseback in the painting again. Nice to have someone believe in you. "Did Xiao find him? Did they win the war in the end?"

"Yes. Liu Bang became the first emperor of the Han Dynasty." Mr. Lam's smile crinkled the sides of his eyes and brought them aglow. "Now, tell me. What stories did you read when you were a child?"

Grace scratched her forehead. Had she read anything entertaining? "Mainly stories from the Bible. My mom gave me a children's version when I was five."

"Besides reading the Bible, any anecdotes about your childhood?"

Why was he interested? She stole a glimpse of him. The sparkle in his eyes made her heart skip a beat. "I love Thanksgiving and Christmas. Every year, our church celebrated together. My mom always asked me to write a letter to Santa, informing him what gifts I wanted. Then, on Christmas morning, the gifts miraculously appeared under the Christmas tree."

He laughed out loud. "How clever. That was how your mother learned about your wish list."

"Yes." Warmth mingled with the sorrow twisting up her heart. *Mom, I miss you so much.*

His face turned serious again. "How was work today?"

Why did he change the subject? Did Wilma complain about her?

"I–I—" She bit her lip. Honesty was always the best policy. "I'm inexperienced and careless, but Wilma caught my errors and helped me correct them."

"It's okay." He patted her arm. "Everyone starts like that. The key is to own your mistakes and keep learning. Remember, conflicts with others, especially with management, should be about resources and the company's long-term goals. All the other stuff is unimportant."

Her shoulders relaxed. He was providing her advice, just like her mom and Nana Wang. "Thank you, Mr. Lam."

"Could you please call me Uncle Lam?" Something tender underlined his smile. "After all, I'm your mom's old friend."

"I... Mr...." Grace couldn't turn away from his face. So much endearment and love in his expressive eyes. "Sure, Uncle Lam."

"Good." He grinned and stood. "Let me get back to my study. I still have some documents to review. See you later."

She directed her gaze to the handsome features of her newly found uncle. "Are we meeting for our first Mandarin lesson this Saturday?"

"I was just about to tell you." He gripped the back of the sofa, leaning over it, his voice gentle. "I have errands to run. Why don't you go out with Kevin to enjoy the day?"

Go out with Kevin? Was Uncle Lam encouraging her to date Kevin?

On her way back to her room, she continued to marvel at Uncle Lam's kindness. Mom was right. He seemed to have her best interests in mind.

In the hallway, she halted and looked out at the night sky. As the stars twinkled, peaceful contentment comforted her. For the first time since her arrival, this mansion felt like home.

The phone rang when she entered the door. She rushed to pick it up. "Hello?"

"Grace?" Danny's Peking-accented Mandarin lilted in her ears. "How was your day?"

"Not bad." No need to bother her new friend with job issues. "How about yours?"

"Same old, same old." He let out a small chuckle. "Are you coming to this Saturday night's fellowship meeting?"

"Of course. I look forward to it."

"Would you join me for dinner before the meeting? We could go to the same dim sum restaurant in Causeway Bay." After she said yes, he asked, "Are you free before that?"

Her heart fluttered. She fiddled with the phone's long cord, unsure which she felt more—flattered or uneasy. "Yes."

"Kevin said you love hiking. Have you taken the Dragon's Back Hike? It's Hong Kong's most popular hiking trail with spectacular views out over the ocean."

It sounded benign enough. Plus, she hadn't been there. She jotted down the meeting time and the name of Chai Wan Metro Station.

After the phone clicked, she changed out of her two-piece suit into a T-shirt and jean shorts. Her thoughts turned to last Saturday's Bible study. So nice to belong to a fellowship group again. During her final months in the US, with Mom sick and a busy school schedule, she skipped many of her cell group's weekly meetings.

And a hike in the countryside would do her good, especially after such a stressful week.

The phone rang again. Nana Wang spoke when Grace answered. "My dear Gracie, how was your day? As bad as yesterday?"

"Actually, much better." She sank onto the bed, the plush navy comforter pillowing her, and shared her interactions with Wilma and Mary. "Believe it or not, Mr. Lam advised me on job issues like a father. He also asked me to call him Uncle Lam. Isn't that amazing?"

"Nice." Nana Wang's merry voice floated into her ears. "Perhaps your mom's idea of sending you to Hong Kong was a good one. By the way, your Libertyville bungalow is sold. You'll see money in your account in a month."

"I'll check. Wow, I hadn't expected it to be gone so soon." She exhaled, letting out a feeling of loss, and tried for a chipper tone. "Well, one less concern." Also one less link to her mom. She blinked away the moisture behind her eyelids.

As Nana Wang relayed the details of the sale, Grace pondered her happy days with Mom in that house. They didn't have a large yard like Nana Wang's. Still, Mom packed it with climbing plants to utilize the small space fully. So many cucumbers, spaghetti long beans, and numerous vines. How Grace loved harvesting their hard work in autumn. How she missed having Mom around!

"Are you all right?" Nana Wang was still there. Whoops.

"Yeah." Grace feigned cheerfulness. "I've been thinking. When I return to the US, can I live with you?"

"Of course, my dear. You're like my granddaughter."

Grace, learn to look to the future. She took another deep breath. "Last time you mentioned you might come to see me. Have you decided?"

"Aha, I'm meeting with a Triple-A travel agent this morning. I'd better go now." A rustle came through the line. Was Nana Wang picking up her purse? "Once I have a firm plan, I'll let you know."

After they ended the call, Grace sat at the table, the antique ebony cool and grounding beneath her palms as images of her previous home intruded. The living room with the old carpet Mom bought from Goodwill, the cramped kitchen where Grace helped cook beef stew...

Someone tapped on the door. She glanced at the clock. Almost ten. As she opened the door, Kevin flashed a broad smile. "How was your day? You didn't come home for dinner. Where did you go?"

"My day turned out better than before." Not wanting to invite him into her messy room, she stepped out. "I had dinner at a BBQ duck restaurant."

Her slippers scratched against the hallway's hardwood floor as they walked shoulder to shoulder to a sitting nook nestled within an alcove.

Moonlight filtered through the window, casting a soft glow on the plush cushioned bench, accompanied by soft and fluffy pillows. She brushed her fingers over the hardcover books on the small side table before sitting down.

Kevin turned on the fairy lights above, and a warm sense of serenity enveloped her. He sank into the seat by her.

"You went there all by yourself?"

The table grazed her bare legs as she shifted her body. "Is there anything wrong with that?"

"Not at all." He adjusted his glasses. "Any big plan for this Saturday?"

She brushed away a loose curl. "Danny just called me. We'll go to the Dragon's Back Hike, have dinner, and attend the fellowship meeting at church."

His face dropped at the word *we*. He shot her a stern glance and scoffed under his breath. "Just you and Danny?"

What's wrong with you? It's none of your business. Grace clenched her teeth and swallowed back the words. Instead, she wiggled against the irritating wooden table again. Maybe she shouldn't have worn shorts. "He didn't say anyone else was coming."

"Grace, I—" He raised a hand, then dropped it. "Can I come with you guys?"

Did he mean that? She curled up her lips. "The hike, dinner, *and* the fellowship meeting?"

"Yes." Crimson blotched his cheeks. "That trail is gorgeous. I've only been there once. We can cover Big Wave Bay, Mount Collinson, Stanley, and Shek O. And the best part is, along the way, we'll view waterfalls and listen to leaves rattling in the ocean breeze."

What poetic phrases he'd come up with. No wonder he wanted to be a writer. "You described it so well. Of course, you can join us. I'm sure Danny won't mind."

"If you wish, we can also stop by one of those beaches for a swim." The sparkle in his eyes dimmed slightly. "Also, Shek O has a variety of seafood restaurants and a fabulous ice cream joint."

Did Kevin think of his friend Wendy? Perhaps they wouldn't swim in the ocean. The prospect of indulging in locally caught seafood already captivated her. But more importantly, Kevin would attend the fellowship meeting. He seemed genuinely interested in learning more about the gospel. Would he become a Christian soon?

"Grace?" He scooted closer, his leg brushing against hers. "How do you feel about us?"

His husky voice shivered over her. She blinked, at a loss for what to say. How did she make him understand her concerns? No, it wasn't prudent to mention them. She took a deep breath, striving to compose herself and maintain a calm tone. "Let's talk later. It's late, and I have to work tomorrow."

She yawned to feign exhaustion, then trod away, leaving him alone in the nook.

Chapter Thirteen

The next two days blended into a cycle of endless Excel sheets, emails, meetings, and phone calls. Grace kept her head down and put forth her best. Before she realized it, Friday ended the workweek.

Afternoon sunlight filtered through the office's film-coated windows and reflected off the white ceiling. Well, her work situation had improved. She no longer made so many careless mistakes, and Mary even invited her out to lunch today.

Should she go home for dinner? She longed to see Kevin while also dreading it. After rubbing her temples as if she could iron out her tangled emotions, she left Ah Tang a message, telling her she wouldn't be back for dinner.

All right. She'd enjoy half of a BBQ duck by herself tonight to celebrate the successful completion of her first week in the company. As she licked her fingers, Mom's laughter echoed in her head again. "One of these days, food will be your downfall."

Grief thudded through her heart, and her toes tingled inside her sneakers. She'd do anything for Mom's spaghetti and meat sauce one more time.

Mom will never be with me again in this life. I'm left all by myself in this world. As moisture blurred her vision, Mom's note popped into her mind, and she whispered the words again. "'Please look heavenward with hope. We'll meet again. I'm sure of it.'"

Yes, full of hope. At least she still had Nana Wang.

Precisely why dating Kevin wouldn't be prudent. They'd yet to share the same belief about heaven. Plus, she didn't plan to stay in

Hong Kong for long but would return to Illinois to take care of Nana Wang.

Grace strolled toward the bus station for home.

Back in her room, she changed out of her business attire.

Uh-oh. She forgot to tell Danny that Kevin would join their Dragon's Back Hike tomorrow. She called him about the change in plans, but he didn't sound surprised.

Good.

After putting down the phone, she pulled the curtain away and peeked into the garden.

Light from the nearby lamppost filtered through the tree branches, casting irregular patterns on the walkway. The mesmerizing silhouettes seemed to sway and dance in an eerily inviting way. She stepped out and descended the stairs. The summer breeze shifted, sweeping a pleasant scent into her nostrils.

Was that a seven-son flower?

Her slippers scratched against the path's hard surface, and her long shadow reached into the lawn.

Lord, thank You for this magical setting...

Her silent prayer went awry, and the hair on her nape tingled.

Someone was watching her.

A few feet away, a tall man leaned against the arbor adorned with climbing wisteria, his gaze hovering over her. Something red flickered in his hand, and a trace of smoke mingled into the sweet, flowery aroma.

Then the bean-like sparkle drew an arc in midair and fell on the grass.

Grace gawked at the cigarette butt. Would it spark a fire?

A light chuckle reverberated. "Don't worry. The dew will take care of it, and the gardeners will pick it up tomorrow morning."

He strutted toward her and halted. "You're more beautiful than they told me." His English sounded American. The younger version of Uncle Lam twisted his sensual mouth into a grin as his unscrupulous gaze fixated on the V-shaped neckline of her T-shirt.

Grace took a step back. "And you are?"

"Christopher Lam." He mocked a bow. "I hope I didn't scare you."

"No, you didn't." She didn't smile back at Uncle Lam's son. "But I don't appreciate your behavior."

"You're so uptight." He threw a sideways glance at her and laughed. "Have I offended you?"

"You have. Don't you know it's not proper to be so blatant when you first meet someone?" She jammed her hands on her hips and jerked her chin toward the smoldering cigarette butt. "Besides, smoking is bad for you. And you shouldn't mess up the lawn and expect someone else to clean up after you."

He shrugged and held up his palms in a stop motion. "Whoa, what a feisty chick."

"A chick?" Grace gritted her teeth. "I'm at least three years older than you."

"I'm so sorry. I intended it as a compliment." He aimed his view at the sky. "Such a beautiful night. Would you like to walk around the garden?"

A tiny crease formed between his eyes, making him appear innocent and helpless, like a lonely child seeking a companion to play with.

Oh, he was just a young college freshman. She mirrored his posture and looked up. The bright moon had moved beyond the ginkgo tree. "Do you often ask strangers to keep you company?"

"Not really. Only when I'm at home and accompanied by a beautiful lady." He eyed her, probably studying her reaction. "Ah Tang said you're from the US. What brought you to Hong Kong?"

He sounded sincere. She squinted and walked along with him. "I thought Ah Tang and her colleagues had figured out everything about me. Didn't they tell you?"

"As much as I love Ah Tang, I don't buy into her gossip." He chuckled again. "Do you know I grew up under Ah Tang's care?"

What did he mean? Mrs. Lam passed away three or four years ago when Christopher went away to boarding school in California. Grace lowered her brows, a knot tightening in her stomach. "Didn't your mom take care of you when you were a child? What happened?"

"Ha, you care about me." A smirk crinkled up his chiseled face. "Be careful. Don't you know men will say what they think women want to hear? You fall too easily and too quickly. Is that how my dad keeps you here with him? Have you questioned his motives?"

A shiver coursed through her back. "How can you talk about your father like that?" Why would she doubt Uncle Lam's intentions? Her mom had told her Uncle Lam would keep her best interests in mind, and she trusted Mom. Grace would trade anything to have a father like him. Yet, no. Papa died before she was born.

Christopher arched a well-shaped brow. "Why not? I spoke the plain fact. Ask around, and you'll learn that my father is the most notorious womanizer in town."

Their conversation was straying into uncomfortable territory. So far, all Uncle Lam ever showed her was fatherly kindness. She'd better bring them back to her original query. "You're the only son. Your mother must have loved you very much. Were you joking when you said you grew up under Ah Tang's care?"

"My mother loved me?" He swept his loafer in an arc across the grass, knocking dew loose. "I'm not sure. For as long as I can remember, she was agitated and mentally unstable. She was also drunk most of the time and needed others' care. How could she take care of me? If she loved me, she hid it well, for I never experienced it."

What sort of person was his mother? Poor child. Growing up with rich and famous parents, he sounded like an orphan.

They followed the serpentine path and meandered into the area near the koi pond. Grace scuffed the cobblestones with her slippers. Under the moonlight, his shadow and hers blended.

He gestured for them to sit on the bench. "My family is a bit atypical. Don't you think?"

Tender sympathy expanded in her heart. "Why did you say that?"

"You see, my dad works hard but also plays hard. He's proud of his status as the most eligible bachelor in Hong Kong. You can't consider him an ordinary person, can you?" He let out a small cough. "As for me? My goal is to enjoy life as much as possible. So far, Dad's the only thing preventing me from achieving my goal."

Could he be serious? "Don't you have a good relationship with your father? I think he loves you very much."

"Is he capable of love?" He examined his hand. "I'm not as convinced as you are."

Did losing that first love impact Uncle Lam so profoundly that he refused to let anyone—even his son—take over her spot in his heart?

Love is as strong as death. She mumbled under her breath, "Song of Songs, chapter eight verse six."

"What did you say?"

"Nothing." Three individuals—Christopher, Mrs. Lam, and her mom—were victims of Uncle Lam's love for that mysterious girl. "Kevin mentioned your dad once loved a girl, but she passed away young and he never got over it."

"Yeah, Ah Tang told me that as well. It's a myth my dad created to cover up his liaisons with all those women." He waved as if trying to brush away the unpleasant topic. "I couldn't care less, as long as Dad doesn't keep bugging me to study architecture."

She snuck a peek at him. "You don't like architecture? What's your major? Are you at Stanford?"

"I wasn't good enough to get accepted into Stanford, and Dad was totally pissed." He massaged the back of his neck. "I'm studying music at Santa Clara University now."

"A music major?" What a surprise! "What do you play?"

"Violin, like my dad. Although people told me he plays well, I've never heard him play. Isn't that odd?"

Uncle Lam had shared how he and Mom used to play duets and even performed for others on special occasions. "Why doesn't your dad play any longer?"

Christopher scrunched his nose. "How would I know? He's a mysterious man. I don't understand him at all."

With mixed emotions simmering, she shifted on the hard bench. "Do you love him?"

In an uncomfortable silence, the crickets seemed louder. Then he touched his forehead. "I'd be lying if I said I don't love him. He's all I have in this world. Well, Ah Tang and many others, including my grandma and uncle on my mom's side, love me. Still, Dad is in a different category. I wish he'd accept me as who I am and not try to mold me into someone like him."

Accept and love me for who I am. Ah, the quest never ceased. Such a simple request, yet so difficult to achieve.

She brought a palm to her heart, cupping it against the burden for his salvation pounding there. Another lonely soul sought unconditional love, something rare in this world because everyone was needy. No one but the self-sufficient Almighty God could love with no strings attached.

Somehow, Christopher came across as someone she'd known for years. "Tomorrow two friends and I will go to the Dragon's Back

Hike. In the evening, we'll attend our church's fellowship group meeting for young people. Are you free tomorrow? Do you want to join us?"

"Hiking and church?" He slapped his hands together. "Sure. I have nothing planned anyway."

Nice. She curled up her lips. "Great. Let's leave home after breakfast. I'll tell Kevin tomorrow morning. He won't mind." She yawned and stood. "Good night. See you tomorrow."

Back in her room, she sat by the table and dialed Nana Wang's number. Her beloved friend asked about her job again.

After Grace shared her workweek, she scooted forward in her antique chair, the hand-carved ebony armrests cutting into her elbows. "Guess what? I just met Christopher, Uncle Lam's son. We had a long chat. He said his goal is to enjoy life as much as possible. But he sounds like a young man lost in this wild and scary world."

"How old is he?"

Nana Wang pitched her voice higher than usual. Why? Was she concerned about Christopher as well? "He's a college freshman, perhaps three years younger than me."

"Hmm." Nana Wang hesitated. "Try to stay away from him. Mr. Lam may get upset if he finds out you've befriended Christopher."

Did she hear that right? Grace pressed the receiver against her ear. "I don't understand. He needs to know God, and I can help him. I've invited him to go to the fellowship meeting with us tomorrow."

"Just be careful. I'll pray for you." A sigh rushed through the line. "Remember what your mom taught you? Always ask this question in whatever you do, 'Is it pleasing to God and helpful to others?'"

"Of course." How could she forget? What she was doing didn't sway from Mom's teaching. Well, maybe Nana Wang was overly worried about her. "Have you booked your flight? When are you coming? I'll make arrangements with Uncle Lam and Mr. Cheung so you can stay with me."

"I'll arrive sometime between mid to late July." The scuffle of papers flipping distracted Grace. What was Nana Wang doing? "I'll email you the flight information."

"Okay."

After the phone clicked, Grace folded her arms on her knees and rested her head on them.

Lord, so many things I don't understand. Please give me wisdom so I can share the gospel with my new friends. They need You in their lives.

Chapter Fourteen

Early Sunday morning, Kevin sat at his desk and squinted at the computer, his mind circling back to Grace. If both Dad and Mr. Lam could tell he was courting Grace, she should have perceived his feelings, right? What else did he have to do?

His fingers glided over Danny's notebook. *Okay, just read two more pages.*

May 21, 1989: Glad to be home. On television last night, Li Peng, premier of the State Council, declared martial law. Rumors circulate that more than a hundred thousand troops have been transferred to Beijing, but they're blocked by citizens outside the city. It's not clear why the government called the People's Liberation Army to Beijing. Mom was worried and begged me not to go to the protests anymore. I assure her everything will be okay.

May 23, 1989: Chong, Jintao, and I participated in the parade. Quite a few officials, cadres, and folks from the scientific and industrial circles joined the procession, about one million people in all. We want Li Peng to resign from his position. Our protests have been peaceful so far.

May 24, 1989: Today's news shocked me. Three men from Hunan, Chairman Mao's hometown, smeared his portrait on the Tiananmen Rostrum with paint-filled eggs. We don't agree with what they did. At the same time, I harbor a deep sympathy for them and their parents. The three, about my age, have been handed over to the Beijing

Municipal Public Security Bureau. They face uncertain fates, but for sure, a long jail term awaits them.

Kevin dropped the notebook and leaned back in his chair. Why did he find Danny's notebook dry? Facts with minimal emotion made it dull and uninteresting. He'd need to rewrite it to resonate with readers. But, how?

He rubbed his temples and shifted his mind toward a more pleasant incident.

The foursome outing yesterday went better than he'd expected.

All the way, Danny behaved like last time. He complimented Grace's appearance, teased her, and cracked jokes to make her laugh. Yet she seemed uninterested in the special attention.

And Christopher? Would he cause trouble? Grace appeared to treat him like a younger brother.

The playboy-in-training surprised everyone. He hiked with them and also attended last night's Bible study where they discussed the subject of spiritual beings. Their leader, Li something, explained how the Bible's teaching differed from the Chinese folk religion rooted in the belief that the dead transformed into ghostly entities.

Christopher had waved a hand and responded that he believed in the existence of evil spirits. He then described how he took part in a game called The Dish Spirit.

A chill crept up Kevin's spine as Christopher's words echoed in his mind. "The four of us used a small porcelain bowl and a large plate of rice. We flipped the bowl upside down. Then we each laid a finger on the plate's edge, closed our eyes, and chanted, 'Dish Spirit, please come.' Faint noise rose as if something was moving. My friend commanded, 'Please call up Dr. Sun Yat-sen. We want to see the signature of the first president of the Republic of China.' A few minutes later, the sound quieted down, and we chanted again, 'Dish Spirit, please leave.' Afterward, we lifted the bowl. On the rice was Dr. Sun's signature, just like the one in our textbook."

Li had inclined her head. "Most likely, you guys didn't call up Dr. Sun. Satan and many evil spirits under him exist in the spiritual realm. They can appear as deceased people to disturb us. By the power of the Holy Spirit, we can rebuke them."

She'd gone on to share her own experience. Once she succumbed to play The Dish Spirit at a party. Whenever she placed her index finger on the plate, the game wouldn't work. The Holy Spirit within her must have stifled the work of the evil spirit.

Li then warned the group to avoid paranormal games and said, "Sometimes, believing in no God by itself is a belief."

Well said.

Why did he believe in atheism? Was it possible he'd taken up his college professor's idea as his own? One classmate, who claimed to be a Christian but didn't act as one, also drove him further away from Christianity. Yet, his recent interactions with Grace and other Christians... Maybe he ought to reexamine his thought process.

Someone tapped on the door.

"Dad, could you get it?"

The knock persisted. Dad must have stepped out. Kevin stood, stretched his arms, and shouted, "Coming."

As he opened the door, Christopher strolled in uninvited.

Speak of the devil, and the devil shows up.

Kevin darted his gaze around them. Nice. Dad had tidied up their room before he left. "You're up early. Any big plans for today?"

The unexpected guest plopped down on the carpet and yawned. "Not sure what's going on here. Both our dads are going to church with Grace. Are you going too?"

The clock struck eight. Kevin rolled his neck from side to side, working out a kink. No way would he have time to write more. "Yeah. How about you?"

Christopher splayed out his legs and stared at the ceiling. "Do you think my dad is courting Grace?"

Kevin clamped his cold palm to his forehead but couldn't subdue his irritation. "What makes you think so? It's nonsense." His bangs tickled the back of his hand as he pulled it away. Had Ah Tang continued to spread groundless gossip? He ought to set the record straight and let everyone know he had Dad's and Mr. Lam's blessings to court Grace.

Christopher waved in the air. "If not, why is he going to church with her? Also, I flipped through the tabloids in the servants' quarters. The notorious womanizer who used to appear on the magazine covers every other day hasn't shown up there for two weeks."

Kevin clenched his teeth. "Grace's mother was your dad's good friend. Mr. Lam is treating her like a daughter."

"Yeah, right. A daughter. The way he looks at her..." Christopher sat up. "Maybe a bit more than a daughter."

Gross! Sick! Kevin forced himself to remain quiet, then pounded a fist against his thigh, fury burning through him.

"Ha, your face is turning red. You're angry." As his eyes crinkled up, Christopher pointed a finger. "You like her, don't you?"

Like? More than like. *I love her.* Heat spread to Kevin's ears, and he turned his head sideways.

"Hmm." Christopher snickered. "Dad has a formidable competitor this time. From the way she looked at you during the hike, I bet Grace also likes you. She's the first girl immune to my dad's wealth and position."

Whoa? Really? Kevin sank to his knees beside Christopher and grasped his friend's arm, his voice trembling. "You think she likes me?"

"Even though you're older than I am, I'm more experienced with women than you are." Christopher's grin widened. "Usually, my hunches about a woman's interest are accurate."

If Christopher was right... But no, Grace had dodged his advances more than once. Last night, after they came home, he'd asked her again what she felt about them, and she hadn't answered.

He dropped his hands and clenched them at his sides. What to do? He adjusted his glasses, his mind clouding. Well, at least they would attend worship together today. "We'd better go to breakfast now if we want to make it in time for church."

***

Grace sat with her friends in the last row inside her church's sanctuary. Nice to have them attend worship again. Even Christopher came.

She stole a glimpse of Uncle Lam and Mr. Cheung on her left side. Kevin said they both attended the fellowship group meeting geared toward business people yesterday.

Lord, thank You. I pray they'll know You soon.

Kevin fidgeted next to her. As his leg brushed against hers, electricity shot through her. Heat tingled in her cheeks, and she shifted away from him.

Focus on the hymns. The worship team singers soared on the stage, and praises of the Almighty echoed in the room. The women behind her lifted their voices and celebrated the goodness of God.

Yet, how could she? With Kevin so close, her mind kept wandering.

She'd dressed up for worship again, albeit with no makeup. Kevin had commented that her jade-green day dress and silver sandals fit her well. And he'd said he liked her curls hanging loose.

His compliments had warmed her heart. Still...

During the past few days, he'd twice asked how she felt about them, and she hadn't answered him. Should she tell him her concerns or continue to dodge his advances?

Lord, please give me wisdom.

After the worship team finished, Pastor Hong ascended to the podium. "Today we'll study Mark chapter five verses one to thirteen about the demon-possessed man."

The familiar passage talked about a man troubled by demonic spirits. He lived among the tombs outside of the city, so out of control that no one could get near him. Jesus sought him out and healed him. But the evil spirits moved into a herd of two thousand pigs and caused them to drown in the Sea of Galilee.

The pastor's sermon aligned with their discussion in the Bible study group last night about the spiritual realm. Unlike before, Kevin hadn't asked any challenging questions and even nodded after Christopher shared his experience.

Did Kevin now believe in God?

She rubbed her forehead and redirected her thoughts toward the sermon. When he twiddled his hands in his lap, the slight movement caught her attention again.

Concentrate. Please.

At last, Pastor Hong said the benediction. Grace rose and exited the church's main entrance with Uncle Lam, Mr. Cheung, and Kevin, while Christopher and Danny lingered behind them.

A woman, tall and curvy, rushed up. Her carefully made-up face looked familiar, except for the sternness in her eyes.

She pointed a manicured finger at Uncle Lam, her red nail polish a perfect match to her lipstick. "Someone said you were here. Indeed! I've been trying to reach you for two weeks. Why didn't you answer my call?"

"Hi, Lily. What a surprise." Uncle Lam took a step back. "I've just returned from out of town."

Grace eyed the newcomer, then Uncle Lam. Why did he lie?

Mr. Cheung shifted forward, shielding Uncle Lam. "Ms. Ching, nice to see you in person. I'm Dave Cheung. We've spoken over the phone before." His voice remained low and steady. "Our SUV is right over there. If you don't mind, could we talk inside the car instead of blocking people's way here?"

Ms. Ching? She must be Lily Ching, Uncle Lam's girlfriend.

"Don't you dare play coy with me." Lily hissed and thrust a hand onto her hip. Then her gaze fell on Grace. "So, you found this new chick. That's why you're avoiding me?"

A chill crept down Grace's spine. She sent Kevin a pleading glance, and he hastened to her side.

"Ms. Ching, it's not what you think." Mr. Cheung held out his palms as if protesting.

Lily pushed him away, stared Grace up and down, and raised her arm.

Would the out-of-control woman strike her? *Lord, please help me.*

The woman lifted Grace's chin. "No makeup? How old are you? You look like someone's kid sister."

What inappropriate and intrusive behavior! A knot tightened in her stomach. Grace bit her lower lip and racked her brain for a reply.

"Ms. Ching, I'm Kevin Cheung, Dave Cheung's son. It's a pleasure to meet the most famous movie star in town." Kevin drew Grace away from the intruder. "This is Grace Feng, my girlfriend."

Grace forced a smile. "Ms. Ching, nice to meet you. You're so beautiful."

"You're Kevin Cheung's girl?" Lily let out a little laugh, and her expression softened. "I'm jealous of your unblemished skin. Maybe I should try the natural look too."

As Christopher and Danny joined them, Mr. Cheung turned to Lily. "Although the young people plan to have lunch together, Mr. Lam and I are heading home. If you like, you can come with us."

He motioned for Old Moy to drive up to them, and the three of them left in the Mercedes-Benz.

Relief weakened Grace's knees. Lily seemed the sort of woman capable of physical aggression.

Thank You, Lord, for Kevin's quick response.

When she glanced at him, he flashed a bright smile. Heat rushed to her face. Once again, he'd saved her from a potential disaster. But why would Uncle Lam date such an unruly woman?

"What happened?" Christopher waved in the air as if asking for a replay. "Why was Lily Ching here?"

Danny's jaw slackened. "Was that Lily Ching? Wow. She's more beautiful than in the movies."

"Femme fatale." Kevin chuckled. "Attractive, but also dangerous and manipulative."

Christopher nodded. "I have no idea what attracts my dad to her. From what I've heard, she's the most difficult actress to get along with."

"She's charming and talented." Danny raised his hand. "I like her movies."

"Somehow, she looks familiar." Grace squinted. Perhaps she'd seen Lily's movies.

As they strolled along the sidewalk, Christopher paused in front of a newsstand and pointed toward a magazine display. "Now you've mentioned it. You and Lily Ching do look alike, especially the eyes."

Grace moved forward and scrutinized Lily's profile. To be more precise, she looked like Mom. Both had almond-shaped eyes and full lips and similarly shaped noses. With makeup, Lily's complexion was lighter than Mom's, but they seemed otherwise comparable in appearance.

Did Uncle Lam date Lily and Mom because he tried to find someone like his first love who died young?

Kevin tugged at her sleeve. "A penny for your thoughts."

"Er... Nothing." She shook her head hard. "I hope Lily doesn't cause trouble for your dad and Uncle Lam."

Chapter Fifteen

Kevin peered into the room. Okay, Dad wasn't around. He returned his attention to Danny's notebook on his desk and flipped to a new page.

June 3, 1989: Hundreds of hunger-strike tents remain at Tiananmen. Thousands of people are still demonstrating on the square.

Disturbing news: Armed troops, more than ten thousand soldiers together with automatic weapons and tanks, approach Beijing. Rumors circulate that soldiers sympathetic to the democratic movement have donned civilian clothes and sneaked into the square to inform the protestors.

In the evening, Chong, Jintao, and I decided to go to the square to check it out. Zhou, a friend who remained at the square after the hunger strike, said the news is correct. A few hours ago, troops used tear gas in Liubukou, not far away from Tiananmen.

We discussed what to do next. It isn't right to leave like cowards at this moment. Nothing we can do except embrace our fate.

Another factual account with little emotion. Kevin dropped the notebook, unsure whether he wanted to read the next day's event—a description of the gruesome massacre in Danny's own words.

Well, no hurry. *I can continue tomorrow.*

He sneaked into the hallway. Should he knock on Grace's door? What should he say? "I'm sorry I told Lily you're my girlfriend. Could we make it official?"

No, too forward and awkward. He'd wait and see if she sought him out.

"Kevin, what are you doing here?" Mr. Lam spoke behind him.

Kevin clutched his forehead. Why didn't he notice Mr. Lam's presence? "I, uh..."

Mr. Lam patted his shoulder. "Thank you for coming to our aid earlier today. Without your quick wit, I don't know what Lily might have done."

"I..." Kevin's face burned. *Calm down. No need to feel embarrassed.* "I'm glad I was able to help."

"Do you have a moment? Let's sit and chat." Mr. Lam gestured toward the nook. "I can tell you like Grace. Have you asked her out yet?"

Kevin jerked his head up. When did Mr. Lam become so direct? "Um, no, I haven't. We're just good friends. For now."

"That's understandable. Just don't wait too long. Learn to seek the moment." Mr. Lam let out a chuckle. "Your dad mentioned that, if you had a regular job, you'd gain confidence in dating. Have you thought more about the job I offered you the other day?"

Not again. Kevin bit his lip, struggling to keep his cool. "Yes, I've thought about it. Not sure I'm ready for something like that yet."

"I believe it'd be good for you. You'd learn a lot and gain new experience." Mr. Lam winked, then flashed a mischievous grin. "Plus, a guy with a stable job becomes more attractive in certain girls' eyes. Why don't you think it over some more? We can discuss it again later."

Both Mr. Lam and Dad must have underestimated Grace. She wasn't the type of girl who didn't return his affection because of his lack of a steady income. Or was she?

And what about their hypothesis that Lisa Lam and Grace's mom were victims of Mr. Lam's love for that mysterious girl? "Ah Tang said you once loved a girl, and she died young. Is that true?"

Humor vanished from Mr. Lam's face, and a coldness fogged his eyes. He turned and stormed away.

What had he just done? Groaning, Kevin slumped against the wall. Too late now to take back the uncensored words.

Dad approached from the other end of the hallway. "Son, are you okay? You don't look well."

"I may have offended your boss." Kevin chewed his lower lip, then relayed the conversation, except for the job offer. "I hope my imprudence won't affect your position here."

"Didn't I tell you to be careful?" Dad's deep frown pinched his brows together. "Yeah, my original guess about Grace and my boss was wrong. But too many mysteries remain between them. Think twice before asking about their pasts."

Right. Mr. Lam's history with Grace's mom indeed involved mystery.

While he remained silent, Dad gestured for them to walk back to their room. "Did Mr. Lam encourage you to ask Grace out?"

Kevin nodded.

Dad laughed, his forehead smoothing out again. "Well, it seems the big boss knew something I didn't. You should listen to him."

What if I ask her out and she declines? A tightness in his chest made Kevin shudder. No, he couldn't take that risk.

Dad bumped their shoulders. "You're silent. Are you worried she'll say no because you don't have a steady job?"

Why did Dad have to bring up the unpleasant subject all the time?

"Let's not go into that today." Kevin resisted the urge to roll his eyes like an ill-behaved child. "Did Lily Ching cause trouble for you and Mr. Lam after you guys left us?"

"Yes and no." As they entered their room, Dad waved and eased himself into a chair. "She got into the SUV and continued to rant about her displeasure. She yelled and hit the window with her fist. At that point, Mr. Lam asked Old Moy to stop the car. He told her they were through and ordered her to leave."

Kevin sagged his mouth open. From what he knew, Lily didn't belong to the category of women who accepted defeat easily. "And she obeyed?"

"Yes." Dad tapped the desk. "She had no choice. Mr. Lam said if she continued to cause a scene, he would contact the media and provide them with the details of why they ended their relationship. If she cooperated, he would let her break the news to the media herself."

Wow. No wonder Mr. Lam became successful in the business world. He knew how to handle manipulative people in difficult situations. With a new appreciation for how much he could learn from Dad's boss, Kevin crossed his arms over his chest. Maybe he ought to accept the job offer. "Mr. Lam asked me if I'd be interested in joining his company's PR team."

Dad stood and grasped his arm, his eyes gleaming. "Son, this is it. The moment I've been waiting for. When will you start?"

He flung away Dad's hand. "You got excited without asking me what the nature of the job is."

"Why is that important?" The light in Dad's eyes dimmed as they bored into his. "A position in Mr. Lam's PR team speaks volumes. You'll become an excellent communicator, both verbal and written, and have opportunities to build lasting relationships with many key players in town. You'd be insane not to accept his offer."

While Kevin kept quiet, Dad shook his head. "So, you turned him down?"

"Mr. Lam was kind enough to give me time to think about my decision." Kevin scratched his forehead. If only he could reach inside and scratch at the perplexity clogging his mind. "Dad, don't you think it's odd? We've been living under the same roof for over a year, and he said nothing about me working for his company. All of a sudden, he wants me to work for him. Could this have something to do with Grace?"

"Now that you've mentioned it, it does seem suspicious." Dad patted him on the back. "I suspect Mr. Lam is eager for Grace to date you. The job offer is his way of drawing you and her closer together."

Nice. Why hadn't he thought of it? Mr. Lam was a sly one. They had to give Dad's boss credit. "But what about my writing?"

"Son, you can still write while working for Mr. Lam, right?" Dad winked at him. "Just think about how this position will help you find a way into Grace's heart."

Perhaps Dad was right. He should try it.

The phone rang, and Dad went to pick it up. "Hi, Angela." With a spreading grin, Dad waved to dismiss him.

Angela Zhou from church? Kevin strolled toward his makeshift office before turning back to Dad. What was going on? Why did Dad sport a goofy smile like a teenager?

Without finding obvious answers, Kevin picked up Danny's notebook and walked out.

***

The summer solstice took place yesterday, bringing excessive heat and rain. Two weeks had passed since Grace started her job. Last Friday, she received an acknowledgment from her boss that her project was going well.

As she settled into her cubicle, her stomach fluttered. Would Kevin visit their building today? Since the Lily Ching incident the Sunday before last, her relationship with Kevin seemed... changed again.

He no longer pestered her with questions about what she thought about them but still sought her out to discuss the Bible. Besides, the entire household continued to attend Sunday worship and Saturday Bible studies.

Lord, I pray once more for Your mercy that all my friends get to know You and follow You.

Last night, Kevin proclaimed he finished reading the New Testament and asked her which Old Testament book he should read next. She'd replied without hesitation, "The book of Isaiah. It covers specific prophecies about the Messiah."

Then he told her Mr. Lam had offered him a job, and he would start working on the first Monday in August. "In the next few days, I may go to your building to familiarize myself with the surroundings."

"Congratulations!" She'd stretched out her hand while stifling her uncertainties. "How come you didn't tell me before now?"

He shook it and thanked her. "I just finalized the deal with Mr. Lam yesterday."

So, Kevin would become her colleague. They might attend meetings together. She'd get to know him even better. But...

Was she disappointed that he no longer pursued his dream of becoming a writer, or was she relieved that he'd chosen to explore other possibilities and grow in different ways?

She hugged her arms around her chest, her fingers gripping her shirt as if she could hold onto something tangible. "Have you given up writing the book about the Tiananmen Square Incident?"

"Not really." He'd turned his head away. "I'm still in the process of researching and writing it. That's why I negotiated with Mr. Lam to start in August. It'll give me time to put together a draft."

Her desk phone rang, interrupting her musing.

"Grace." Wilma spoke with an underlying sense of urgency. "Please come to my office."

Grace twisted her watch into view. Not even nine. Why did Wilma want to see her so early on a Monday morning?

As she entered her boss's office, two individuals, an older woman clad in high fashion and a middle-aged man in three-piece business attire, turned in their seats. Wilma introduced them as Mrs. Connie Dong and her son, Stanley, and emphasized that Connie owned a sizable stake in Mr. Lam's company.

Uh-oh. Grace's chest hurt. She must have made errors to render a visit from an important shareholder. But what could have so displeased the Dongs?

The visitors' gazes fell on Grace's face, and their eyes widened. Then Mrs. Dong pointed at her. "Christopher was right. You look just like his other women, except you're much younger. No wonder his pictures haven't appeared on tabloid covers recently. With a chick like you under the same roof, he must be having lots of fun and living life out of the public eye."

Surely, she wasn't talking about me. Or referring to Uncle Lam. Otherwise, the woman must be insane. Normal business owners wouldn't insult their partners and new employees with such disrespectful talks.

Grace narrowed her eyes, tension radiating from her body. "Excuse me. I'm not sure I understand you."

Mr. Dong stood and surveyed her up and down, a smile tugging at his lips. "It's no secret he prefers a certain type of woman. You're the best example of it—beautiful, young, and innocent. Has he made you an offer you couldn't refuse?"

Haziness overwhelmed her, and Grace took a step back. She glanced at her boss, whose expression registered shock. "Wilma, what are they talking about? It doesn't seem to have anything to do with my work. Why are they even here?"

A knot of muscle trembled in Wilma's jaw. She clenched her fists as if steeling herself for the task ahead. "Connie and Stanley, the office is no place to discuss personal matters. We need to focus on our work and maintain professionalism. Certain topics should be discussed in a more private setting."

The color rose to Connie's face. She spoke through clamped teeth. "We aren't talking about personal matters, are we? He took this girl into his house and let her work under you. As a shareholder, I have the right to know whether the company's policies and procedures are being followed and that the rights and interests of our shareholders are being protected."

Stanley inclined his head. "This arrangement may subject the company to potential legal or financial liabilities."

Legal or financial liabilities? Grace crunched her eyebrows. Of all the exaggerations... She was just Wilma's insignificant new assistant.

"Connie." Wilma placed a palm on the desk, her voice calm. "Since you raised an issue about the company's policies and procedures, I suggest you bring it up to the board. You can discuss your concerns with other board members."

With that, Wilma stood, guided Grace out of the door, and spoke in a low voice. "Grace, why don't you return to your cubicle? I'll continue the discussion with Connie and Stanley."

Grace trod back with her shoulders sloped and her face scorched. The two visitors had wronged her with their words and actions, with no justifiable reason. Why was she left alone in this unfriendly city?

"Are you all right?" Mary leaned over the thin wall separating them. "You look rather pale. Did Wilma give you a hard time again?"

"No." Grace shook her head hard. Mary's concerned tone undid her shredded dignity. "A certain Mrs. Connie Dong and her son wanted to meet me in Wilma's office. I didn't quite understand what they said to me. It has nothing to do with work." Moisture gathered behind her eyelids. She swallowed to squelch the lump forming in her throat. "Do you know who she is?"

"You don't know who Connie is?" Mary let out a snort. "Everybody in Hong Kong knows she's Sam Lam's mother-in-law. Since her daughter's death, she and Mr. Lam haven't been on good terms."

What? Grace shot up to her feet, then sat back down. That woman was Christopher's grandmother? No wonder she said, "Christopher was right."

Connie and her son accused her of having an inappropriate relationship with Uncle Lam. How heinous and sick!

Kevin's hypothesis about the victims of Uncle Lam's love for that mysterious girl flashed across Grace's mind. Alongside Christopher, Lisa Lam, and her mom, she joined the list today.

Did secrets in Uncle Lam's past affect them all?

She palmed her cheek, then raised her head high. "Mary, thanks for the information. I'd better get back to work. Wilma expects me to complete a new spreadsheet today."

Mary flashed a thumbs-up. Then her head disappeared from above the cubicle wall.

The day passed with no further incident. Grace dragged her exhausted body to dinner, then slipped into her room. Sitting in the antique chair, her shoulders arched with a load of heaviness on her chest. She shut her eyes and whispered, "Lord, I'm weary and confused. Please give me the strength to accept whatever You have planned for me."

A trace of peace crept into her heart. No matter what happened, God was with her. If she left Hong Kong, it had to be in God's will, not because of Connie, Stanley, or anyone else.

She opened her eyes and dialed the familiar phone number.

After she relayed to Nana Wang what'd happened, her beloved friend offered encouragement, then commented, "I can understand why Mrs. Connie Dong feels threatened. As the only heir, Christopher, her grandson, will inherit everything Mr. Lam owns. She doesn't want him to remarry, especially to a young woman who could bear him more children and take away from Christopher's inheritance. She may also feel that, if Sam remarries, it's a betrayal of her daughter's memory. Tension must have already existed between her and Sam."

"But it's totally untrue!" Grace's shoulders stiffened further. "Does Connie really think Uncle Lam intends to court and marry me?"

"With the unique arrangement for you, someone like her may draw that conclusion."

She rubbed her neck, the phone receiver almost slipping from her hand.

"Hello?" Nana Wang's voice wavered.

"I'm still here." Grace's neck remained stiff from the tightness of her grip on the phone. "Uncle Lam has done nothing improper. My mom trusted him. And now, I trust him too. He has my best interests at heart. He even suggested I should date Kevin."

"I agree. Take his advice and go out with Kevin. Ignore anyone with a perverted, twisted mind."

"Sounds like you want me to start a relationship with Kevin as well," Grace teased.

A light tap on the door sounded.

"Um, someone is at my door. Let's talk later." She put down the phone and went to answer the knock.

Kevin strolled in, and his gaze, full of concern, bored into hers. "You were awfully quiet during dinner. Something must be wrong. Can I do anything to help?"

Moisture rushed to her eyelids. Should she tell him what had happened? She blinked back the heat in her eyes, holding back the words as well. "Thank you. I feel... overwhelmed. That's all."

Yet, uncontrolled tears welled up.

"Oh, Grace." He drew her to his chest.

The simple act of his touch conveyed a profound sense of solace. She closed her eyes and let herself surrender to the moment, the weight on her chest easing as she leaned against him. His strong arms wrapped around her with a tenderness that melted her defenses. He smelled of clean laundry with a hint of cologne. The warmth of his embrace formed a sanctuary, an embrace that seemed to cocoon her fragile soul from the chaos of the world. Despite the unpleasantness of her day's experience, a wave of tranquility washed over her, soothing the raw edges of her heart.

Then his warm mouth fell on hers.

With an avalanche of thoughts tumbling through her mind, she pushed him away.

"What are you doing?" Her screech reverberated off the walls in a strange echo.

"I–I..." Crimson crept into his cheeks, and his face crumpled. "I thought you wanted me to kiss you."

She shook her head, her heart pounding. "No. This isn't right."

"I misinterpreted your signals." He stepped back and ran a hand through his long hair. "I'm sorry. I didn't mean to make you uncomfortable."

She took a deep breath, still shaken by her unplanned first kiss. "Let's forget this happened. Okay?"

He flashed a sheepish smile and dashed out of the room.

She slumped into the chair nearby, squeezed her eyelids tight, and focused on her breathing, counting each inhale and exhale. As her heart rate slowed, she opened her eyes, but the memory of the kiss lingered.

Her stomach tightened with a quiver of an inexplicable new emotion.

What was it?

She couldn't answer.

Chapter Sixteen

The last Friday of June arrived. Rain turned the trees along the streets lusher and greener, and women's skirts shrank to above the knee.

While strolling toward the dim sum restaurant in Causeway Bay, Kevin narrowed his eyes at the overcast sky. Did Grace take an umbrella?

His relationship with her appeared to be moving in the right direction until...

Before he tried to kiss her, she'd trusted him and opened up her deepest concerns. He often sought her out after she came home from work, and they chatted—only the two of them—in the hallway sitting nook. Against sounds from falling raindrops on the windowpanes and the rumbling thunder, they laughed and talked about everything and nothing.

Then, when he placed his lips on hers, she pulled away and grew distressed. Afterward, she kept her distance, refusing even to look at him as if he were a deadly plague.

He'd told her he'd now secured a steady job, but it didn't seem to make a difference. As he suspected, Grace wasn't the type of girl to care whether he had money.

What was her real concern? Perhaps he'd moved their relationship too fast, and she wasn't ready for physical intimacy.

Or was she in love with someone else?

Maybe she felt unsure about her employment situation. Last night, Dad mentioned how Connie Dong confronted Grace at work and raised an issue with the company's board. Mr. Lam called an ad hoc board meeting this afternoon to resolve the problem. After such an unpleasant experience, anyone would develop a heightened sense of anxiety or fear.

Oops. Grace might question whether she should remain in Hong Kong.

As he entered the restaurant, Danny waved from a corner table on the left. "Kevin, over here."

Although the place wasn't crowded like on weekends, the diners' voices and clattering plates still assaulted Kevin's ears.

Why did Danny ask him to lunch today? Did his friend succeed in securing Grace's affection and want to tell him in person? *Please let that not be the case.* Kevin strode over, his heart hammering. "Today is Friday. Why aren't you at work? Comp time again?"

Danny didn't answer and slid the chair open for him. "I saw the tabloids this morning. The news has it that Lily Ching broke up with Mr. Lam. Does that have anything to do with the chaos in front of the church two weeks ago?"

"Ah, that." Kevin waved, eased himself into the chair, and relayed what Dad had told him.

Danny's eyes widened. "That simple? Wow, I'm impressed. Mr. Lam is good at dealing with tough situations."

"He is." Kevin scanned around him. A family occupied the table next to them, and the other tables nearby stood idle. Okay. Nobody was eavesdropping. "I was just as impressed."

"Mr. Lam sounded ruthless. Didn't you say he's kind and generous?"

"I know. It's odd. He usually plays the role of Mr. Nice Guy with his girlfriends." Kevin shoved the hair off his forehead. Should he tell Danny he would soon work for Mr. Lam? "It's even weirder. During the past month, my dad and Mr. Lam not only faithfully attended church worship but also participated in a fellowship group for working people."

"Incredible. Is the most eligible bachelor in Hong Kong becoming a Christian?" Danny poured tea for him. "The tabloid covers no longer display his pictures. Except for Lily Ching's press conference to announce her breakup with him, the media seldom mentions his liaison with starlets anymore. What's causing his change?"

Kevin shrugged. So, Danny made the same observation. It'd been like that since Grace's arrival. Why? How could her presence inspire such a dramatic change? From all he knew, she'd done nothing other than invite all of them to church. Oh, yes, she now called Mr. Lam, "Uncle Lam." Perhaps her unique way of trusting others with unconditional love cast powerful effects on people around her, just like what had happened to him. Yet, he'd betrayed her trust by kissing her in her vulnerable emotional state. He'd tried to convince himself he misunderstood her, but in truth, he'd taken advantage of the situation. What could he do to repair their relationship?

Danny sank back in his chair. "How about your dad? Is he going to church just to keep his boss company?"

"I'm afraid my dad has become engrossed with Christianity as well. He and Mr. Lam plan to get baptized together soon." Yeah, so unlike the dad he knew.

"Isn't that wonderful?" Danny grinned.

"Maybe. Dad used to be an agnostic but now believes in God's existence. How can a person's view be transformed in mere weeks?"

A server swung by with a cart, and Danny ordered for them. "Tripe stew, your favorite." After the waiter placed the dish on their table, he scooped a spoonful for Kevin.

"Nice. Thanks." Kevin bit into the tripe's chewy texture, savoring the sauce's unique taste. He worked it around his mouth, then swallowed it down. "Mr. Lam is organizing a private yacht party next weekend and has invited Dad along with Angela and Amelia Zhou."

Danny raised a brow. "The spinster sisters from our church?"

"Right. The nurse and the nephrologist. The four of them now attend the same Bible study group." Kevin took another bite. "I suspect they're double-dating."

"Are you serious?" Danny's jaw slackened. "Who is dating whom?"

Kevin shut his eyes and rubbed his hand along one temple. "I believe my dad is dating Angela. They've been calling each other almost every night. I often hear Dad's muffled laughter even from my desk in the closet."

Yet, the part involving Mr. Lam and Amelia puzzled him. Amelia was intelligent, with a pleasant appearance, but no beauty. Didn't Mr. Lam prefer a particular type of beautiful woman? Had he changed in that regard as well?

"Aren't you happy for your dad?" Danny patted his arm.

Kevin shifted in his seat. "Yes and no. Dad once said he didn't remarry because no woman would love a poor widower like him. Angela seems the first person interested in him for who he is and doesn't mind what he has or doesn't have." He moved a palm to his brow. "They're moving forward at light speed. It's unreal for people their age."

Danny picked up his chopsticks and pointed them at him. "I don't think it's possible to control the speed of falling in love."

The speed of falling in love! His friend sounded like a philosopher. *Are Danny and Grace falling in love?* Kevin grabbed a pork bun. "Are you talking about yourself? Who is the lucky girl?"

"Nobody." Danny shook his head. "I'm leaving Hong Kong in two weeks."

"What?" Kevin dropped the pork bun, stood, and gripped the chairback. People from the next table eyed him.

"Sit, please." Danny tugged at Kevin's sleeve.

He sat back down. "Where are you going?"

"Sorry, I didn't tell you before, but I wasn't sure I'd get it." Danny tapped his teacup. "Operation Yellow Bird applied for a special visa for me to go to the US. The application has gone through. Remember my friend Yan? We'll go to LA together."

Danny wasn't after Grace? He'd misunderstood his friend. "I can't believe it." Stunned, Kevin scratched his chin. "I had it all wrong. I thought you were interested in..."

Whoops. An unfortunate slip of the tongue.

"Interested in Grace? She's a unique person. I must admit, I tried to court her in the beginning." Danny squinted. "Besides, Grace likes you more than she does me."

"You think so?" Kevin jerked his head up, his bangs flicking into his eyes. "How can you tell?"

"Well, she radiates a lovely glow when you're around." Danny chuckled. "Plus, she always laughs at your jokes even when they aren't funny."

"Thanks. I appreciate it." Not exactly a compliment, yet it carried joy and warmth. Then a more unfortunate thought intruded. Maybe she did like him prior to that kissing incident. Now... Kevin squirmed. He'd goofed and terribly flubbed the line. "The problem is, every time I tell her how I feel about her, she dodges my questions. My dad said it was because I didn't have a steady job. I didn't think so."

"I agree with you. She isn't the type of girl who considers a decent salary a requirement for courtship." Danny picked up a shrimp dumpling. "She's probably holding back because you aren't a Christian."

"What do you mean?" Kevin scrunched his forehead, his long bangs tickling his brow.

"Just a hunch." Danny chewed slowly, his voice muffled. "Grace may only date Christians."

Was that her concern? Somehow, the idea never crossed Kevin's mind. "If I believe in God, she'll accept me?" He pushed the remaining tripe pieces on his plate with the chopsticks, his appetite diminishing. "It's not prudent to become a Christian just to date her."

Danny swallowed his mouthful of food. "I'm glad to hear that. She'd be able to tell whether your faith is genuine, anyway."

A chill crept into Kevin's heart. "You weren't born into a Christian family, right?"

"No." Danny sipped his tea. "I became a Christian after I came here."

Kevin clattered his chopsticks to his plate and adjusted his glasses, tumultuous feelings roiling him. He'd secured a regular job, and Grace still hesitated to settle into a steady relationship with him. Danny must be right that she only dated Christians. But... "When did you find out you'd become a Christian? Did you experience a specific aha moment?"

Danny set down his teacup. "Every person has their own spiritual path. For me, it happened at home when I was reading Jesus' parable about the father and his two sons. Suddenly, the Bible verses spoke to me. I confessed I was like the prodigal son and needed Jesus in my life."

"That was it?" Kevin braced an elbow on the table with his chin on his palm. "What happened afterward?"

"Nothing dramatic overnight." Danny lifted his gaze toward the ceiling. "I became more sensitive to sin, and my faith fluctuated over a wide range. Later, I learned that the transformation of my life by the Holy Spirit is a long process that ebbs and flows. Time and again, I found myself falling so low, making me question my salvation."

It didn't sound complicated. Kevin lowered his head, his long hair tickling his cheeks. "Don't you have to study the Bible, attend church, and receive baptism to become a Christian?"

"Yes and no. Those steps are important but not sufficient." Danny's soulful, midnight-black eyes gleamed. "A Christian is a person who has confessed his sin and established a relationship with God through Christ's sacrificial death on the cross. As in any relationship, spending quality time together is critical. God is always there for us. We tend to stray off course when we become distracted by external influences. The Bible, church, and baptism are ways to help us get closer to God."

Sins? Why must they harp on that? Kevin kneaded his brows. "Confess my sins? I consider myself a decent person."

"By your standard, you are." Danny's gaze bored into his. "Before God, we're all sinners. Even if we don't sin by commission, we sin by omission."

"What does that mean?" Fighting the impulse to shield his eyes from Danny's stare, Kevin ran his fingers through his hair and pushed the strands away from his face. Christian jargon used to irk him. Somehow, it no longer irritated him.

Danny tapped the table. "We may not do things that displease God, but often, we don't do things that please Him, which is equally bad. We've all sinned against God because human nature is self-seeking."

Kevin jutted his chin. "That's such a high standard." Despite his defiant response, he rubbed his neck, his muscles tightening to protest his uncertainty.

True. In the past year alone, how many times he didn't do what he ought to do? Self-seeking was the correct word for him. He focused mostly on his interests and goals and seldom considered the needs of others outside his circle of family and friends.

Sin by omission.

If that was God's standard, he'd sinned miserably. Still...

"God is holy. He won't accept anyone who harbors sin." Danny gave his hand a gentle squeeze. "If we confess our sin and accept Jesus as our Savior, the Holy Spirit will help us establish a relationship with God. Do you want to confess your sin to the Lord today?"

"I–I—" Kevin drew his eyebrows even tighter. "No, I'm not ready. This is such a serious decision." He must experience God first. "I need to think about it more."

"No worries. I understand." Danny dropped his arm. "You mentioned Grace gave you a Bible. Have you been reading it?"

"I've finished the New Testament." Kevin stretched his lips in a sad attempt at a smile. "Grace suggested I read the book of Isaiah because it covers specific prophecies about the Messiah."

"Excellent suggestion." Danny inclined his head. "About the book on the Tiananmen incident, what progress have you made?"

"I'm working on it. Thank you for your notebook. You provided me with a unique personal account. As I read the information about what the Chinese government did back then, I can't help but ponder what will happen to Hong Kong after 1997." Heat rushed to his face, and frustration seethed from his clenched jaw. "I feel like I'm standing at the juncture of history and witnessing the fall of a unique place, the Pearl of the Orient, my hometown."

Danny pressed his fingers to his temple, the pain on his face almost too much to witness. "Even though I only live here for three years, I've fallen in love with this special locale."

Kevin gaped at him. "Then why are you leaving?"

"Because—" Danny's voice dipped, and tears glimmered in his soulful eyes. His misery appeared like an immense, invisible cloud. "I'm a coward. I fear persecution from my government."

A few simple words. Yet, as if all hope had been drained out of him, Danny's leaden tone fell heavily between them, and his sorrow weighed on Kevin.

Danny loved China. He could have gone to Europe or the US under the political asylum protocol after he escaped from Beijing, but he lingered in Hong Kong. He once admitted he dreamed the Chinese government would change their attitude toward democracy.

Now that dream seemed dashed. After three years, China still denied anything bad ever happened in Tiananmen.

What a burden for someone to bear. The motherland Danny so loved had betrayed him. It was as if his mother sold him into slavery.

The horror emanating from this realization was almost palpable to Kevin. Would it be his fate along with many others in Hong Kong after 1997?

Kevin brought a palm to his chest. If Danny learned he'd accepted a job offer from Mr. Lam, what would he think? He let out a dry cough, trying to clear the lump lodged in his throat. "Have you told anyone else your decision?"

"Not really. I'm concerned about Yan's and my own safety. Please keep it quiet as much as possible." Danny picked up his teacup, then set it down again. "I won't be going to church anymore. If people ask about me, please tell them I'm busy. Once Yan and I arrive in LA, I'll call Pastor Hong myself."

Okay, Kevin got it. Even though Hong Kong was still under British rule, the Chinese exerted an increasing influence on his hometown. The recent implementation of a controversial national security law, the promotion of Chinese culture and language in the school system, the intertwined economy with the mainland... All pointed toward an obvious message. Hong Kong was no longer a safe place for dissidents like Danny.

Driven by an unidentifiable inner emotion, Kevin leaned forward to hug his friend. "I'll miss you. Take care."

Danny returned the hug, his eyes glistening. "Stay safe, man. I'd better go. A realtor is coming to my studio this afternoon. Lots of things to do." He asked for the check and paid. Before he left, he tapped Kevin's shoulder and mustered a slight smile. "I hope to read your book soon. Keep in touch."

Kevin stood to watch his friend stroll away. Two questions, together with a crushing despondency, pressed on his core.

Was it a mistake to accept Mr. Lam's job offer? At this historic juncture, why did he still worry more about pursuing his personal interests and goals?

***

Friday afternoon, the PowerPoint slide on Grace's computer screen blurred out of focus again. During the past hour, she tried to stay on task, but her thoughts kept turning to her first kiss, *stolen* by Kevin a few nights ago.

He said he'd misinterpreted her signals. Had she sent him an unspoken cue, beckoning him to kiss her? The incident with Connie Dong earlier that day might have confused and overwhelmed her. After Kevin offered her comforting words, she did cling to him and stay in his arms, didn't she? Maybe she'd misled him. He apologized, showing the courage to admit he'd made a mistake. No matter what, she'd have to stay away to avoid falling under his spell again.

The way he made her feel... She placed a finger on her mouth. The warmth of his lips seemed to linger on her skin. Her heartbeat picked up, and heat radiated from her face. Part of her desired to be close to him, to feel his embrace and never let go. Another part of her wanted to keep a safe distance. There was no future for them. He wasn't a Christian, and she didn't plan to stay in Hong Kong. They'd best remain friends.

With a sigh, she returned her attention to the computer screen. Uncle Lam had summoned an ad hoc board meeting in response to Connie's challenge. The board asked Grace to prepare a presentation highlighting her background and the projects she'd completed so far as Wilma's assistant. Uncle Lam had assured her that, although it was up to the board to make their decision, she possessed the necessary degree and skill set for her position.

Five minutes before two, she entered the conference room. Uncle Lam gave a brief account of the matter and signaled for her to begin.

After her presentation, the three board members Grace hadn't met, two older men dressed in expensive suits and a stunning middle-aged woman in a simple blouse and skirt, smiled, seemingly impressed.

"Her qualifications may be acceptable." Connie raised her hand. "My issue is whether Sam has violated the company policies. He offered her a position in the company and asked her to stay in his house. Isn't it unusual for an employer to ask a new hire to live in the same house with him? Especially since she's a beautiful young girl. This type of arrangement could lead to abuse or exploitation of the employee and must be avoided. We ought to investigate Sam's motives."

All gazes fell on her. The two men's expressions turned stern, while the woman flashed a kind smile. "Grace, I'm May-May Ying. You did an excellent presentation." May-May's voice sounded gentle and warm. She turned toward Uncle Lam. "Sam, could you please explain?"

Grace sucked in a quick breath, relieved to find a friendly face. Yet, now she realized the impropriety of the situation. Why hadn't she considered the wrong implication? True, she wasn't well experienced in the business world, but Uncle Lam should have known better. Why did he take the unnecessary risk? How would he respond?

He maintained his calm expression. "Grace's mother, Susan Feng, was a classmate of mine since my high school days in California. Susan passed away a few months ago and asked me to help Grace as much as I could. Since Grace came from the US and didn't know anyone here, I thought she could stay in my house until she became more familiar with Hong Kong." He dipped his chin. "I admit I should have taken more time to consider how others might misconstrue this arrangement."

Uncle Lam tapped the enormous oval table, the sound thudding in time with Grace's heartbeat. "Connie, thank you for raising your concerns. I believe all board members agree Grace's skill set makes her an ideal candidate for her current position. If her living in my house is a source of discord for the board members, we can solve it by having her find an apartment."

Except for Connie, all the other board members nodded. They set a deadline for Grace to move out before the end of July or risk having her employment terminated.

A knot tightened in Grace's stomach. Where could she find an affordable apartment in one month? She might as well quit her job and go back to the US. At least Nana Wang would welcome her return.

Hadn't she prayed that, if she left Hong Kong, it must be up to God's plan, not because of Connie or anyone else? Now, others dictated her next step.

"Before the meeting adjourns, I have a question to put to the board," Uncle Lam interrupted those who were starting to stand. "Will it be acceptable for Kevin Cheung to join the company while he continues to live with his dad, Mr. Dave Cheung, at my house?"

May-May Ying, already tucking paperwork into her satchel, paused and folded her hands atop it. "I know Dave and Kevin Cheung well. Kevin is a talented young man. When his dad became your personal secretary and butler, I approached Kevin about whether he would like to work for us. He declined. I'm glad he's changed his mind. Since he's been living in your house for quite a while now, it's unreasonable to ask him to move out just because he agreed to join your team."

The other board members, including Connie, didn't have objections. Though happy for Kevin, Grace clenched her teeth, suppressing the sensation of injustice that consumed her. After the board members left, her energy drained away, and she slumped into her chair.

Uncle Lam walked out with others, then returned to the conference room. "You look pale. Don't worry. I know an excellent place for you to move to. Remember Angela and Amelia from church? They have an extra bedroom and will welcome you. The rent will be quite affordable."

The two aunties from church? Yeah, they'd become her dear friends in Christ, but she hadn't expected them to take her in.

"Come with me to my office." He guided her out. "I'll call Amelia right away."

While he talked on the phone, Grace sat up straighter in her chair. Wow. He seemed close to Amelia. Were they dating? When did that start?

Amelia's cheerful voice boomed over the speakerphone. "My sister and I would be delighted to have Grace stay with us. Don't worry about the rent. Whatever she can pay should be fine. When will she move in?" She giggled. "Sam, that yacht party you're organizing for next weekend. Is Grace coming? I'll give her the keys then, and she can move in any time she likes."

Ah, the yacht party. Uncle Lam invited everyone, including Kevin and his dad. Grace had turned down the invitation because Wilma gave her a new assignment and expected it completed soon. Plus, she couldn't spend an entire weekend on a yacht with Kevin. It wouldn't do them any good.

"Well, now that you've mentioned it." Uncle Lam crinkled up his lips. "Grace can't go. Maybe the Saturday after the party?"

"Sounds great. Why don't you bring her to our flat in the afternoon? I'll show her the room and give her the keys. If you two have time, stay for dinner with me. It so happens all the Bible study groups on that Saturday are canceled in preparation for the annual children's vacation Bible school during the week of July thirteenth."

A grin stretched his sensual lips wide. "How about Angela? Will she be home?"

Laughter burst from the speaker, filling the room with warm, joyful energy. "Guess what? She'll be going out with a guy you know well."

A guy Uncle Lam knew well? Who was that? Grace scratched her forehead. Well, it was none of her business. But she now had a place to live and could keep her job. Plus, she needed to get away from Kevin. Staying under the same roof with him wasn't prudent.

Thank You, Lord, for Your guidance. Even the problem with Connie is under Your control. Help me trust in You.

Oh no. How about Nana Wang's visit? Well, she'd worry about it later.

Chapter Seventeen

In the members-only marina, Kevin opened his eyes wide at the sheer size of the vessels, all luxurious and shiny. Envy infused his whole person, while heat crept up his neck. What a lifestyle!

They stopped in front of a sleek white yacht with blue trim underlining the name *Susanna* on its side.

"Here we are." Mr. Lam extended a hand toward Angela and Amelia. "Do you need help with your bags?"

The sisters shook their heads, their mouths ajar. Amelia lugged her Pullman. "No thank you. I've got it."

"Very well." Mr. Lam stepped aside. "Welcome aboard the *Susanna*. I hope we'll have a wonderful time together. Let's go inside."

Susanna? Was the name derived from Susan Feng, Grace's mom? Kevin swept his gaze toward the clear sky, brushing aside the question.

The voyage ahead would be full of adventure and fun if Grace had come along. When he didn't see her before they left home earlier today, Mr. Lam mentioned that she received a special assignment from Wilma and needed to complete the project over the weekend.

Yeah, the special project was an excuse. Grace was avoiding him. After the kissing incident, she'd shunned him, finding something else to do or fleeing whenever he was around.

The group walked up to the yacht, and Kevin ran his hands along a section of the smooth hull. The craft's beauty and power seemed to whisper, "I'm something special."

Christopher swung his backpack to and fro, his lips pressed into a thin line. "Dad, what's the living arrangement? I suppose the two aunties will stay in one guest cabin, and Kevin and Mr. Cheung will share another. What about me? Shall I stay in your stateroom or use the third guest cabin?"

Ah, the *Susanna* boasted three guest cabins besides the owner's stateroom?

"You can take your pick." Mr. Lam smiled at his son.

Amelia raised a hand. "Sam, give us a tour."

With a wave to beckon them along, Mr. Lam chuckled. "I'd be happy to. Let's start with the bow."

They left their luggage on the deep side deck and headed toward the front.

Kevin sucked in a quick breath at the panoramic harbor view. The afternoon sun burned brightly, casting a golden glow across the water. The waves lapping the shore and boat hulls lent a gentle, calming rhythm. In the distance, the city's tall buildings gleamed in the sunlight.

On the main deck, they passed a grill and bar in the outdoor dining area and entered a sitting room equipped with a TV and a piano. Then Mr. Lam led them into a luxurious suite.

Christopher eyed the king-sized bed and muttered, "I'll use the third guest cabin."

"Yeah." Mr. Lam's lips crinkled up. "I figured you wouldn't enjoy sleeping in the same bed with your old man." He glanced at Kevin. "Don't worry. All the guest cabins have two beds."

At the bridge, Mr. Lam introduced the captain, a muscular man in his midthirties, and three crew members.

The captain gave a brief overview of the room and equipment. "We're all set to leave."

"Sure." Mr. Lam clapped. "Let's go."

The yacht glided through the calm ocean. Minutes later, the city disappeared from sight, leaving only the vast expanse of blue. From the deck, Kevin surveyed the turquoise water. Nearby, two high-powered fishing boats worked on the South China Sea, their outboard motors humming.

Ah, Hong Kong! Hundreds of islands, numerous fishing villages, and miles of white sand beaches dominated three-quarters of his beloved home. No, he wouldn't live anywhere else in the world.

A crew member started the grill. Soon, the scent of burgers, ribs, and seafood swirled around them. With music in the background and the sun shining, Kevin grabbed a plate of food and sat underneath the enormous umbrella. He chewed on a fresh grilled shrimp, savoring the smoky flavor.

"May I sit here?" A slim shadow appeared across the white tablecloth.

"Angela? Of course." He stood and drew the chair out for her. Today, she'd pinned her hair back in a tight bun. Clad in a teal blouse and black slacks, she looked chic and professional. Dad would be a lucky guy if he could marry her.

"Thank you." She smiled. They sat quietly until she broke the silence, her voice light. "So, your dad mentioned that you've been studying the Bible?"

Kevin stopped chewing. He dipped his chin, unsure of how to respond. He was still trying to get used to the idea that Dad had become serious about Christianity. "Yeah. A little. I've been reading it and trying to understand its different meanings."

She grinned. "Which book are you reading now?"

He swallowed. "I finished the New Testament and have started the book of Isaiah."

She stared into his eyes. "Do you believe in God?"

Kevin coughed, unease creeping up. She sure didn't mince words. "I don't know. Somehow, I've never explored the God stuff until now." He scooped a forkful of fish, his chest tightening further. "Even if God exists, we have many religions. What's special about Christianity?"

He took a bite of fish but couldn't focus on the taste as Grace's words intruded. She'd asserted that the Old Testament gave more than three hundred prophecies about Jesus. He blurted out, "Grace said Jesus is unique because He fulfilled all the prophecies about Him. She also told me I should read the book of Isaiah since it contains specific prophecies about the Messiah."

"Grace gave you sound advice." Her warm eyes aglow, Angela smoothed back strands of hair the breeze freed from her bun. "I also hear you wish to date Grace. How is that going?"

Heat rushed to his cheeks. He clenched his teeth, controlling his composure. Did Dad share everything with Angela? This was such a personal matter, and now it was out in the open for Angela to judge. Good thing that he hadn't told Dad about the kiss he imposed on Grace.

"Don't be shy." Angela patted his hand. "Did your dad tell you he and I are dating?" Her face lit up, her beaming smile further warming her eyes. "It'll be great if you and Grace could take things to the next level."

I wish the situation between Grace and me were as smooth as the one between you and Dad.

What could he do to restore his relationship with Grace to where they were before that awkward kiss? He racked his brain for something nice to say, but all he could manage was a small yeah.

Angela hugged him, enveloping him in a motherly embrace. "So, you're okay with your dad and me dating?"

He nodded. "I—"

Amelia strolled toward them. "Ah, you two seem quite serious. What are you chatting about?" She cocked her head toward her sister. "Angela, have you told Kevin that Grace will come to live with us?"

"What?" He shot to his feet. "Grace is moving out of Mr. Lam's house?"

Right. She was trying everything to get away from him.

"Are you well?" Angela gaped up at him. "You look pale."

"I—" Knots tightened inside of him. He sat back down. "When did she make that decision?"

Angela frowned. "Only recently. I thought you knew."

He ran a shaky hand through his hair. He hadn't expected this— not at this point, not ever. With Grace in the same house, he'd hoped to rekindle their relationship. Now, everything had changed. He took a deep breath and met Angela's gaze. "When will she move?"

Amelia put a comforting hand on his arm. "Before the end of July."

He had to figure out what to do, fast. The food on his plate no longer appealed to him. He pushed against the table to stand up again. "Excuse me."

As he dashed into the sitting room, someone trailed him. Dad's worried voice sounded. "Son, are you sick?"

Moisture gathered behind his eyelids. He sat and stared at his sandals to hide his emotions. "Do you know Grace is moving out of Mr. Lam's mansion into Angela's flat?"

Dad sighed. "Angela mentioned it yesterday. I should've told you right away."

Kevin swallowed hard, the lump in his throat not budging. "Dad, I want to be with Grace, but she's avoiding me. Once she moves out, I'll forever lose my chance with her." He turned sideways, tears stinging his eyes. "I don't know what to do."

Dad gripped his shoulder. "Son, don't panic. Grace won't move until the end of this month. Once we get back home, try to talk to her again."

"If she..." His chest seemed constricted, each breath a struggle. If she said no, what could he do? "My friend Danny said Grace will only date Christians. I want to be honest with myself. I won't claim to be a Christian just to court her."

"Honesty is the best policy with anyone." Dad drew back his arm and kneaded the back of his neck. "Have you tried prayer? I learned from Angela that, if we pray with a sincere attitude, God will answer and guide us."

Kevin jerked his head up. "Have you prayed? Did God answer you?"

"I have." Dad responded without hesitation. "In the beginning, I found the Bible study boring. I asked God to help me. Strangely enough, I began to understand the Bible better, and now I can't get enough of studying His Word."

Kevin gaped. Was Dad serious? He'd always been a practical, no-nonsense kind of guy. What caused his change? Angela! Of course.

"Well, I haven't eaten yet. I'd better get back to the buffet." Dad stood. "God is real, son. I'll pray for you and ask God to open your heart and mind so you can know Him."

With a heavy weight pressing on his chest, Kevin watched Dad stroll away and fought the urge to cry. No, he wouldn't and shouldn't shed tears. He was no longer the teenage boy he'd been when Wendy died. If he survived back then, he could live his life without Grace by his side, right?

He stifled a groan and returned to his cabin. His Bible, Grace's gift, lay on the nightstand. He flipped it open to Isaiah chapter nine. As he read, verse six jumped out. "For unto us a child is born, unto us a son is given; and the government shall be upon his shoulder: and his name shall be called Wonderful, Counselor, The Mighty God, The Everlasting Father, The Prince of Peace."

Suddenly, the words came alive. Goose bumps crawled all over him. He couldn't control his body from shaking. Could anything be more explicit? The Almighty God, the Everlasting Father, was born as a baby into human history.

He kneeled with tears in his eyes. "O God. Forgive my unbelief. You, the creator of the universe, were born as a helpless baby, experiencing all the limitations we humans face."

Too much to fathom. Yet, it was written clearly in black and white.

As he reflected on guilt woven deep within his spirit, Jesus' words in the Gospel books flashed across his mind. He removed his glasses and rubbed his temples, his heart pounding. "Lord, You gave Your life as a ransom to redeem me from Satan. The evil one can't accuse me anymore."

The burden weighing on him since Wendy's accident vanished. "Lord, thank You..."

He kept on praying, oblivious to the time.

Pitter-patter, pitter-patter...

The persistent noise roused him. He opened his eyes, blinking away the gloom in his room. Why was it so dark? Was it evening already?

Thunder cracked in the distance. Raindrops smacked louder and louder. The ship rocked. Even inside his cabin, the wind's howl was deafening.

Right. Typical monsoon season in July. One moment, a clear and beautiful sky. The next, unpredictable weather could carry a typhoon.

A faint tap sounded. He opened the door, and Angela stood outside. "Your dad said you might be in your cabin. Are you all right?"

"I'm fine. Is everything okay?" He followed her up to the sitting room. "How serious is the storm?"

Amelia sat with Mr. Lam on the couch. Christopher and Dad stood by the piano. As he and Angela approached, Mr. Lam waved. "According to the captain, the monsoon wind funneling through Taiwan Strait can create dangerous conditions. We've been beating into thirty-knot winds and three-meter seas for a few miles to get away from the center of the storm. If the condition persists for the next twenty minutes, we'll turn toward the protected waters of Snake Bay."

Kevin peered outside. Water crashed against the hull, and spray plumed into the air. A hazy gray hid the sky's previous vibrant blue.

Then a towering wave slammed into the yacht, throwing him down on the carpet.

The lamp flickered, someone screamed, and Angela prayed aloud.

Kevin tried to scramble up to his feet, his stomach churning. Another violent jolt flung him across the floor. His tongue flicked across his dry lips, and something cold coiled around his core. *Are we all going to die today?*

The light went out. The darkness seemed to stretch on forever, like a vast emptiness with no end in sight. He laid a palm on his chest. *God, I believe in You. My life is under Your control. If we survive today, I'll dedicate my life to serving You.*

A simple prayer. Yet, an inexplicable peace spread through his whole person. A few more minutes passed. Then the electricity returned. Moments later, the sea calmed.

Christopher shouted, "Hooray! We managed to escape the storm."

Kevin sat up and looked around. Small pieces of furniture were scattered and knickknacks overturned. Angela sprawled on the floor, her face contorted. Dad kneeled by her side, his features taut. Amelia cowered in Mr. Lam's arms, and Christopher's hands latched on the piano, the tendon on his neck stretched.

"Is anyone hurt?" Mr. Lam's eyes widened like a frightened rabbit's.

No one responded at first. After a moment, Angela straightened up from her crouched position. "Praise the Lord. All of us seem okay."

Amelia pulled away from Mr. Lam, crimson spreading across her cheeks. "Whoa. It's a miracle. We've just experienced a storm of immense power and magnitude, and everybody made it out unscathed."

Dad helped Angela to her feet, and Christopher let go of the piano.

Joy surged through Kevin's veins. A newfound appreciation for the power of nature and the God who created it developed.

Lord, thank You for saving our lives and also our souls. You are here with us.

Chapter Eighteen

Dreams spread across the shadowy valley. Voices burst into a chorus of emotion.

Kevin opened his eyes. The midmorning sun streamed through the window, illuminating the room with warm, golden light. The dreamscape remained vivid in his mind. Some faces appeared familiar, while others seemed strangers. Together, they weaved a web of happiness and sorrow around his core.

He flipped his bangs and remembered he'd just cut his hair short earlier. Six days had passed since his encounter with God on the yacht. Oh, what a difference a week made! He not only altered his appearance but also experienced a profound internal change. One minute, a strange sense of peace and joy flooded him. Then the next, his mood swung to the other extreme. Doubts and fears, with all his transgressions, flashed across his mind. His past with Wendy, his tendency to tell white lies, his uncontrollable desire for Grace, his penchant for procrastination...

Dad's concerned voice rose. "Son, are you taking a nap? Why don't you go to bed?"

Kevin furrowed his brows. This was the third consecutive day he'd fallen asleep on his desk. Why couldn't he focus on his writing? After starting his new job in August, he wouldn't have time to write like now.

Yet, how could he concentrate? Shame gripped him when his faith fluctuated. Did he deserve God's forgiveness? "Dad, I don't know what's going on with me. Since that day on the yacht, I thought I connected with God. But I waver. At times, I question whether I've been saved."

Dad's lips crinkled up, his half smile soft. "I experienced that too. Angela told me being a Christian doesn't mean we won't sin. As new Christians, our inner struggle seems worse than before. We become more sensitive toward sin with the Holy Spirit's help."

Kevin scratched his cheek. His eyebrows loosened somewhat. "Danny said the same thing."

"Yes." Dad drew a chair to sit by him. "He told you Grace only dates Christians, right? Have you shared with them about your faith?"

Should he tell Dad that Danny was leaving Hong Kong in two days? It might jeopardize his and Yan's safety. And Grace might think his conversion to Christianity was a ruse to court her. No, he must not tell her himself. "I haven't. I'm not sure how Grace will react."

"Hmm." Dad drew out the sound in a thoughtful tone. "It's awkward for you to tell her. Maybe Angela and Amelia can help. Mr. Lam and Grace will go to their flat later today and have dinner with Amelia. Since we won't have Bible study tonight, Angela and I plan to go to a concert." He twisted his watch into view. "Let me make a quick call."

Kevin waited for Dad to stroll away, then pulled out Danny's notebook.

June 4, 1989: I'm still shaking. Who could have believed today would end like this? Nothing seemed unusual this morning, just hot and humid. My throat still burns—from the tear gas or the actual tears clogging it? I don't know. I don't even know how to write about what happened. It started so normal. We stayed put in Tiananmen Square, along with a few thousand people. Many waved banners and sang songs. In the evening, gunfire broke out, and the air became thick with tear gas. I started running with others as fast as I could. Broken banners littered the square, and the approaching tanks vibrated the ground. My steps faltered. I yelled for Chong and Jintao but didn't hear any response. From where I stood, the scene shocked me. Hundreds, perhaps thousands, stood shoulder-to-shoulder in a human chain to block tanks from entering the square. Were my good friends among them? The tanks didn't stop and kept advancing. I debated whether to join them. It was the most difficult and devastating moment of my life. Then I started running again.

Kevin dropped the notebook and swallowed against the knot forming in his throat. On June 5, 1989, when he turned on the TV, the news overwhelmed him. Later, stories leaked out, divulging the full horror of the event. Still, when an eyewitness revealed the details in his own words, it conjured up a different meaning. Those who hadn't made it faced a terrible death. And the survivors endured so much pain and remorse. Danny said both his friends didn't make it out of Tiananmen Square on that day. How their parents must have felt after the news reached them! What happened to their girlfriends? Did Chong and Jintao have a chance to say farewell to their loved ones?

I ought to tell Grace I love her before it's too late.

A persistent knock sounded. Had Dad left the room already? Kevin stood. "Coming."

When he opened the door, Christopher stepped in and gaped at him. "What happened? You cut your hair short."

Kevin touched the back of his neck, raking the bristly parts at his nape the wrong way. "Um... it's about time."

"Did the storm we experienced on the yacht have something to do with it?" Christopher brought a palm to his chest. "The howling of the wind was horrible. I was afraid we were all going to die. It was a miracle we made it through."

"For sure." His prayer on that day flashed across Kevin's mind. *Thank You, Lord. How great is Your mercy.* "Moments like those reminded me of the fragility of life and how I should make every day count."

His thoughts turned toward the Sunday worship led by Angela the next day. She cited Acts 27 and talked about Apostle Paul's shipwreck journey to Rome. "Angela's sharing last Sunday further strengthens my conviction. I envy Paul. Driven by a steadfast purpose to serve God and humanity, he maintained an unshakeable composure in the face of death."

"Ha, you sound like a preacher, like Pastor Hong." Christopher edged away and diverted the conversation. "Are you all pumped about your new job in my dad's company?"

"Not really." Kevin yawned, a sudden exhaustion hitting him after the emotional overload. "Why?"

"Nothing." Christopher plopped down on a chair. "You probably know already. Grace is moving out. My dad is taking her to Amelia's flat this afternoon. Ah Tang is wrong about Dad and Grace."

"Didn't I tell you that?" Kevin rolled his eyes. Oh well. No way would he have time to write more today.

Christopher jerked his gaze up toward the ceiling. "Seems my dad is dating Amelia. Do you think he's serious about this relationship?"

Kevin scratched his forehead, brushing aside his short bangs. "Why don't you ask and see what he says?"

"I'm confused." Christopher scuffled his slippered feet. "If Dad remarries, what will become of me?"

In front of him sat a confused and frightened teenager. Brimming with tender care, Kevin laid his hand on Christopher's shoulder. "If your dad remarries, he isn't replacing you with someone else. He'll love you the same."

"Do you believe so?" Christopher glanced at him, then lowered his chin. "I once thought my dad didn't know what love is. How wrong I was! I still desperately want his love and approval." Moisture glistened in his eyes. He blinked hard. "You're facing a similar situation. Don't you mind your dad remarrying?"

"I've already given him my blessing." Kevin grinned, a gentle heat coursing through him. "I'm happy he has found Angela. It's a beautiful thing when someone loves you for who you are. I believe her sister is like her. She loves your dad for who he is, not because of his wealth or status."

"How does one change so fast in such a dramatic way? Last summer when I came home, Dad played the field like always." Christopher crossed and uncrossed his legs, then slapped his knees. "Somehow, it must have something to do with Grace. I just don't know how and why."

"If Grace had anything to do with it, it was because she invited us to church. By studying the Bible, we, including me, have all gone through a time of self-reflection and growth." Kevin paused. Yeah, what an amazing period since Grace's arrival—they'd experienced "Amazing Grace," indeed.

"Thank you for listening. Sorry to have bothered you. I'd better leave now." Christopher stood. "I'm meeting some friends for a picnic on Lantau Island."

"Will you go to church tomorrow?"

Christopher waved as if to brush aside an unpleasant subject. "Maybe."

Kevin watched his friend leave. *Lord, I pray Christopher will know You too. And I need Your guidance to find a way into Grace's heart.*

***

Lush greenery, palm trees, and purple bougainvillea flowers surrounded Grace. What an oasis in the center of the bustling city! She followed Uncle Lam into the lobby. "Wow. The marble floors and glass walls create such a pristine and airy feel."

"You like it?" He waved to encompass the vast space. "The building has various amenities, including a gym, pool, and spa. Several restaurants and cafés on the second floor also offer a variety of cuisine."

"Is this one of your creations?" She opened her eyes wide at the detailed pomegranate-motif decorating the ceiling.

He nodded, an enormous smile curling his lips. "Yeah, a project I completed a few years ago. I've always wanted to ensure that my buildings are functional and aesthetically pleasing." He led the way toward the counter where two security guards stood. "We need to check in first."

As they exited the elevator onto a hardwood floor, murals depicting ancient gods and goddesses lined the hallway. The intricate designs and luxurious touches made her gasp. She'd thought his mansion was the best. Well, this place must rank the second best. "Now I'm worried. How much do I have to pay every month?"

"Amelia said whatever amount you feel comfortable with." Uncle Lam rang the bell.

The door swung open. "Welcome. Nice to have you here." Amelia stepped aside to let them in. "Please, make yourself comfortable. Can I get you anything?"

Grace relaxed her shoulders. Warm sunshine filtered through the floor-to-ceiling window to highlight comfortable furniture and inviting artwork. The place felt like home already. "No thank you. I'm fine for now."

Uncle Lam took a seat on the plush sofa. "Amelia, why don't you show Grace around your apartment?"

"Of course." Amelia grasped Grace's hand. "Let's go to the kitchen first."

After showing off the modern kitchen with lots of storage and workspace, Amelia took her to an enormous room. "Your future home. It has its own en suite bathroom, walk-in closet, and dressing table."

Light and airy, the room also offered large windows overlooking the Hong Kong harbor, and its walls—a pastel pink, perfect for a girl—brought warmth to Grace's heart. "This is wonderful." She leaned against the table. "Um... How much is the rent?"

"Don't worry. Whatever amount you can pay is fine." Amelia chuckled and drew her to sit on the bed. "Call me Auntie Amelia. I have something to tell you."

"Yeah?" Her curiosity piqued as Grace plopped down beside her new auntie.

Amelia's gaze fell on her face. "Kevin accepted Christ as his personal Savior. Has he mentioned it to you?"

"That's incredible!" Grace slackened her jaw. "No, he hasn't. When did this happen?"

"During our yacht outing last weekend, we encountered a severe storm. That might have been the trigger. After we came back, he confided in his dad about his change and how he struggled as a new believer." Amelia smiled. "You've been part of this change. You ought to congratulate and encourage him."

"Absolutely. I'll be sure to do that."

Indeed, God worked in mysterious ways. Yet, heat crept up to her cheeks, even while something cold coiled in her stomach. Since the kissing incident, she hadn't allowed herself to get near Kevin. What would happen to them if she sought him out? Would he think she was trying to make a move on him?

"Well, let me know how it goes." Amelia pushed off the bed and checked the nightstand alarm clock. "We'd better get back to Sam. He's probably ordered food for us."

In the living room, Uncle Lam was setting down the phone receiver. "Ha, what took you so long? Girl talk?" He winked at

Amelia. "I ordered your favorite Shanghai cuisine from downstairs. It should be here soon."

After the food arrived, they settled at the dining table. Amelia raised her teacup. "To Grace and her future home here!"

"To Grace's success in Hong Kong!" Uncle Lam hoisted his teacup. "Now, when will your friend, Ms. Wang, arrive?"

At the mention of dear Nana Wang, a gentle embrace of comfort enveloped Grace. "Nine more days. She'll arrive on July twentieth." She sipped her tea, savoring the earthy flavor. "I can't wait to see her. I've already told Wilma I'll take that day off." She turned toward Amelia. "Nana Wang won't leave until the end of July. After my move on the last Saturday of this month, is it okay for her to stay with me here for a week?"

"Of course." Amelia scooped up a spoonful of pork and plopped it on Grace's plate. "Try this. The best sweet-and-sour pork in town."

"I love their xiao-long bao." Uncle Lam snatched a steamed dumpling with his chopsticks. "Amelia, thank you for introducing me to Shanghai cuisine. I didn't know it could be so delicious."

Amelia giggled and placed a chunk of steamed fish with ginger and scallion on his plate.

Over the next forty minutes, they consumed the five dishes with occasional chitchat. Grace stole glances at Uncle Lam and Amelia. The two didn't say anything special. Yet, from the way they interacted, something sweet was happening between them.

Thank You, Lord. With Amelia's help, Uncle Lam will draw closer to You. Please continue to guide him as he seeks You.

Her thoughts turned to Kevin, and her grip on the chopsticks tightened. What was he doing now? Without their regular Saturday Bible study gathering, did he stay at home and write?

What would happen if she talked to him one-on-one tonight? Would she lose control of herself? Since childhood, Mom had taught her that honesty was always the best way to deal with difficult situations. No matter what happened, she must be honest with him— and with herself. They belonged to two different galaxies. Traversing was impossible.

At eight thirty, Amelia urged them to leave since they all had to get ready for Sunday worship tomorrow. After getting out of the Mercedes-Benz, Grace bid Uncle Lam good night and trudged toward the garden. Light from the lamppost filtered through the tree branches, casting a glow on the bushes. Still, the gentle murmur of the wind rustling through the leaves failed to subdue her edginess. *Take a deep breath. You need to remain calm when knocking on Kevin's door.*

Underneath the arbor supporting climbing wisteria, a long shadow meshed with the moonlight and dappled shade. Jasmine sweetened the air, and the crickets' distant chirps brought the background alive.

"Kevin?" Grace sucked in another deep breath, her heart pounding. The figure stepped forward, the moon's reflection in the night sky illuminating him. She blurted out, "What happened to your hair? Did you get it cut?"

As he approached, his eyes sparkled. "Yes. I'll start my new job soon. It's time to change my hairstyle."

"You look nice." A lump formed in her throat, and she coughed. "Congratulations! Amelia said you've accepted Christ as your Savior."

The corners of his mouth rose like the dawn mist dueling with the sun. "Yes. I'm thankful for God's love and grace. I also want to thank you for your help in my faith journey." He plucked a flower, a purple camellia. "For you. No matter what, you'll always remain in my memory as the most special person I've ever known."

Heat rushed to her cheeks. She took the flower, the soft petals caressing her fingers. "Thank you."

"Grace." His gaze bored into hers, his breathy voice barely more than a whisper.

Her chest tightened as she looked into his eyes. "Yes?"

"I love you." He waited.

The air seemed charged with electricity. She wanted to say she loved him too, yet the words wouldn't come. Tears pricked her eyes as an uncensored response bubbled to the surface. "Kevin, I care about you and will never forget you, either. But you belong to Hong Kong, and I don't. A year from now, I'll return to the States. Then what will happen? There's no future for us."

The smile drifted from his face, confused and sad lines taking its place. Was he trying to process what she'd said?

Oh, how she wished she could drop into his arms and comfort him. Still, she must speak the truth. "I'm sorry."

He turned his head sideways. "I thought..." His voice trailed off, and he dashed away.

As she watched him go, sorrow pulsed through her veins. *O Lord, why does my heart hurt so? Am I in love with Kevin?*

Chapter Nineteen

Kevin tossed and turned in desperation, unable to sleep or shake the pain. Yesterday, he'd professed his love for Grace, only to receive a cold, senseless response. What did she mean by saying she'd leave and there was no future for them?

He'd thought she felt the way he did and the only hindrance between them was his faith issue. Wasn't their relationship something special? Now he'd accepted Christ as his Savior. Why couldn't she stay in Hong Kong if she cared about him?

The pain intensified in his abdomen as if someone had punched his gut. He scrambled off the bed and tiptoed along the floor.

Light seeped in through the slit in the curtains, and Dad's voice rumbled through the dimly lit room. "Kevin, it's still early. Where are you going?"

He froze in his tracks. "Out for a walk. I couldn't sleep."

Dad sat up in bed. "I heard you restless all night. What happened? Are you worrying about starting your new job in August? It's still over three weeks away."

Kevin walked back and slumped down by Dad. "Last night, Grace came back from Angela's flat and congratulated me on my accepting Christ as my Savior. I professed my love for her, but she turned me down."

Dad put an arm around his shoulder. "Did she explain why?"

Heat rushed up Kevin's throat, and he swallowed hard. "She said she's returning to the US in one year and there's no future for us."

"That's a tough situation, son." Dad blew out a breath. "I can understand her concern. She doesn't have any relatives here. It's natural for her to want a support system back on her home turf. It doesn't mean you can't make it work if you're both invested in the relationship. Are willing to go to Illinois?"

Caught off guard, Kevin stiffened. Surely, his father hadn't suggested such a solution. Right. Dad had once told him that, if possible, they should leave the city before 1997. The handover of Hong Kong to China involved great uncertainty and change. While he was applying for universities, Dad wanted him to make a new start in Australia, but Kevin couldn't bring himself to do it. His birthplace had been the backdrop of his entire life.

He paused. No, he wouldn't leave Hong Kong. Not when Dad asked him to go to Australia for college and not now with 1997 fast approaching. "Dad, I'll stay put. I'm not leaving Hong Kong."

Dad exhaled sharply. "May I know why you're so insistent?"

"Because this is home, where I belong. After my experience on Mr. Lam's yacht, I'm more convinced than ever that I should make my life count by helping others, not only for my ideology but also for the new conviction from God." Kevin gripped his forehead under his short bangs, his voice quavering. "Staying in Hong Kong to encourage my fellow Christian brothers and sisters during the most difficult time this city has ever faced will bring me more fulfillment."

"Then I have nothing else to say." Dad shifted away. "Remember, love is a choice. You can choose to love Grace, even if she doesn't return your sentiment. Just keep on loving. Who knows? By God's mercy, something wonderful may happen."

Was Dad right? Yeah, he would keep on loving Grace, even if she wasn't ready to love him back.

The morning light filtered through the curtain with a soft warmth. Kevin glanced at the clock on the wall. Wow, time to get ready for breakfast. Today would be the first Sunday in church since he accepted Christ as his Savior. Would he understand Pastor Hong's sermon better?

***

Grace curled up her legs to her chest and pressed the phone against her ear. "Hi, Nana Wang. It's me."

"Hello, dear Gracie. What's up? You don't sound well."

Tears rolled down her cheeks as she fidgeted in her chair. "Last night, Kevin professed his love for me, and I turned him down."

A distressing silence fell in the room. The only sound came from the slight crackle of the phone line. "Are you still there?"

"Yes, I am." Nana Wang's voice sounded softer than usual. "I'm sorry to hear that. Are you okay? Did you tell him why?"

She wiped her face with her free hand. "Yeah. There's no future for us. I don't belong to Hong Kong. I want to return to the US and stay with you."

"I understand." A sigh whooshed over the phone line. "No matter what, I'll always support your decision."

"Thank you." Sunlight streamed in the window and warmed Grace's face. "Eight more days, and you'll come to Hong Kong. I can't wait to see you."

"Same here. Love you very much."

"I love you too." She dropped her feet to the carpet. "Last time you asked about where you would stay after I move out of Uncle Lam's house. Don't worry. I've already asked Amelia. She said you can stay as long as you wish."

"I'm sorry to have caused you extra trouble."

"No trouble at all. You booked your flight before all this happened." The muscles in Grace's shoulders eased up. She described in detail the Zhous' flat—the awesome harbor view, the spacious kitchen, and the inviting pink room. "It's perfect for me."

After she hung up, she hugged her arms across her chest. How was she going to face Kevin today? Was he still upset? They must ride in the same car to church. Oh, why did she care so much about his feelings?

For sure, she'd fallen in love with him. When did *that* happen?

She tightened her grip around herself, holding in the sorrow. A heavy weight pressed over her. Between her commitment to Nana Wang and her love for Kevin, she would hurt someone dear to her no matter what she chose. How she wished she could split into two persons!

Lord, is there a solution to my dilemma?

With tension on her whole body, she squared her shoulders and strolled toward the guardhouse. When she rounded the corner, Kevin stood with his dad, Uncle Lam, and Christopher, waiting for Old Moy to pull the SUV over. He glanced up, and their eyes met. He gave her a small smile and waved her over.

Laughing out her relief, she smiled back and rushed to join the group.

***

At the guardhouse, Kevin forced a smile as Grace's gaze locked with his. Good. Her lips crinkled up in response. The ride to church was quieter than usual. Even Christopher, usually quite talkative, was subdued today. Mr. Lam and his son engaged in small talk about the junior's activities, and that was about it.

As Old Moy pulled up to the church, Kevin's heart fluttered. He took a deep breath and walked inside. Following the others, he moved toward the front. Angela and Amelia Zhou were waiting for them.

The worship team led songs in Mandarin, followed by Pastor Hong's sermon based on Matthew 5: 38–48. The pastor preached about how to love your enemies. He began by stating that it wasn't easy to show kindness to those who had hurt us, for it went against human nature.

Kevin shivered, thinking of Danny's account of the June Fourth massacre. Had Danny left Hong Kong already? When your government—something that was supposed to protect you and love you—hurt you the most, how did you accept the betrayal?

Pastor Hong's assured voice rang through the sanctuary. "On the cross, our Lord uttered in agony, 'Father, forgive them, because they do not know what they are doing.' To follow Jesus, we should take up the cross. This means we must be willing to make sacrifices for our faith and to put God first in our lives. It may also mean to suffer for our faith and to face persecution if necessary. We should offer forgiveness to those who have wronged us, just as Jesus did. We forgive, because of Jesus."

Every word pierced Kevin's heart. After 1997, if he stood up for what he believed, would he receive persecution just like Danny and his friends?

On the yacht, he'd dedicated his life to the Lord. Before, he wanted to stay in Hong Kong for his own reason. And now? A calling larger than himself, greater than he could have imagined. Maybe it was better for Grace to return to the US. At least the government there respected the rights of its citizens more than in

China. *Lord, teach me to be obedient no matter what happens between Grace and me.*

After the benediction, he bowed his head. Joy, like a gentle stream, flowed into his heart. Yes, God was here. The Holy Spirit was here.

The postlude ended. Someone tapped his shoulder. He raised his gaze to Angela's smiling face. "Kevin, are you all right? I saw the distress on your face earlier this morning. Your dad mentioned a few things about your interaction with Grace last night. Now you seem at peace."

Kevin turned his head sideways. Amelia had apparently pulled Grace away to a corner. "Yes, I am." He adjusted his glasses, refocusing on Angela. "God has comforted me during the worship. I need to obey His guidance. Please pray for me."

Angela glanced at the dispersing crowd, then back to him. "Of course." She squeezed his shoulder. "Whenever your dad and I pray together, we pray for you. God is with you, and so are we."

He surveyed the empty pews and the stained-glass windows. Swallowing the lump in his throat, he muttered, "I'm so glad Dad has found you."

***

"Grace, how did it go with Kevin and you? Did you have a chance to congratulate him?"

"I... We..." As Auntie Amelia cornered her, Grace leaned against the wall. The weight that had dissipated from her chest during the worship returned, and she cringed over what happened last night. "We talked."

Amelia switched her handbag from one hand to the other. "That's it?"

"Yes." Could she share the details? No, it wasn't fair to Kevin. If the Zhou sisters wanted the facts, they must hear them from Kevin.

"What did you talk about?" Amelia's gaze bored into hers.

Her cheeks burning, Grace surveyed the dispersing crowd. What were Kevin and Angela talking about? Did he share the details with her? "We talked about... our future."

Where was her straightforwardness? Hadn't she always emphasized transparency among friends?

"Care if I guess?" Amelia's lips crinkled up. "Kevin professed his love toward you, right? Don't be shy. You two make a cute couple."

"Amelia." Heat spread to her ears, and a lump rose in her throat. "Kevin did profess, but I..."

"Yes?"

Grace turned her head away, unable to look Amelia in the eye. "I turned him down."

"What?" Amelia's voice rose to the next octave. "No way! You can't be serious. We all thought you care about him as much as he cares about you."

"I do care about him." Grace dragged her sandal across the hardwood floor. "But Kevin belongs to Hong Kong, and I must return to the US next year. There's no future for us."

"You're such a rational girl." Amelia shook her head. "You need to take risks and allow some leeway in your life. You and Kevin are both young and have time to figure out a way to make things work. You'll never know if you don't try."

While Grace kept quiet, Amelia continued. "May I ask why you must return to the US?"

Moisture rushed to Grace's eyelids. "Nana Wang's done so much for my mom and me. I want to tend to her needs when she ages."

"It's admirable to take care of her." Amelia scrunched her nose, her intelligent eyes sparkling. "Have you talked to her? If Nana Wang learns you give up a potentially fulfilling relationship because of her, what will she think? Also, even if she wants you to take care of her, why can't she come to live in Hong Kong?"

Somehow, such ideas had never occurred to Grace. Focused on fulfilling her obligations, she hadn't considered other options. *Lord, are You talking to me through Amelia?* But Nana Wang had never lived outside of Illinois. "Oh, Amelia, please pray for me. I'm so confused."

Amelia drew her into a hug. "We've all been praying for you and Kevin. God has answered part of our prayers and led Kevin to start his faith journey. Please keep an open mind and see how God guides you."

Tears welling up, Grace rested her head against Auntie Amelia's bosom and wrapped her arms around the older woman.

Thank You, Lord, for such caring sisters in Your family. Let Your will be done and lead me down the right path.

Chapter Twenty

Uncle Lam had canceled the Mandarin class again. Lucky her, a free Saturday with nothing on her agenda except for tonight's fellowship meeting.

If only Nana Wang would come today! She had so much to share with her beloved friend. Although they talked over the phone often, phone calls could never replace face-to-face togetherness.

But Nana Wang wouldn't arrive until Monday morning. Okay, two more days.

Grace succumbed to a twinge of loneliness and dialed Danny's number. Nobody answered. He hadn't attended worship or Bible study for a while. Did he work overtime, even on weekends?

In one week, she'd move into Angela and Amelia's flat. Oh, for sure, she would miss this mansion with its gorgeous garden. With a shake of her head, she walked out of her room and strolled toward the koi pond.

Would she run into Kevin? *I hope not.*

"Morning, Grace." Christopher crossed the bridge and approached her. "Isn't the sunshine wonderful? Any big plans for this splendid day?"

She turned her body just enough to look at him. "Not really."

"What? Where is Kevin?" He held up both hands and exaggerated looking around for someone, a shrewdness dancing in his bright eyes.

During the past week, she and Kevin remained cordial, but neither broached the subject again. She jutted up her chin. No way would she tell Christopher what happened between her and Kevin.

"Interested in going out?" He gave her another glance, then winked. "Just you and me."

No harm in an outing with him alone, right? He was like a kid brother. Besides, if she stayed home, she risked running into Kevin. "Where?"

"Have you ever had grilled abalone? It has the most delicate texture and flavor of any food I've ever tasted. I know an excellent seafood joint that serves the best abalone in town." His grin spread out, revealing a dimple with a hint of recklessness. "How about we ride a motorcycle together? Let me check with Old Moy. Perhaps I can borrow Dad's Lamborghini."

Abalone and a Lamborghini motorcycle? She'd never ridden a motorcycle before, not to mention a Lamborghini. As she pondered his description of abalone, saliva pooled in her throat. *Oh, Grace, one of these days, food will be your downfall.* Well, maybe not today. "All right. Just make sure we make the fellowship meeting at seven."

He raised his fingertips to his right temple and saluted. "Yes, ma'am. Your wish is my command."

Following Christopher, Grace entered the ten-car garage and stretched her eyes wide at Uncle Lam's car collection—Jaguar, Mercedes-Benz, Rolls-Royce...

Old Moy didn't raise questions and surrendered the key. She giggled, then swatted at Christopher's arm. "I suspect this isn't your first time asking for the use of the bike."

"What makes you think I'd want it for anything other than transporting you to a memorable day?" He jiggled the key in her face.

As he pulled it out of the garage, Grace brushed her fingers against the leather seat. "Wow. Such a beautiful piece of work." Painted a solid shiny black with yellow lightning bolts on either side of the tank, it looked classy yet fierce. How would it feel to ride such a wild beast? The fun in her life included Bible study, food, music, church friends, travel, and school, now work, though not necessarily in that order. To be certain, zooming around on a Lamborghini motorcycle was off the list.

He chuckled. "You like it."

Heat flashed across her cheeks. How did he read her emotions so easily? "I've never been this close to a motorcycle before. It's..."

Her gaze shifted back and forth between him and the bike. "Is it safe?"

His boyish grin widened his handsome face, the dimple winking at her again. "Since it's your first time, I promise to keep it under the speed limit." Perhaps detecting her doubts, he gave her hand a gentle squeeze. "Life is short. Don't be so upright all the time. Live a little. This will be an adventure."

Right, what was the big deal? As much as she liked order and serenity, something different from her predictable routine seemed benign enough, especially after her recent run-in with Kevin. And she would move out soon.

He handed her a blued helmet and smirked. "Put it on. Let's ride off on this death machine."

The bike rumbled.

Her heart pounding, she raised her voice above the noise. "What next?"

"Throw your right leg over behind me." After she obliged, he glanced back. "Wrap your arms tight around my waist. I don't want you to fall off."

He laughed. She didn't think it funny and clutched at him for dear life as the beast grumbled down the road.

A delightful aroma swirled around. Must be from the shrubs laden with pink flowers. Odd. Why did it smell different from when she was walking?

While the machine picked up speed, the gentle summer wind turned brisk and blew stray hairs back from her face. Nice to have on the helmet. Otherwise, her hair would become a tangled mess.

The road curved, and he and the bike leaned into the bend. Were they going to fall? She leaned with him. He straightened just in time, and they sped down the street.

Cars, pedestrians, and buildings zipped by as they weaved through the traffic. Gradually, the road grew emptier.

Awesome. They'd left the town center. For a moment, her body seemed unconnected to the ground. She shut her eyes and let the wind carry her soul upward, toward the blue sky.

A sky as clear as the day she climbed Mount Arbel in Israel. The hike up to the most iconic viewpoint over the Sea of Galilee took them hours. Mom had still been active and full of energy. At one point, Grace stepped on a sharp stone. The air rushed past as her feet slid out from under her. Mom sprinted over and caught her forearm. As they toppled together, her mom used her body to shield her against the impact of the hard ground.

Heat scorched the back of her eyelids. *Oh, Mom.* How she missed the moments they'd laughed and shared secrets. An icy chill slithered through her, and the loneliness, even with her arms around another human being, almost undid her. Then Mom's words echoed in her head. "Gracie, everything that lives must die one day. In Christ, we have hope, because death isn't the end. Through death, we'll receive the eternal inheritance the Lord has promised."

The bike slowed and stopped, interrupting her dismal reverie. Christopher dismounted and removed his helmet. She followed.

With a teasing chuckle, he reached up and tucked a tress behind her ear. "Are you okay? You aren't crying out of fear, are you?"

"No. It was far better than I'd imagined." She shifted away and faced the white-sand beach to hide her emotions. "Where are we?"

"Repulse Bay. Riding always helps me clear my head. Well, if there's such a thing as a clear head for me." His eyes twinkled. "Come, let's go to the ocean."

The beach wasn't overly crowded. A group of children swam nearby. Their cheerful laughter buoyed her. Yeah, life was good. Yet, without death, would life be meaningful?

They took off their shoes, giving in to the sea's invitation. Warm sand received and reflected the subtropical sunlight. Christopher immersed his hands in the gentle waves. "Grace, do you think my dad is serious about his relationship with Amelia Zhou?"

Ha, Christopher made the same observation. She raised one brow. "Why do you ask?"

"I forgot you didn't go to the yacht party." He stood up and shrugged. "They seemed close, talking in whispers and exchanging coy glances. But Dad loves beautiful women, and Amelia is no beauty. Even weirder, he's no longer playing the field and appears content to spend his time with her."

"Beauty is in the eye of the beholder. I think Amelia is gorgeous and intelligent." She patted his hand. "You should be happy for your dad. I suspect he's found someone interested in him as a person, not his wealth."

"I guess," he mumbled and pointed toward his left. "Look over there."

A few feet away, a couple engaged in a passionate kiss, and an imprint of lipstick on the man's cheek shouted out their love for each other.

As she glanced at the lovebirds, Christopher picked up her fingers. "Grace, I like you a lot. Will..."

Uh-oh. *Not again. Definitely not with Christopher.* Her shoulders stiffened, and she withdrew her hand. "Look at the boat over there."

In the distance, a sail glided across the blue canvas. After a glimpse at the ocean, he turned back to her, his voice as low as a whisper. "You're so beautiful. I can barely take my eyes off you."

She took two steps away from him. "I don't appreciate what you've just said."

"You don't like me?" Christopher squinted. "Are you in love with Kevin?"

Was she in love with Kevin? She'd told him they didn't have a future together. Grace shook her head hard. "Don't say anything to spoil the day. I like all my friends. You guys have become an important part of my life. Somehow you come across to me like the kid brother I've never had."

"Kid brother? Just because I'm three years younger than you?" He muttered under his breath, then lifted his face toward the sea again. "I know I'm not worthy of your affection. I–I have many character flaws. For one, I don't have the tenacity to work hard."

"You're still young and full of potential." Once he connected with God, he'd find his way in this world. She leaned forward, an expansive warmth rising in her chest. "Tell me. If you had no limitations, what would you do in your life?"

He fixed his gaze on that distant boat. "I'd sail around the world with someone who loves me as I am." His attention returned to her. "How about you? What's your dream?"

What was her dream? She pressed a hand to her heart as if she could reach inside and capture it. "I'm very practical. As a Christian, I believe my life is entrusted to me by God temporarily. All I need to do is to follow His guidance step-by-step."

"That's why you came to Hong Kong without any hesitation? Did you think God wanted you to come? Will you stay here for the rest of your life?"

She winced. She'd come to Hong Kong only because of Mom's request. No, she didn't plan to stay. Her roots weren't here. Her whole body stiffened, and she rubbed the rising goose bumps from her arms. No matter what—she would return to the US to take care of Nana Wang.

Her taut muscles sagged. She'd never expected to become entangled in a serious relationship. Now, she'd grown to care for Kevin deeply. Every time she thought of leaving him, her heart broke a little more. But if she stayed, she'd be living in a constant state of conflict.

Christopher eyed her again and burst into a chortle. "Boy, what are we doing? I've never discussed anything so earnest with a girl before."

She wiped her forehead and remained quiet.

"Come on." He bumped his shoulder into hers. "Don't give me that awful look. Cheer up." Restrained laughter rattled his voice. "Before we go to our next stop to enjoy abalone, let me take your picture."

She forced a smile. After the photo session, he sauntered toward the bike with the swagger most teenagers displayed.

Yeah, he was still a boy.

A short, smooth ride later, he stopped before a Japanese grill joint. "I've been to a lot of restaurants. This one serves the best seafood in town."

Did his life revolve around food, parties, and perhaps women? Poor child. He'd had no one to guide him onto the path toward a God-given purpose.

When their orders arrived, Grace had to agree that every dish— grilled whole abalone, steamed scallop on the shell, and the sashimi boat—was beyond anything she'd ever tried.

"Wow." She devoured everything on her plate. "You're right. Abalone is rich, naturally buttery, and a bit salty..." She ran out of words to describe its texture and taste.

He gawked. Maybe shocked by her healthy appetite. "I'm glad you like it. I'll tell Ah Tang to cook them for you at home before you move out."

Nice to be loaded with money. Back in Illinois, she could never have afforded to eat like this. At the same time, a voice whispered. *Man does not live on bread alone, but on every word that comes from the mouth of God.*

She blurted out, "Matthew four verse four."

"What did you say?"

"Er... Nothing." She twisted her watch into view. "It's not even two thirty. Shall we go home?"

"Home? Are you kidding?" He glanced sideways with a provocative smile. "I thought you wanted to go straight to the fellowship meeting."

She shrugged. "There's nothing else to do."

"You're three years older than I am? Why do you know nothing about fun things in life?" He signed the credit card slip and stood. "Have you ever played pool? I know a place in Causeway Bay near your church. Let's go."

"Pool? Billiards? No, I've never played the game." She narrowed her eyes. "Wait. Don't we have a game room at home with a pool table?"

"Playing at home differs from going to a billiards bar."

"Don't gangsters populate those places?" The words were out of her mouth before she could stop them.

He hugged his stomach and unleashed an earsplitting burst of cackles. "Are you sure you're three years older than I am? You sound like a middle-school girl."

That's the difference between growing up in a Christian family versus not. She swallowed back the words.

He wagged a finger at her. "Tsk-tsk, it's about time you see what the real world looks like."

They returned to the town center. Inside the bar, Grace slackened her jaw. Loud music boomed through the spacious room. Young women about her age shot darts at the board, smoking, chatting, and laughing. Men and women on the barstools sipped liquor and cheered one another.

It seemed as if young people from the whole of Hong Kong had gathered here.

Christopher lit up a cigarette, then said something. She pointed at her ears, a tight knot forming in her stomach. As the smoky air swirled around her, her throat tickled. But music, laughter, and clinking glasses, mixed with the click of the billiard balls, drowned out her cough.

Her lungs ached from the oppressive particles. Why did others appear unfazed? Was she so out of touch with the real world? She took a deep breath and faced a wall lined with trophies, awards, and memorabilia from past tournaments.

Christopher went to the bar and ordered a draft beer, then pulled her toward a young couple standing by a pool table. He put down his drink and shouted, "Can we join?"

The two smiled.

When her turn came, she latched onto Christopher's arm and whispered, "I've never played this before."

While the strangers watched, Christopher grinned and showed her how to hold the cue stick and bend over to make the shot. She hit the cue ball hard, and it jumped off the table, rolling on the wooden surface.

Her cheeks burned, but the others nodded with encouragement.

The people were nicer than she expected, and Christopher's enormous smile showed his delight at being here. For sure, they lived in two different worlds.

Amidst the commotion, she chuckled at the irony. *O Lord, I like my world with You in the center much better.*

Yet, without understanding her friends' worlds, could she share the gospel with them?

Lord, I thank You that Kevin has accepted You as his Savior. Please open Christopher's mind so that he gets to know You soon.

Chapter Twenty-One

"Kevin, have you seen this?"

At Ah Tang's higher-than-usual voice, Kevin jerked up his head. The noon summer sun, high in the sky blazing through the gentle breeze, radiated warmth on his face. He leaned back against the ginkgo tree trunk. "Sorry. What did you say?"

Ah Tang dropped a pile of tabloids on the lawn next to him. What was she up to?

His gaze shifted to the magazine covers, and he sat straight to flip page after page of pictures depicting Grace and Christopher together. In one, the young man hugged her from behind with his hands holding her, and both bent over a pool table. In another, they rode a Lamborghini motorcycle with her arms wrapped around his waist.

A sharp stab lanced his core. No wonder she turned him down.

Her statement was a mere cover-up, and Danny's hunch about her only dating Christians had no merit. Like most women, she aimed high for a certain type of man—handsome, heir to a vast fortune, and a lot of fun to be with. With a strong jawline, dark-brown eyes, and a muscular physique, Christopher could pass for a movie star. As Mr. Lam's only son, he would inherit everything. He was also always up for new adventures.

How long had she been dating Christopher?

Ah Tang smirked. "Well, well, Grace will become Mrs. Lam after all. I didn't expect it to be Christopher. Like father, like son. For sure, they both prefer women with Grace's look."

Kevin adjusted his glasses to fix his gaze on the beautiful couple in the tabloids. His shoulders stiffened, and his feet froze in place.

A cry of pain ripped from his throat. "That playboy can't be serious about her."

"Who knows?" Ah Tang shrugged. "Grace seems smart. Maybe she'll help Christopher settle down. It'll be a good thing."

The thought of Grace succumbing to someone without dreams and aspirations threw a heavy punch into his gut. Nausea surged through him. But was there any difference between him and Christopher? Before he accepted Christ as his Savior, he also drifted through life with only a vague ideology but no real purpose. At least, Christopher's family was rich.

"You don't look good." She gave his arm a gentle squeeze. "I was right before. You care about Grace, don't you?"

His whole body shaking, Kevin forced himself to stand up. "I..." He dashed to his room.

Dad was reading by the table. When Kevin entered, Dad shot to his feet. "Are you all right? You look ghastly."

Kevin's hands still trembled. He slumped on the carpet, his chest heaving. Was it pain or fury? He spoke through clenched teeth. "Grace is dating Christopher."

"Whoa, you saw the tabloids." Dad came to his side. "Since early this morning, the phone has been ringing off the hook. Almost everyone acquainted with Mr. Lam called to confirm whether Christopher and Grace are engaged. The reports detailed their outing on Saturday, showed them returning home with her arms around his waist on a bike, and hinted they already live together."

While Kevin remained silent, Dad patted his shoulder. "We know it isn't true."

Kevin's muscles relaxed a bit. He cocked his head, squinting to see a ray of hope. "You don't think they're dating."

"As usual, the tabloids try to manufacture a juicy story out of thin air." Dad's face scrunched into a puzzled expression. "Something is out of the ordinary. Wayward news about Christopher and his girlfriends never bothered Mr. Lam. This time, he became enraged. To be honest, I've never seen him so furious."

Mr. Lam seething? That was odd. Although he and his son didn't see eye-to-eye, he didn't balk last year at the numerous pictures of Christopher's pool parties with young girls crawling all over him.

Kevin scratched his forehead. "After church yesterday, Christopher said he was going to a friend's party. Where is he now?"

"He stayed out all night." Dad rubbed the back of his neck, his voice strained. "I'm afraid there's an ugly scene in store for us when he comes home."

"How about Grace? Didn't she take today off to pick up her friend from the airport?" Stomach churning, Kevin adjusted his glasses. "Was Mr. Lam upset with her?"

"Grace may have left already." Dad clutched his fingers together. "Mr. Lam didn't mention anything about her."

Had Grace seen the tabloids? She'd said she was too practical to read nonsense. Still, this time, the gossip focused on her. If she was home, he'd better tell her. "Dad, I have something to take care of. I'll see you later."

He paced in front of her room for almost ten minutes, raised his arm a few times, but failed to muster the courage to knock.

Would she say it was none of his business? Or worse, that she and Christopher were dating?

A shout from the living room broke the tranquility. Mr. Lam's roar thundered through the hallway, covering the squeak of Kevin's rubber soles against the hardwood floor. "You scoundrel! I don't care about your reason or excuse!"

A baritone, much like Mr. Lam's, but higher in pitch, yelled back. "I thought you were serious about dating Amelia now. Why are you furious about Grace and me together? You still want her for yourself?"

As Kevin entered the living room, Mr. Lam slapped Christopher across the face. The son brought a palm to his cheek, his eyes bulging, his chest heaving. He gawked at his father like a caged animal ready to fight for its life.

"How dare you say such a thing?" Mr. Lam's now-icy tone sluiced through the room, the words spoken slow. "I don't care if you fool around with anyone else. Just. Leave. Grace. Alone."

Raising his fist, Christopher lunged toward his dad.

"Stop!"

Christopher froze midstride, his face contorting.

Grace rushed in, followed by an older lady in a blue dress.

"Please don't." Grace wedged herself between the father and son, her delicate appearance in pink exuding vulnerability.

The older lady—Nana Wang?—surveyed the room, her eyes widening and perspiration beading her temples.

Mr. Lam thrust a hand toward Grace, then lowered it. As if someone punctured a balloon and the air whooshed out, the fury on his chiseled face deflated. "Did... did Christopher... did you—?"

***

What was all the commotion about? Why were Uncle Lam and Christopher behaving like bulls about to gore each other to death? The tabloids on the coffee table caught Grace's attention. Intimate pictures of Christopher and her together brought a sickening feeling to her stomach.

Her knees wobbled. "Are you upset because of the tabloids? Christopher and I didn't do anything improper. Please listen." She lifted her chin. "He treated me like his sister. He took me to Repulse Bay and taught me to play pool. Then we went to the fellowship meeting. That was all we did on Saturday."

A cry—no, a moan—escaped Uncle Lam's lips. He slumped on the sofa and wrapped his arms around his head.

When Christopher remained motionless, Grace grasped his hand and drew him to sit beside her. "Uncle Lam, your son needs you to love him as he is."

She gestured for Christopher to speak, yet the young man shook his head. She elbowed him and motioned at her mouth again.

With his shoulders squared back, Christopher cleared his throat. Still, a choked sound preceded his words. "Dad, I'm sorry for what I said about you and Grace."

Uncle Lam jerked up his gaze. "Son, I apologize. I've misjudged and wronged you. Can you forgive me?"

Tears welled up in Christopher's eyes. "This is the first time you've apologized to me."

As Kevin slipped away, unease slithered up Grace's spine. She stood and crooked her index finger to beckon him to stay.

"Are you sure?" he muttered. "I feel like a nosy bystander."

Nana Wang led him to the sofa. "Grace needs you." She sat across from Uncle Lam. "Mr. Sam Lam, I'm Margie Wang. Nice to meet you."

Uncle Lam forced a smile. "I'm sorry for the unexpected scene at our introduction. Grace has told me so much about you. I'm glad to meet you in person."

"May I call you Sam? I feel like I've known you for years." Nana Wang's eyes misted. "The first time I heard about you was more than twenty years ago when Susan came to live with me."

Grace dropped her jaw. If Nana Wang knew about Mom's relationship with Uncle Lam, why did her beloved friend dodge her questions?

As Uncle Lam kept quiet, Nana Wang's eyes bored into his. "Sam, I figure you haven't told Grace how you two are related. Am I right?"

Uncle Lam shifted his feet and looked away. "No, I haven't."

Grace's heart thudded, and something closed around her throat. What did Nana Wang mean? Grace was his old friend's daughter. Wasn't that all?

Nana Wang stood up. "Grace, you deserve to know the truth." Her kind eyes grew misty. "I'm sorry I didn't tell you sooner. Your mom and I wanted to protect you since it involves a painful past Susan tried to forget."

Grace gasped. What had her mom kept from her? Didn't Mom always teach her to be honest and transparent in everything she did?

"This may come as a shock." Nana Wang grasped Grace's hands. "Sam Lam is your father."

"No!" Bile rose in Grace's throat. She flung away Nana Wang's arm and shot to her feet. "Impossible! My dad passed away before I was born. Mom never lied to me."

Uncle Lam also rose and took a step toward her. "Grace, it's true. You're my daughter."

She spun around and glared. "I don't believe you."

Her hands fisted, but she couldn't fight so many emotions. Was it true? Had Mom lied to her? And Nana Wang...

Grace trusted them both, but they had betrayed her trust.

How could her mom, a devout Christian who taught Grace to abstain from sex before marriage, conceive her out of wedlock with a man who had never bothered to contact them?

Her fists clenched tighter, her blood boiling. She dashed out of the room.

"Grace..."

Mingled voices called her name. Ignoring them, she kept darting forward. Her surroundings turned into hushed greenery. The rustle of leaves offered the only sound. She kept running, her heart

178

pounding and her breath coming in short bursts. By the pool, her feet slid out from under her. She sprawled on the tiles. The hard surface scratched her bare legs. Coldness radiated up through her body into her core. Moisture burned in her eyes as the blue sky blurred.

A pair of arms reached down to draw her into an embrace. Kevin's warm breath tickled her neck as his familiar scent enveloped her. "Grace, are you okay?"

With his deep voice reverberating through her body, she leaned against his chest, and tears trickled down her cheeks. "Why did everyone betray me? Even my mother and most trusted friend lied to me."

"Oh, Grace." He hugged her tight and stroked her back. "They must have had their reasons. Maybe they thought it better for you."

"Grace?" Nana Wang's gentle voice rose against the birdsong in the nearby trees. "Your mom and I wanted to protect you."

Uncle Lam also came to her side. When he stretched a hand toward her, she flinched. She wasn't ready for a father like him—a father who never made an effort to learn about her.

"I understand." He exhaled a weighty breath. "I didn't know you existed until I received your mother's letter."

She jerked up her gaze. "How is that possible?"

"I'll explain." He inclined his chin. "Your mother's last wish was for you and me to know each other, and I'm here now. I'm sorry for all the pain I've caused you and your mom."

The sorrow in his eyes was too much. A part of her wanted to scream, to push him away. Another part wanted to wrap her arms around him, to uncover the mystery behind him and Mom.

"No wonder I've felt a special connection with you." Another warm palm rested on Grace's shoulder, and Christopher's baritone intruded. "I've always wished for an older sibling. My dream came true today."

"This isn't the right place to delve into our past. It's a long, complicated story." Nana Wang tugged Grace away from Kevin. "Let's get back to the house."

Grace wiped the tears. So much remained unsaid. Yet, Christopher's words brought something new into her chest. From being alone in this wide world with only her and her aging friend, now she had two blood relatives, a father and a kid brother.

Could she embrace them amid the betrayal in their tangled past?

Chapter Twenty-Two

Grace paced in the spacious, unfamiliar bedroom, her brows drawn tight.

Night had fallen. Moonlight stained the floor-to-ceiling window with irregular patterns of gray and white. A floor lamp in the sitting area threw just enough light on her two companions on the sofa.

Where did the time go? One moment, she was with everyone near the pool. The next, she followed Nana Wang into Uncle Lam's master suite. The interim period melted into a haze like a dream. How did Nana Wang and she fall into slumber under such a circumstance? For her friend, it must have been the jet lag. What about her? Did the physical and emotional fatigue overwhelm her?

Good thing Christopher and Kevin steered clear of this meeting. She must face her mom's past alone.

"Grace, please come sit by me." Nana Wang crooked a finger, beckoning her to sit with them.

No. She couldn't sit on the same sofa with him—Mr. Lam, Uncle Lam, *Dad*. Not yet.

How could she call him Dad? He didn't deserve to be her father. If he loved Mom as he'd proclaimed, why hadn't he ever tried to find her?

Uncle Lam stood and approached. He rubbed his nose, his gaze miserable, his usually straight shoulders sloping. "You've got to believe me. The last news I had of your mother was that she'd committed suicide. I knew nothing of your existence."

"What?" Grace retreated a step and bit down on her lip, her widened eyes training on the familiar stranger before her.

He advanced and grasped her hand. "Come with me."

She jerked her arm but failed to dislodge herself from his grip. As he pulled her toward a writing desk against one wall, her body grew cold and rigid. He opened a drawer and took out a faded yellowish paper. "Read it."

Grace picked up the one-sentence note in her mother's handwriting and whispered the words written there. "'How does one bear to live when evil has destroyed all hope?'"

Oh, Mom. What anguish! Grace loosened her fingers, the note falling to the floor.

The moon remained bright, yet an evening wind wailed like a broken heart. Branches rattled into the eerie hush.

What desperation!

Teardrops warmed her cheeks. Still, how could her mother, so full of faith and hope even when confronting cancer, consider suicide?

"No!" she yelled in between sobs. "No way would Mom have considered killing herself. This tells me nothing. She could have written it on a gloomy day while she was dating you."

"I found this note laid on top of her other belongings." Uncle Lam crossed to a nearby bookcase and pushed a button. It swung open to reveal a room. "Follow me."

She stole a glimpse at Nana Wang. Her friend hung her head low, appearing to isolate herself from the two of them. "Nana..."

Nana Wang jerked up her head and waved. "Go with him."

Uncle Lam guided Grace inside and flipped on the switch. Her vision adjusted to the strong light.

Paintings covered the walls. An easel stood in a corner with a half-finished product. They all depicted a young girl, *Mom*, in a series of actions—licking an ice cream cone, clamming on the beach, dancing in the rain...

Discordant with their surroundings, three battered boxes claimed the center of the plush carpet.

"Susan—" Uncle Lam sucked in a breath, then opened the torn cover of one of them. "She put her note here."

His mention of Mom's name, simple yet so sorrowful as if wrung out of him in a moan, plucked at Grace's heart. She stooped, picked up the album on the top,- and opened it to reveal pictures of Mom with Uncle Lam.

181

Nana Wang walked in. "Didn't you return to Hong Kong after your graduation? How did you obtain Susan's belongings?"

Uncle Lam didn't answer. He plopped down on the floor and covered his head with both hands.

Grace rummaged through the first box. Album after album displayed Mom, Uncle Lam, and occasionally others. Mom's clothes filled the second box, and knickknacks occupied the third.

He'd treasured Mom's belongings like the most precious gems. "If you loved my mom, why did you leave her?"

Uncle Lam tilted his head up, his eyes misty. "My father, your grandpa, called me. He said he was seriously ill and couldn't come to the US for my graduation ceremony. He urged me to come home immediately."

Nana Wang sat by him, her expression unreadable. "What happened after you went home? You called Susan a few times and mentioned certain issues. You said you expected to resolve them in two or three weeks and get back to her. Then you... vanished."

"My father wasn't sick. He wanted me to marry his friend's daughter to strengthen his real estate business."

The misery in his tone, intense like the darkest night, choked up Grace's throat. She fell to the carpet, letting her weary body wallow in the anguish brought upon by the information.

Nana Wang rubbed her temples. "Susan called you almost every day after she found out she was pregnant. Why didn't you answer her calls?"

A groan ripped from Uncle Lam's lips. "I was in the hospital. I contracted bacterial meningitis and almost died."

Grace cupped a palm to her mouth, a tightness creeping into her chest.

Nana Wang's eyes widened. "You were hospitalized?"

Uncle Lam wiped his face with a hand. "I was there for almost two months."

"How about the letter your father sent to Susan, informing her you were engaged to Lisa?"

Uncle Lam's jaw slackened. Then he roared, a knot of muscle trembling in his jaw. "What did you just say?"

Grace jammed both hands into her armpits, her shoulders tight.

Nana Wang narrowed her eyes. "You didn't know your father wrote to Susan?"

"My father...?" A tendon erupted on his neck. Another loud cry burst from him and dwindled into a groan. "Oh, Dad, what have you done?"

The question hung in the air. In the heavy silence, Grace's legs quivered as she drew her knees up to her chest. What a horrible, unexpected turn of life. Oh how her heart ached for this man.

"After you left the hospital, did you become engaged to Lisa?" Nana Wang's relentless voice echoed in the small room.

"No." His tongue flicked across his parched lips, a pulse twitching in his neck. "As soon as I recovered enough to travel, I booked a flight to San Fran. But it was too late."

Moisture glistened in his eyes, and he turned his head away. "I rushed to Susan's apartment. Her roommate told me she'd left without leaving an address. I went into her room and discovered she'd neatly packed everything into these three boxes."

A lump wedged in Grace's throat. In her mind's vision, a young Uncle Lam—no, Dad—sat on Mom's empty bed, his face pale and contorted, his body shaking. Shivers ran up her spine. *Oh, Lord, how he must have suffered.*

"When I opened the boxes, I found this note. For two weeks, her roommate and I searched everywhere." His voice cracked. "We filed a police report. A policewoman told us if Susan had committed suicide by jumping off the Golden Gate Bridge or from a cliff into the Pacific Ocean, then her body might never be found."

Desolation! Wretchedness!

Grace's eyes burned, and tears tickled her chin. Her soul connected with Uncle Lam's as if they were tangled silk fibers spun from the same silkworm's mouth.

"How long did you stay in the Bay Area?"

Warm empathy emanated from Grace's soul for the man Nana Wang interrogated. Now, she knew where she got her naturally curly hair from. Her father!

She crawled to the third box and picked up a lavender hairbrush. Light purple, Mom's favorite color. When Grace was little, her hair became frizzy on rainy days, and Mom would comb it with a lilac brush identical to this one.

A half smile tugged at his lips. "The brush was a gift I bought for your mom." Then he returned his focus to Nana Wang. "I lingered as long as my work visa allowed me to stay in the US legally. I tried all I could to collect any tidbit of news about her. But nothing. In the end, I became convinced she'd died."

"Her body was never found because she didn't die." The words dropped slowly off Nana Wang's mouth. "I was visiting a friend in San Jose, and she took me to view the magnificent span linking the San Francisco Peninsula to Marin County, the famous tourist attraction once dubbed 'the bridge that couldn't be built.'"

Grace stopped fiddling with the brush bristles in her lap. "You met my mother there?"

Nana Wang nodded. "As we were about to leave, a girl with an expression so desperate and hopeless wandered toward us, alarming my friend, a social worker. We struck up a conversation and convinced her to spend the night with us. The next day, Susan accepted Christ as her personal Savior. A week later, I bought her a plane ticket, and she returned to Chicago with me. The rest is history."

So, Nana Wang saved their lives. Grace flung away the brush and hugged her beloved friend. "If it weren't for you, I wouldn't be here today."

Nana Wang tucked the curls behind Grace's ears. "God loved you even before you were born." Her attention shifted back to Uncle Lam. "When did you marry Lisa?"

Grace stiffened, waiting.

"Two years later, my father suffered from a stroke. According to Cantonese folk belief, the wedding of a family member would bring him comfort and even a cure. As his only son, I had no choice but to marry Lisa." He glanced at Grace. "Do you know about this Chinese tradition?"

She shook her head.

He tapped his hand against his knee. "Your grandpa did live for two more years, long enough to see the birth of his grandson."

She twittered her fingers together. "Christopher?"

"Yes." Uncle Lam turned his dazed eyes toward the ceiling. "One thing has puzzled me till this day. Why didn't Susan go back to her father? He was a well-to-do businessman in Taiwan. Susan was his only daughter. She didn't even mention him in her last note."

Under Grace's palm, Nana Wang's warm body stiffened. "Do you know about the incident in Taiwan involving a noted democracy activist, Peng Ming-min?"

Uncle Lam stretched his eyes wide, and so did Grace. She blurted out, "Did he have anything to do with Mom?"

"In an indirect way." Nana Wang's soft nod ruffled her white hair. "Peng, a well-known law professor, was arrested in 1964. Under the pressure of international public opinion, the authorities released him but kept him under surveillance. His relatives and friends were also implicated, and none of them could find work to make a living. Then in early 1970, with friends' help, Peng managed to escape to the US. The Taiwanese government arrested several individuals who had helped him, including Susan's father. He died in jail about the same time your mom found herself pregnant."

So many unfortunate events befell Mom. No wonder the book of Job was one of her favorites. Grace had once commented that the story seemed unlikely, and Mom replied, "My dear Gracie, I do believe in Job's story. I know people who have experienced life's brutality like him."

Yeah, Mom spoke from her own experience. Grace spun toward Uncle Lam. "You never forgot my mother?"

"Susan, Susan—the name still has its charms even today. I've whispered that name on each of my sleepless nights. I've uttered it with moans and longing." He touched her face. "Then you came. I saw her in you. Her voice, her steps... But my Susan was dead. Oh, what a cruel trick life pulled on me."

How horrid that trick was!

"Uncle Lam—" Grace brought a palm to cover his hand on her cheek, unsure what she was feeling.

He wetted his lips. "Grace, you're my daughter. Could you please call me Dad?"

"I–I—" How should she respond? She eased back from his touch and rubbed her neck. "Dad..." She tested the name. "You got upset seeing the pictures of Christopher and me together because you were concerned about incest? Why didn't you tell me earlier you're my father?"

"That's the first time you've called me Dad. Thank you, Grace." His eyes sparkled. He hugged her, and his warm breath tickled her ear. "I should have. But I had to consider certain factors. Once I announce your link to me, I must show proof to many who come forward to oppose me. In preparation, I requested a DNA test. The result arrived recently. I was about to tell you and make the announcement. Then the tabloids..." He paused and exhaled. "I'm sorry I kept this from you until now."

Yeah, Connie Dong would be the first to issue a challenge. With money involved, people became ruthless. Grace leaned against his chest, feeling lighter than air. "I often wondered how it would feel to call someone Dad." His embrace muffled her voice. "It's beyond what I've ever imagined."

Time seemed suspended. Then he pulled away and wiped his eyes. "Let's get going, sweetheart. We've got a lot to do." His stare seeped into hers. "First things first, are you willing to stay in Hong Kong with me?"

She glanced at Nana Wang, her heart torn. Yes, Grace would love to live near Dad. But if she stayed here, who'd take care of her beloved friend?

Nana Wang wagged a finger at her. "Don't worry. Now that I've seen this gorgeous mansion, I can see myself settling down easily."

"You amaze me." Grace smiled and turned to Dad. "The letter my mom asked me to hand deliver to you. What was in it?"

"Come with me." He led them back to the desk in his sitting area and opened another drawer to retrieve a paper. "Here it is."

Someone tapped on the door. While her dad went to answer it, she pocketed the letter.

"I'm sorry to intrude." Kevin walked in. "I just want to make sure Grace is all right."

Warmth flooded her chest. *How blessed I am to have somebody as kind as him.* And now she could return his affection. "I'm fine."

"Grace, why don't you go with Kevin for now? I'm sure you two have a lot to discuss." A hint of a chortle echoed in Dad's words. "We can resume our discussion about your stay in Hong Kong later."

Chapter Twenty-Three

Grace followed Kevin downstairs, her body thrumming. "Thank you for coming. After how I treated you last week, I didn't think you'd still care about me."

He crinkled up the corners of his mouth. "You can't get rid of me so easily." His gaze lingered on her. "Let's go to the garden. I have something special for you."

A sweet, earthy scent swirled around them. What a pleasant, warm summer night after her emotional roller coaster. The stars twinkled, and under the crickets' chorus, the bushes came to life.

Kevin hooked her arm with his and led her toward the koi pond. "Close your eyes, please."

She complied and let him guide her forward.

A moment later, he released her. "Ready?"

Grace opened her eyes. On the garden bench stood an enormous glass jar. Hundreds or perhaps thousands of tiny lights danced within. "Wow. Where did you catch so many fireflies?"

"Shh." He laid a finger on her lips, then removed the lid. The insects rushed out and flew around them, forming a glowing circle.

Mesmerized, Grace lifted a hand toward the sky, the heaviness in her chest easing. "You remembered me telling you about the fireflies?"

Kevin stuck his eyeglasses into a pocket and bent down toward her. Heat pulsed through her veins. When their lips met, passion exploded, sending electric currents of delight through her soul. Like flying, she soared high above the clouds in a paradise theirs alone.

A small moan escaped her throat as he broke the embrace. Then his husky voice caressed her ear. "I love you."

Breathless, she searched his eyes, her heart swelling. She didn't say the words back but drew his head down and teased his lips with hers.

He returned the favor, his palms molding her waist. Surrounded by a blanket of bliss, their embrace seemed locked forever. At last, he pulled away again, his smile wide. "From how you responded, may I guess you love me too?"

She grinned, her eyes misty. "Yes, I do."

"Do you still plan to return to the US next year?" He squinted.

A soft breeze swept strands of hair against her cheeks. *He's teasing me.* "What if I say yes?"

He gave her a mischievous wink. "Well, I must conclude there's no future for us and have no choice but to break up with you."

"How dare you?" She tickled his armpit.

"Of course, I dare." He chuckled and squeezed her into another hug. Then his tone turned serious. "Care to share what happened between you and Mr. Lam... Well, I guess I should say your father?"

After she relayed the details, she rested against his chest again. "Before you walked in, Dad gave me the letter I hand delivered to him. I'm dying to find out what's in it. Let's go to our favorite nook where I can read it with you."

Soon, they settled into the plush seat. Light from the lamppost shone through the window and lit the area with a warm, inviting glow. She settled into the soft cushion, her heart vibrant. "We sat here and chatted so often. I never imagined this moment would come."

He nuzzled her neck. "Unlike you, I've dreamed about holding you in my arms for a long time."

She giggled and snuggled up to him, content in his embrace. "Are you ready for my mom's letter?"

"Let's do this first." He tipped her chin up and moved his mouth to hers.

The brief, sweet peck was enough to send her into a new blissful state. "Do it again."

"Your wish is my command." He gave her ear a slurpy smooch, then returned to her lips.

As he broke away, a new wave of longing swept over her. "I'll never get enough of your kisses." Her fists clenched at her sides, and she leaned into him. "One more, please."

He chuckled, his eyes sparkling behind his glasses. "I'm glad you liked it so much. But we should read the letter."

With a sigh, she pulled out the letter and unfolded it, and he peered over her shoulder to read along.

Sammy,

For over twenty years, I've buried this name and our shared past deep within my heart. I thought I'd forgotten the anguish of your betrayal. I'm wrong. I've forgiven you, yet the wound remains, only covered by the scars of time.

For our dear Gracie, I'm compelled to write my last letter to you from my deathbed. I've also requested she hand deliver it to you after I die. Our daughter is kind and smart, the greatest gift God has given me through you. I know you have your own family now and may not wish to be told of the existence of a daughter whom you know nothing about. Even though you cast away our relationship like broken glass, Gracie is a constant reminder of our time together and how much I used to love you. Besides my salvation, our daughter has been the most important thing in my life. I have tried to give her the best of my love, time, and advice. I understand you don't share my sentiment. If you resolve to turn her away, please do so gently for the sake of the love we once shared. I haven't told her about you because I don't know how you'll react and I don't want to give her false hope.

In case you decide to accept Gracie, please try to persuade her to stay near you. I was once lost, and God found me. My prayer is that, through her, you'll accept Jesus Christ as your Savior.

Yours always,
Susan

Tears welled up in Grace's eyes. "Till her death, Mom thought Dad betrayed her. No wonder she never spoke about her days in California. She bought Hong Kong tabloid magazines in Chinatown from time to time. I suppose she kept track of Dad's news." She buried her head in Kevin's chest as his arms wrapped around her. "Even when she wrote this letter, she doubted Dad would take me in and tried to protect me."

He held her tight and murmured, "Such a tragic turn of life. Mr. Lam never loved anyone besides her. He thought your mom was dead and sought her look-alike in other women. None of them could replace her. So, for years, he never found true love. Your mom would have been touched by his devotion had she known." He stroked her back. "No wonder he changed so much after your arrival. He found out his beloved Susan not only lived but also bore him a beautiful daughter."

Grace raised her gaze. "You think so?"

"Yes, you're the driving force for all of our changes. Without you, I'd never have stepped out of my comfort zone. Thank you, my dear Gracie." He kissed her teardrops away. "Another reason is the church. Mr. Lam heeded your mom's advice and went to church with you. Meeting God and Amelia further opened his soul."

An inexplicable warmth soothed her heart, her sorrow dissipating. She teased his lips again, then whispered, "God has been so good to us. He deserves all the praise."

"Yes, He does. Isn't it amazing how much God will do when we open ourselves to Him?" Kevin's large hand caressed her cheeks. "I have one more thing to ask you. Aren't you worried about 1997? Many doubt China will keep its promise to leave Hong Kong the same for fifty years." His grip bracketed her face. "In line with my dedication to serving the Lord, I believe God is guiding me to remain in Hong Kong. After 1997, if we stand up for what we believe, we may suffer persecution like Danny and his friends."

She cupped her hands over his, taking in his familiar scent. "Remember Pastor Hong's recent sermon? It's never easy to follow Jesus. As Christians, our lives are guided by God's callings. I'm convinced God brought us together. If He calls you to serve in Hong Kong, I'll stay and support you." She nestled against his body, relaxing into contentment. "Plus, I want to stay close to my dad. I doubt he plans to leave Hong Kong because of 1997."

A misty light shimmered in his eyes, framed by his eyeglasses. "You're an incredible blessing from the Lord."

She smirked, feigning exhaustion when he kissed her again. "You're making me breathless."

"I suppose I'll just have to keep going." He bent toward her.

She placed a finger between them, blocking his advances. "I also have a question for you. Since you mentioned Amelia, do you think my dad is serious about marrying her?"

He brushed away her finger and held her chin. "I hear wedding bells already, the first one for him and Amelia, the second for my dad and Angela, and the third"—he leaned closer and whispered against her lips—"for us."

She murmured her response, "In that particular order?"

"Hmm. If you can't wait, maybe we go first?" He covered her mouth with his.

Epilogue

Hong Kong
June 30, 1997

Kevin checked the time on his cell phone. Forty-five minutes to midnight. When Grace walked in and snuggled herself against him, he wrapped an arm around his wife's shoulders and kissed her lips. "Are the twins asleep?"

Before Grace responded, Angela, sitting on the other leather sofa, wagged a finger. "Tsk-tsk. You two still behave like newlyweds."

Kevin's dad pulled Angela into his arms. "Want me to follow suit?"

Angela giggled and pushed him away. "No, I'm good."

Grace's dad, cozied up with Amelia on the loveseat, erupted in hearty laughter. "Dave, your wife is shy, but her sister isn't." He drew Amelia closer and planted his mouth firmly on hers.

Christopher spread his body down on the plush carpet and shut his eyes. "I can't believe you all still act like lovebirds. How long has it been? Kevin and Grace's Luke and Nathan are almost four years old."

Warmth crept up Kevin's chest. His wife remained as lovely as when he first sighted her. "It feels like our wedding day was yesterday. Time flies."

"Time does pass by fast." She brushed a curl away from her face. "Here we are, sitting together in the family room, about to witness a historically significant event."

Nana Wang chimed in from her seat next to Grace. "I looked it up on the internet earlier today. Tonight marks the end of British rule. After a hundred and fifty-six years, Hong Kong will revert to the Chinese government under the 1984 Sino-British Joint Declaration."

"You're still as sharp as always." Grace patted Nana Wang's arm. "Age hasn't slowed you down."

Nana Wang held up a palm. "Hey, I'm only seventy-eight years young."

"Wow, look at the new administrative center in Victoria Harbour. What a crowd." Christopher moved toward the TV. "And listen to the steady beat of traditional Chinese drums accompanying the dragon dance."

Eyeing his brother-in-law with pride, Kevin flashed a thumbs-up. "Only a musician would hear the drum among all the noises." Yeah, Christopher had come a long way. He stopped partying, quit smoking, and started taking his studies seriously. After graduation, he came home and joined the Hong Kong Philharmonic Orchestra. He now also taught music at a local school and performed in many concerts, both in Hong Kong and abroad. On special occasions, Grace and Sam played with him. More importantly, he became a devout Christian, just like his sister and father.

"Speaking of music and lovebirds..." Grace flashed Christopher a smile. "My dear bro, aren't you dating a colleague at the Orchestra? I forgot. What does she play again? When can we expect the wedding bells?"

"Gloria plays the harp." Christopher sat in front of the TV. "Don't worry. When the time comes, you'll all know."

The clock struck eleven thirty.

"Shh." Grace's dad placed a finger over his lips and motioned for the family to be quiet. "The ceremony is beginning."

On the TV, a group of Chinese military officers marched up the step. Then British officers approached from the other side. As the emcee made the announcement, representatives from both sides, including UK Prime Minister Tony Blair, Chinese Premier Li Peng, the prince of Wales, and the last governor of Hong Kong made their appearances. At midnight, the band played the British and Chinese national anthems, and a flag ceremony entailing the descent of the Union Jack and the ascent of the Chinese Five-Starred Red banner took place.

Christopher pointed at the TV screen. "Did you see the expression on Prince Charles's face?"

"Indeed," Amelia responded. "I'd say he looks bewildered, puzzled."

Kevin traced a finger along his jawline. If he were Prince Charles, how would he have felt? More than a hundred years ago, Prince Charles's ancestor, the mighty Queen Victoria, raised the British flag all over the world. For a long while, Britain was dubbed "the empire on which the sun never sets."

But from today on, the British flag would disappear from Hong Kong forever. What a strange turn of history.

Mixed feelings—the hope of a better future mingled with anxiety—gripped Kevin as he stared at Prince Charles on the screen. With great change and uncertainty ahead of the Pearl of the Orient, how did other Hong Kong people feel? He shifted toward Sam. "Dad, didn't you receive an invitation to take part in tonight's ceremony? Why did you choose not to attend?"

Sam exhaled and ducked his head. His long fingers massaged the back of his neck. "I have mixed feelings about the event. On the one hand, I'm glad Hong Kong returns to China. On the other, it's difficult to know how to react to the changes in our city. For the first time, Chinese soldiers, armed with rifles and clad in the standard olive-green uniform of the Chinese People's Liberation Army, marched onto our turf. Definitely something to behold."

Amelia patted Sam's arm. "We decided not to attend because we don't want to appear to support or oppose either party. It's best for everyone to take a step back and observe the changes."

Angela leaned toward her sister. "Although we weren't invited, Dave and I feel the same way. For one thing, even after so many years, the Chinese government still hasn't admitted they did anything wrong during the Tiananmen Square incident. I doubt their sincerity and honesty when it comes to human rights and international relations."

"For sure, things won't remain the same, even though China promises to leave Hong Kong alone for fifty years." Sam let out a sigh. "Speaking of changes, Kevin, have you finalized your plan to study for your Master of Divinity degree at the Chinese University of Hong Kong? When will your last day of work at our company be?"

Kevin nodded. "Although a difficult decision, both Grace and I think it's the right thing for me. We've been praying about this for quite a while, and I'm ready. My last day will be at the end of August."

"And you, Grace?" Sam's eyes bored into his daughter's. "Will you continue to work for the company?"

"Of course." She straightened her shoulders. "After rotating through different subsidiaries, I've developed a clear picture of the organization. Remember the plan we formulated together to move the company forward? If you have time, we should meet next week to go over it again before we submit it to the board for their review."

Sam grinned. "Let's do it. I'm proud of you, Grace."

Christopher shot up from the carpet. "Dad, you should be proud of your son-in-law too. He's just published his novel, *A June Day at Tiananmen*. I've read it. His fictionalized retelling surrounding the protests of 1989 makes a brilliant book."

Excitement pulsed through Kevin. After years of hard work, he pieced together the lives of three characters who experienced the chaos and violence of the Chinese government's crackdown on the student demonstrators. His book traced their steps before, during, and after the protests, as they explored several issues, including the consequences of authoritarianism and the moral dilemmas of being loyal to the country or to their conscience.

Sam's smile widened. "I am, indeed, so proud of him." He stood to shake hands with Kevin, then winked at Grace. "You and Kevin have been busy. Any plans to expand your family? All of us grandparents are dying to have a granddaughter bouncing on our knees."

"Oh, Dad." Crimson flushed her cheeks. "We're not there yet."

Kevin drew her into his arms, nuzzled her ear, and whispered, "Maybe we should start working on that tonight."

The End

Do you know the characters in this book (e.g., Danny) also appear in Ruth's other books? Check out *Blazing China, Detour to Agape,* and *Love Under Holy Skies.*

A Note from the Author

Hello and thank you for sharing this journey with me. Writing this book was a special and emotional experience, and I cannot say how honored I am that you joined me through these pages. If you like the book and have a moment to spare, I would appreciate a short review. Thank you for your help.

About the author

Although I grew up in Hong Kong and Taiwan, my family members live in different parts of the world, a common phenomenon for most Chinese my age because of political conflicts.

I work for a small biotech company and have published 120+ scientific books and papers (under my legal name).

While I am relatively new to the realm of creative writing, I'm thrilled that I was chosen as a featured author by the Minnesota Anoka County Library in 2025 and by the Suffolk Virginia Authors Festival in 2026.

One of my books, *Echoes over Stormy Sea*, has won several awards, including being recently chosen by readers as a winner in the HOLT Medallion Contest.

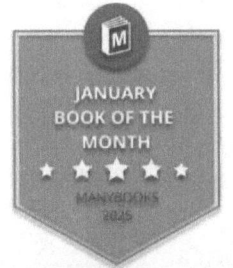

Amazon Best Sellers

Our most popular products based on sales. Updated frequently.

I currently live in the Midwest with my husband, a retired pastor. We served together at three churches from 1987 to 2020. Our grown son works in a nearby city.

Check out my other books.

The Way We Forgive (Women's fiction): https://www.amazon.com/dp/B0BQ5LNLNB

Blazing China (family saga): https://www.amazon.com/dp/B0CD9P49HW

Detour to Agape (sequel to *Blazing China*; contemporary romance): https://www.amazon.com/dp/B0CD9P29GJ

Prestige of Hearts (contemporary romance): https://www.amazon.com/dp/B0CV4FL3CH

Center of Enigma (Paradise PA Mystery Book 1; mystery/suspense/thriller): https://www.amazon.com/dp/B0D9R2M134

Essence of Illusion (Paradise PA Mystery Book 2; mystery/suspense/thriller): https://www.amazon.com/dp/B0DFVPKW3N

Allure of Elegance (Paradise PA Mystery Book 3; mystery/suspense/thriller): **https://www.amazon.com/dp/B0FCP1BV32**

Series Page: https://www.amazon.com/dp/B0DFNXPSGW

Love Under Holy Skies (contemporary romance): https://www.amazon.com/dp/B0F362Q7T8

Echoes over Stormy Sea (Action/Adventure; Dual-time Odyssey Book 1): https://www.amazon.com/dp/B0DPGQ6TZP

Thunders over Idle Land (Action/Adventure; Dual-time Odyssey Book 2): https://www.amazon.com/dp/B0F49GFHW6

Fire Between Two Skies (Action/Adventure; Dual-time Odyssey Book 3): https://www.amazon.com/dp/B0G2YZZ8LG

Series Page: https://www.amazon.com/dp/B0F4LKXS2W

Zenith of Tea (Historical romance)
https://www.amazon.com/dp/B0GNNFT2XM

Nonfiction (under Ruth Wuwong):

Are your health and finances linked? A Christian Entrepreneur's Quest:
https://www.amazon.com/dp/B0BQ5JXFYY

Wander Or Not: https://www.amazon.com/dp/B0CXJ79MWF

To connect with me, please go to www.ruthforchrist.com.

Follow me on social media:

Amazon: https://www.amazon.com/author/love.respect.grace
Goodreads:
https://www.goodreads.com/author/show/42632055.R_F_Whong
Bookbub: https://www.bookbub.com/authors/r-f-whong
Twitter/X: https://twitter.com/RWuwong
Instagram: https://www.instagram.com/ruthwuwong
Facebook: https://m.facebook.com/ruth.wuwong